WARM UP

CATHRYN FOX

Discover other titles by Cathryn Fox at www.cathrynfox.com. Please sign up for Cathryn's Newsletter for freebies, ebooks, news and contests: https://app.mailerlite.com/webforms/landing/c1f8n1

ISBN ebook: 978-1-989374-52-8
ISBN Print: 978-1-989374-51-1

1

KENNEDY

I briefly shut my eyes, blocking out the noise of the campus pub, and let the soothing sound of my guitar fall over me as I strum. Most of the time I'm up here on stage, singing and playing to myself, the students crowding the place are too busy drinking, gossiping, or fighting to pay me much attention. Not that there is a lot of fighting. The owner Jimmy doesn't put up with that kind of nonsense, and once you're kicked out of the campus Tap Room, you're kicked out for the semester.

As I finish strumming, I take a breath and open my eyes, a rare sense of peace deep in my soul—peace that's quickly obliterated as I accidently make eye contact with some drunk guy at the bar. I normally don't play here after a hockey game. The place is always loud and rowdy, especially after a win like tonight, but there's no way I could turn down the gig. I need the money, and not just to pay my tuition.

He holds his beer up to me in salute, and I set my guitar down, ready to take a break. I don't date. I don't have time for it. But I especially avoid drunk guys at the pub. Nothing good can come from that. I try to avert my gaze, and that's when it lands on Matt Morgan—not that I know him personally. I don't. But he's the star defenseman for the Scotia Storms and his reputation precedes him.

His gaze goes from me to the drunk guy, then back to me again as he inches forward in his chair, perched on the edge like he's about to pounce. On the drunk guy, not me. But I don't want him involved. While I appreciate his gallant behavior—I really don't see much of that in the pubs where I play—I'm not worth him getting kicked off the hockey team.

My heart jumps into my throat and I practically stumble off my chair as the drunk guy staggers onto stage, two beers in his hand. "Hey," he hollers, and hands a beer out to me. It sloshes over the side, and I quickly move my guitar before he spills on it. "You look thirsty."

"I'm good. Thank you, though." I force a smile and bend to tuck my guitar away. I'm supposed to play for another half an hour, but I want to get out of here before a fight breaks out, and judging by the way Matt and his friends all just jumped from their chairs, I'm about to be in the middle of a bar brawl, and not only do I not want to get hurt, or be the reason anyone gets hurt, I can't lose this job.

"What, you think you're too good for me?" the guy says loudly, slurring his words, and he glances back at his buddies, who are all laughing. He steps closer, sets one of the drinks on my stool and roughly grabs my arm. Heat crawls into my face, and I steal a fast glance around the bar as a hush comes over the crowd, everyone interested in the scene playing out on stage—with me in the middle of it. Kill me freaking now. I tug my hand away, or at least I try. His hand is the size of a baseball glove and he's got one hell of a strong grip.

"Get your fucking hand off her." My gaze flies to Matt. His murderous eyes lock on the drunk frat boy, and it's a good thing he's not directing that stare at me. I'd probably fall dead right before his eyes.

Frat boy smirks as he turns to Matt. With his attention diverted, his grip loosens and I'm able to snatch my hand back. I stand there, my heart crashing against my ribs. "Please stop," I plead, but my voice gets drowned out by the guy standing over me.

"Yeah, what are you going to do about it, asshole?" he taunts, setting the other beer down and fisting his hands.

"I don't want any trouble." I back up and stumble on the microphone cord.

Matt cracks his knuckles. "I'd be happy to show you."

He stalks toward the stage, and I hold my hands out, palms toward him. "Please, I don't want any trouble."

Matt jumps onto the stage and squares off against the frat boy, but it's not a fair fight. Nope, not a fair fight at all. While the frat boy is big and tall, Matt is bigger and taller, and his body is pure muscle and strength.

"Back the fuck off and leave her alone," Matt says.

Frat boy snorts. "Or what?"

Matt turns to me, his gaze moving over my face. Something in his eyes soften as he takes in my fear. "Kennedy," he says and the fact that he knows my name momentarily shocks me. But that's not the only thing that has my pulse jumping. I don't think I've ever seen such kindness in a man's eyes before. "You need to get off this stage," he tells me, before turning to his buddies and gesturing for them to help me.

Boots hitting the stage reach my ears as Matt turns back to the frat boy. "Listen, I'm not going to fight you. You're drunk, and you'll only end up getting hurt. But if you bother her again, I won't go easy on you," Matt says and I'm grateful that he's not going to pummel the guy in front of me. I also like that he's not throwing around his brawn, when he so easily could.

"Fuck you," the frat boy yells, and draws his fist back. Only problem is, I'm standing close, and his elbow gets me in the eye.

"Owe," I cry out, my hand flying to my stinging eye as I drop to my knees. With my eyes closed, I can't see what's going on around me. I can only hear the commotion of Matt dragging the guy off the stage, Jimmy cursing as he comes running out from his office, and the crowd cheering Matt on as he drags a kicking and screaming frat boy outdoors.

"Pack it up," Jimmy orders, as tears fill my eyes.

"It wasn't her fault," Matt's friend, and fellow hockey player, Chase explains.

Jimmy waves his hand around. "You know the rules. You fight, you're out. None of you are welcomed back until the winter semester."

My heart falls into my shoes as my mind races. I can't lose this gig. I instantly begin to calculate my expenses. If I cut my food bill down any more than it is, I'll only be able to buy crackers. I swallow hard. I guess I've lived on crackers before, but there's more than me to think about these days.

"Jimmy," I plead. "Please. I'm sorry. It won't happen again."

"It wasn't even her fault," Matt argues as he comes back inside and jumps up on stage. He crouches down next to me. "Jimmy, it wasn't her fault."

Jimmy folds his arms across his chest, a good sign that he's not open to hearing my side of things. "You know the rules."

My body shakes despite my best efforts to keep myself together. Usually, I'm shivering because I'm always cold, but this time I can blame it on worry and fear. Matt's big arm goes around me and he helps me to my feet. While it's instinct for me to pull away, for the first time in a long time, I lean into him, let his warmth push back the cold racing through my blood—which is so not like me. The last time I relied on a man, or trusted one, it was a disaster. Why the heck am I doing it now? I can only blame it on the adrenaline dump and the fear cutting through me.

Jimmy points to the door. "Out, now."

Matt's arm tightens, hugging me to him as he leads me to the three steps leading to the main floor. "My guitar," I manage to choke out, my throat so tight it hurts. I try to turn back. His hold tightens.

"My buddy will get it for you." I nod and keep my head down, completely mortified as I work to put one foot in front of the other and step into the dark night. The cool September air washes over my skin, and I take deep gulping breaths. Losing this gig might not seem like a big deal to Matt—he's the world's golden child who's never had to work for a thing—at least, that's what I heard about him. But to me, it's food on the table, and not just for me.

"I'm really sorry," Matt murmurs, his gaze moving over my eye, which will likely be sporting a big bruise come morning. "I'll talk to Jimmy."

I nod, but we both know he's wasting his breath. He might forgive Matt—heck, a star on the hockey team brings in business. No one pays attention to the singer in the corner. But if I'm anything, I'm tough and resilient, and prefer to take action over feeling sorry for myself, so that's just what I'll do. Tomorrow, I'll put on my big girl panties and find another job.

"Thank you for helping," I say, my little pep talk giving me a measure of strength.

"That guy won't be bothering you again."

"I...hate fighting." I'm a peacekeeper, and there's not much I can do about that. "I'm glad it didn't come to that."

As my eyes adjust to the dark, and light spills out of the bar as his friends come outside to meet us, I admire the color of Matt's eyes. I'm not sure I've ever seen such a translucent shade of blue before. It's no wonder he has a harem of girls following him around. He scrubs the scruff on his chin, and oddly enough, the scratching sound does the strangest things to my insides. I reach for my guitar, needing something to do with my hands before I extend my arm and see if that scruff is as rough as it sounds.

What would it feel like on my skin?

Whoa, where the hell did that thought come from? I quickly shut it down, and the truth is, I'm well aware of where it came from. Matt is one hell of a hottie, and the second I saw that genuine kindness in his eyes, it tugged at something deep inside me. The simple fact is, I'm lonely. Between my home life, school, and work, there's no time left for anything else. Not that I want anything else. I will absolutely not—I'm talking zero percent chance here—get involved with anyone. Especially an easygoing, life of the party, responsible only to himself guy like Matt. Bringing a guy like that into my life would only lead to disaster, and I have more than me to think about.

"Thanks," I say to his buddy Chase, and force a smile as I hug my guitar to my chest. "I...need to get going."

"Did you drive here?" Matt asks.

"Yeah," I say but quickly remember I chose to walk tonight. It's nice enough out, and I want to save gas until I need it in the dead of winter. After losing this gig, I'm glad I made that decision. Plus, I like my car to be at home, in case of an emergency.

Matt glances around like he's searching for my vehicle. "I'll walk you to your car."

I give a fast shake of my head, and simply say, "You don't need to do that."

The pub door opens again and out walks Sawyer, who was in my English class freshman year, and her friend Daisy. There's another couple with them, but I don't know who they are. Sawyer gives the couple a quick hug, and they say goodbye. Once they've rounded the corner, Sawyer turns to me.

"Hey," Sawyer says. "Are you okay?"

I nod. "I am." It's a lie. I'm not okay. I haven't been okay for quite some time now, but that's my business and I'll get through this like I get through everything else. I'm a resilient East Coast girl.

Sawyer jerks her thumb over her shoulder as her fiancé Chase puts his arm around her, and Brandon—another hockey player—joins the circle. "We're headed to The Lower Deck to grab some nachos. Why don't you come with us?"

Longing wells up inside me. I want to go. I really do. I want to have a normal campus life, but that's not in the cards. "I can't…I just lost this job."

My gaze is on Sawyer, but I'm completely aware of Matt at my side. I don't need to turn to him to know he's staring at me, his intense gaze assessing everything I say and do. I slowly angle my head, and my tight throat tightens even more as my eyes meet his. Wow, I'm pretty sure no guy has ever gazed at me like this before. Being the sole recipient of his focus is rather unnerving…flattering.

"Nachos are on me," he says. "It's the least I can do to make up for that asshole harassing you."

"None of that was your fault."

"Well, he's a guy and I'm a guy and I want to make up for our kind."

"You're not responsible for all mankind, Matt," I say, a little chuckle bubbling up in my throat.

He angles his head. "How do you know my name?"

I arch a brow and stare at him like he might have taken one too many hits on the ice. "Really?"

"You follow the team?"

"No," I say honestly. I don't. I don't have time. "I've heard of you. Who hasn't?" I say lightly, at least I'm trying to be light. God, the last thing I want is for him to think I'm another one of his groupies. But a guy like Matt, he's hard to miss on campus.

"Don't believe everything you hear," he says, and Chase slaps him on the back.

"Only half of what you hear is true," Chase laughs. "The other half. That's true too."

"Hey," Matt shoots back, and pretends to punch him in the gut. Chase laughs, puts Matt into a headlock and rubs his knuckles on his head. The knot in my chest loosens as everyone laughs, the air flowing into my lungs a little easier now as the two fake-fight like brothers and best friends. I watch, transfixed, my heart squeezing a bit as a part of me longs for this kind of friendship, comradery...normalcy. Don't get me wrong. I don't regret the choices or my life, but this... I miss this.

I steal a fast glance at my watch. "Okay," I blurt out. The two guys stop playing around, and Matt fixes his mussed hair.

"Okay, you'll come for nachos?" he asks, like me tagging along somehow just made his day. I guess he's really interested in making up for his kind.

I nod. I was supposed to be playing for another half hour, which means no one is expecting me until my shift was over. What could one little plate of nachos hurt?

"Sweet," Matt says and takes my guitar from me. I'm about to snatch it back, until I realize he's being gallant again. This time around, however, I'm older. I've seen too much and have been through too much to fall for a man because he's charming.

I hope.

2

MATT

We leave the campus pub, and Kennedy keeps pace beside me as we walk along the path leading to the pub with the very best nachos in town. Yes, I've checked out all the places. But I'm currently checking out the quiet girl beside me. I would say she's shy, but I don't know many people who can go up on stage and perform the way she does. Heck, just last year, my buddy Chase, in an effort to win his girl Sawyer, acted out one of her plays. If I didn't think it was completely corny, I would probably say it was rather sweet.

"I'm sorry about the job," I say to her. "I feel responsible."

"Did you make that knuckle-dragging neanderthal drink too many beers, jump on stage and act like a complete jerk?"

I chuckle at her apt description and her dry wit. "No, but I was ready to start a fight, and there's a no fighting rule."

A small smile touches her mouth, a quick flash. If I hadn't been looking, I wouldn't have noticed.

"While I appreciate it, you shouldn't have done that. You have a hockey career to think about."

What? Has no man ever stood up for her before? Does she not think she's worth it? Damned if that doesn't make me want to keep my eyes on her from here on out, and fine, I know what you're thinking. I like my eyes on her, with her long curls, big brown eyes and full kissable lips that look like puffy clouds, she's pretty easy on them.

I inhale deeply and stick out my chest, but I do hope I'm not coming off like a caveman when I say, "I wasn't going to let him talk to you like that, and he had no right to touch you."

"Thank you, Matt."

Fuck, what is it about the sound of my name on her lips that tugs at my dick? She's definitely not the kind of girl to go home with a guy like me, and I think I like her better for it.

"Are you from around here?" I ask her.

She nods. "Born and raised in Halifax." She lifts her head a bit. "You?"

"I'm from Alberta. Moved here for school and hockey. You should come to a game sometime." As I consider how juvenile I suddenly sound, a frown cuts into her smile, like I might have suggested we head to one of the many oyster bars in town and slurp a few raw ones down. Bleh. A shiver races through me. In Alberta, the main protein is grade A grass-fed beef. While I love the East Coast, the restaurants go a little overboard on seafood. Maybe I'm biased because I came from a long line of dairy farmers—those cows are the milk producing variety, however.

"I'll try," she says, her voice lacking any kind of conviction. I get hockey isn't for everyone, but dammit, I don't know why I like the idea of seeing her in the stands quite so much.

We walk along the boardwalk, and Daisy points to the wave, an art structure that mimics a giant wave. "Who wants to race me up?"

"I do," Chase says, and we all slow a bit as they kick off their shoes and jump on the structure, ignoring the well-lit sign that says no climbing. It's kind of a running joke around these parts. Chase is in the lead, until Daisy grabs his ankle. I laugh at their antics. Those two have been in competition since I met them. Apparently, they go way back. Both their fathers, as well as Brandon's have been friends forever. When I moved here, they took me in like I was one of their own. I used to have a crush on Daisy—heck, almost every guy on the hockey team did at one point—but she doesn't date hockey players. Crazy, since she's on the women's hockey team.

A breeze washes in off the Halifax Harbour, and when Kennedy wraps her arms around herself, I instinctively pull her to me and run my hand up and down her arm. Her gaze jerks to mine. I held her earlier when she was shaking outside the pub. Now, though, I'm getting a different vibe.

"I'm sorry," I say quickly and pull my arm back. "I didn't mean to touch without asking."

"It's okay, it just surprised me."

I tug on my hoodie. "Want my sweater?"

She gives a fast shake of her head. It's no wonder she's cold. A good breeze would likely carry her away.

"Say it," Daisy shouts to Chase as she slides down the wave after cheating to beat him to the top.

"I won," he shouts back.

She tugs her shoes on. "No, I won. Say it, Chase, or I'll tell your Dad about that time you stayed home from school pretending you were sick in bed."

"I was sixteen," he calls back.

"I know what, or should I say who, you were really doing in that bed."

Sawyer comes up to us, shaking her head and laughing. "You'd think they were brother and sister with the way they act." She glances at Kennedy, who has the cute little grin on her face, like she's enjoying everything about this. Or maybe she's far more mature than we are and thinks we're all idiots. "They go way back."

We all start toward the The Lower Deck again, passing by guests eating at all the outdoor patios, beneath the moonlight. Kennedy pulls her phone from her pocket and checks the time. Does she have somewhere to be?

We finally reach our destination, and Chase holds the door open as we all pile in. Music reaches my ears as we grab a big table in the back.

"I'll be right back," Kennedy says and disappears down the hall leading to the bathrooms.

Brandon and Chase head to the bar to get drinks and put our food order in while Sawyer and Daisey slide in on either side of me.

"She's cute, huh?" Daisy grins as she flicks her blonde curls from her shoulders.

"Who?" I play dumb and glance around like I'm trying to figure out who she's talking about. A lot of guys are looking our way, their focus on Daisy, but she couldn't care less.

"You're not a dumb-ass, Matt. Stop acting like one," she says. Leave it to Daisy to tell me what she really thinks.

"Yeah, okay fine. She's cute. Lots of girls are cute." While it's true, there really is something different about Kennedy. I can't put my finger on it, but she's not like the other girls I usually hang out and party with.

Not letting it go, Daisy suggests, "You should ask her out."

"Out where?"

Sawyer rolls her eyes hard. "You're right. She'd never go for a guy like you."

"What makes you say that?" I ask, even though I know exactly what she means. I'm a player, a guy who never had any kind of real responsibility. Heck, my parents run a huge dairy farm that has been in the family for generations, and my brothers and sisters all worked it since they could walk. The second my grandfather—the patriarch of the family who pays for everything, even my education and living expenses— learned I was a skilled hockey player, my only responsibility was to make it to the NHL. I became his obsession, really. He hated when I dated, or went to parties, or did anything remotely normal. Maybe that's why I rebelled a little when I first arrived in Nova Scotia a couple years ago, hooking up with a different girl every weekend because I could, because no one was watching my every move. I'll admit, I'm getting a bit played out. But now that's what everyone here expects of me.

Why do you have to live up to anyone's expectations, Matt?

Good question and the answer probably stems from my upbringing. Back home, everyone expected so little of me.

Every time I tried to help out on our million-dollar dairy operation, I was shooed away. Honestly, I love my family, I love that they all worked hard and cut me slack so I could focus on hockey—and I'm happy that I got drafted by Tampa —but sometimes I think they only see a guy who has no life skills beyond the hockey rink. That I am a man of zero substance, who only has the ability to take care of himself.

I became what they expected and haven't proven them wrong, though.

Are you capable of more, Matt?

"So you do want to ask her out?" Daisy says loudly, too loudly. I glance down the hall to make sure Kennedy isn't within earshot.

"I never said that. If you'll excuse me." I nudge Daisy, and she shoves me back before she climbs out of the booth.

As they guys come back to the table with a couple pitchers of beer, I head down the hall, and stop abruptly before I bang into Kennedy. With her phone pressed to one ear, and her finger plugging the other one, she gives me a nervous smile and turns into the wall to speak. Unease works its way through me, and I keep going.

I duck into the washroom, go about my business and wash up, Kennedy still on my mind. She didn't seem upset on the phone, and while I have no idea who she was talking to, she did seem jumpy about something.

I head back to the table and run into a few girls who want to talk, but I'm anxious to get back to my friends—to Kennedy. Okay, so I'm being ridiculous. She's not really my type, and probably only goes out with guys who have substance.

As I reach our table, I overhear Daisy mention to Kennedy that she knows the owner and can check.

"Check what?" I ask.

Daisy shifts to let me into the booth, ever so blatantly forcing me to sit next to Kennedy. She gestures toward the guitar player. "Since Kennedy lost her gig at the pub…" Her voice falls off and she eyes me like it's all my fault. I get it, I'm partially responsible. "We were wondering if they had any openings here."

"Oh yeah."

She nods. "Yeah, I really need the…uh, to play." Why do I get the sense that's what she wasn't really going to say? "For my program," she adds quickly, her head nodding, like she's trying to convince me.

"Hopefully they can fit you in. That's great that you know the guy, Daisy."

Kennedy tugs her phone from her pocket, shields the screen from my eyes, reads something and quickly tucks it away.

"Everything okay?" I ask, as she lifts her long lashes and glances at me. My God, her eyes look huge against her thin face.

She smiles, but it's forced. A part of me wants to press, but what would be the point? She'll go home at the end of the night and I'll go back to watching her from afar. Actually, now that she's fired, and I do feel responsible, I won't be seeing her at all—unless she can get work here. Strange how much I hate that she won't be at the campus pub on the weekends. Jimmy told me not to come back until next semester, but he never bans the hockey players for that long. We're too big of a draw after a game, and that means money in his pocket.

The nachos come, and like the barn cat who always shows up at our place when Mom is cooking salmon, Beckett shoves into the booth, squishing Kennedy against me. I don't hate the way her soft body presses against mine. Nope, don't hate it at all.

Her nose crinkles in apology, but I shrug it off, and don't bother shifting to give her anymore room. I'm a douche like that.

Beckett, our team's goalie and an all-around nice guy, snatches up a cheesy nacho, and darts a glance my way as he says, "Dude, what the fuck did you do?"

"Jesus, does the whole world know?" I know rumor spreads fast on campus, but Beckett wasn't even at the pub when Jimmy kicked us all out.

"Why would the whole world know that you fucked our housekeeper?"

Kennedy stiffens beside me. "What?"

Around a mouthful of nachos, he says, "Yeah, she quit, and that has your name all over it. Straight up walked out right after she made lasagna. I probably wouldn't eat that if I were you."

"Shit."

"We need new rules," Beck says. "The housekeepers are hands off."

I want to protest, tell him I never slept with her. That would be a lie, but it was ages ago and she came on to me. Not that it matters who initiated it. I have no idea why she quit, but I'm one hundred percent sure it had nothing to do with me. Okay, maybe I'm ninety-five percent sure.

"Jesus dude, keep it in your pants," Daisy snaps, and Chase and Sawyer agree.

"Now what the hell are we going to do?" Beckett asks. "I sure as hell can't cook."

"I can," Daisy declares. "Not that you guys could pay me enough to clean your disgusting place and cook for you."

"I...cook," Kennedy says so quietly, I almost miss it.

"Are you saying you want the job?" I ask.

"I mean..." She glances around at everyone as we all fall quiet to hear her. "If you're hiring and the hours are flexible."

Beckett chomps on another nacho and shouts, "You're hired!"

"Wait, what?" I ask, this all coming at me fast. "Do you really want to clean up after a bunch of disgusting hockey players?"

Dark, innocent doe eyes flash my way. "Is it that bad?"

"Oh, it's that bad," Daisy snorts out. "But the pay is good, and this is a great way for Matt to make up for getting you fired."

"Just keep it in your pants this time, dude," Beckett says and Kennedy blushes.

Kennedy turns to Beckett. "That's not...I mean I don't want... I'm not going to..."

"You say that now," Beckett teases.

"Shut up, Beck," I warn and Kennedy turns my way. "If you want the job, it's yours, Kennedy, and no, you don't have to do anything you don't want to do."

She smiles. "It's settled then. I can start Monday and make a lasagna that you're not afraid to eat."

"Sweet," Beck says, and I sit there a little stunned. Kennedy is going to be our new housekeeper, and I have to keep it in my pants? Okay, then. Seriously though, it's not like I had a chance with her anyway. She's too damn good for me.

We all fall into easy conversation, and munch on our chips and drink our beers. Once we're done—and I don't miss the way Kennedy keeps checking her phone, what, does she have a hot date, or a boyfriend waiting?—we clear the booth.

I grab her guitar, and the night air is cooler when we step from The Lower Deck, and everyone says goodnight to head back to their own places. I turn to Kennedy. No way am I letting her walk the waterfront alone, not at this time of night.

"Come on, I'll walk you to your car."

She turns from me and glances into the dark. "No, it's okay. I actually forgot I walked to the pub."

"Then I'll walk you home."

"No, home is a little far from here."

"I'll drive then."

"But it's far."

"All the more reason for me to drive."

"I'm sure you have better things to do." She reaches for her guitar and I hold it out of her reach.

"Nope." Honestly, I can't think of anything I'd like more than to see her home safely. "Do you know how many crazies there are out at night?" She grins and eyes me. "Wait, are you saying I'm one of them?"

"No, I'm not afraid of you, Matt."

"Good," I say, and can't help but think she should be. Her, alone in my room... I can think of all kinds of crazy things I'd like to do to her. I won't, of course. I'd never do anything she didn't want to do.

What if she did want to do it, Matt?

Nope, still not going to. I'm not good for her.

Instead of walking the boardwalk, we head out onto the street where the lighting is better.

"What was it like growing up in Alberta?"

"It was okay. Grew up on a farm. Miss Alberta beef," I say with a laugh. "Ever been?"

"No. Do you have siblings?"

"Yeah, there's five of us."

Her eyes widen, like she loves that idea. "Really?"

"Yeah, I'm the middle child."

She makes a face, a half cringe, half apology. "Sorry."

"For what?"

"You know how needy those middle children are?"

I laugh at that. "How about you? Siblings and if so, where do you fit in?"

"None, just me." There's a longing in her voice.

"It's not all it's cracked up to be." I gesture to the path that leads to Storm House, not that I'm trying to get her to my room or anything. We cut through the tree-lined path, and she steps a bit closer to me as darkness closes in on us.

"I really would love to go out west sometime. I'd love to see the world."

"You could pack your guitar, go from city to city, and play for money on the boardwalks. Busker style." I'm joking of course, and she just laughs.

"That's for the young and free."

"Which we are, of course." It's not that true. We all have obligations. I'm not sure what hers are, but mine is to play in the NHL. It's all that's ever been expected of me. I stop walking when we come to the parking lot of Storm House.

"So this is it, huh?"

"Yup. I'll give you a key so you can come and go as you please," I say. A cool breeze blows in from the water, and she shivers. "That's my truck."

"You drive a truck?"

"You can take the boy out of the farm, but you can't take the farm out of the boy. Come on, let me drive you the rest of the way."

She hesitates for a brief second. "It's not that far."

"You're not the one lugging this thing around," I tease and lift her guitar.

She grins. "I'm quite capable of carrying my own guitar."

"I have no doubt," I say and mean it. I get the sense that Kennedy is the kind of girl who takes care of herself and everyone around her. "But come on, hop in."

She nods and we walk to my truck. I click my fob to unlock the doors and place her guitar on the back bench seat. She slides into the front, and I circle the vehicle and get into the driver's seat.

"Ohmigod, Matt," she shrieks and picks a pair of my boxer shorts up off the floor, holds them up using two fingers, wrinkles her nose and asks. "Do I want to know?" I snatch them from her and toss them into the back. "Is your room this bad? Was Daisy right?"

"No and no and no." She blinks and one eye half closes as she tries to piece that together. "You probably don't want to know, but I'm going to tell you." I start the truck and back out of my spot. "They probably fell out of my hockey bag after our Wednesday night game in Cape Breton. No, my room isn't that bad." I toss her an apologetic look, because it's not that good either. "And no, Daisy was not right. Daisy is never right." She's still giving me the side eye as I pull onto the road. "What?" I ask.

"Nothing."

"Are you telling me I won't find your panties in the passenger seat of your car? Like it's not a thing?"

This time she laughs out loud and I laugh with her. "You're crazy, Matt."

"You're probably right. Where do you live?"

"Just off South Park."

I take a right and head down the street, and she guides me, telling me to stop before I pass a tiny little bungalow tucked in between two bigger houses.

"This is me." She's opening her door before my vehicle is barely stopped. Is she embarrassed to be seen with me? Yeah, probably. "Thanks for the lift and nachos, and the job. I'll stop by Monday after lunch. Will you be there?"

"Yes." I will be now. The door shuts, and she darts in front of my truck and into the house. I sit there for a moment, staring at the front stoop, lit under the porch light.

As a yawn pulls at me, I step on the gas and head back to Storm House. I round the corner and that's when I remember her guitar. She could probably get it Monday, but she probably needs it before then, and I don't want to be responsible for it getting played or damaged by any of the guys in the house. I turn around and pull into her driveway, parking behind a car that looks like it's held together by duct tape.

Her porch light is out as I grab her guitar and hurry to her door. I knock, and wait a second. I knock again, and just when I think she might have already gone to bed, the door opens, and my jaw gapes open—so does hers—as I glance at the girl I just hired to clean our house. The same one I had very inappropriate thoughts about.

At least now I know why Kennedy seems different from other girls and why she doesn't hang out and party with us.

3

KENNEDY

s I walk to Storm House, my phone rings, and I tug it from my pocket, half expecting it to be Matt. Although I don't know why. He doesn't have my number, and after finding me at my door Friday night, my daughter in my arms, there's no way he's going to try to get my number from someone, or try to hook up with me. The shock on his face was blatant, and I didn't miss the way he stumbled backwards. Why wouldn't he, though? He had no idea I was a mother. Most people don't. I keep my private life private. But the sight of me with my daughter, who looks very much like me, totally threw him off.

Just like everything about Matt throws me off. And maybe the chemistry between us is all in my head. Maybe when he put his arm around me to warm me, it was nothing other than him trying to make up for the near fight that got me fired. I'm certainly not his type and everyone knows his reputation with the puck bunnies.

Heck, he had boxer shorts on the floor of his truck and I'm not sure I believe the story that they fell out of his hockey bag. I have no doubt I was sitting on the seat he had sex on numerous times, and probably within the last twenty-four hours. I should probably burn the jeans I was wearing.

Despite all that, Friday night was weird even before he showed up at my door with my guitar. How could I have forgotten it? I guess I was in a hurry to get away from him, and get inside before he tried to walk me to the door. I'm very careful who I bring into my daughter's world. But the truth is, I actually enjoyed his attention, and hanging out with his group of friends. I have friends of my own, of course, but most of them are in the play groups I take Madelyn too. I love my daughter dearly, don't get me wrong, but for one brief moment, I enjoyed forgetting about all my responsibilities. God, that makes me a bad person, doesn't it?

My phone rings and when I see that it's a call coming from The Lower Deck, I put on my best professional voice and answer.

"Hello."

"I'm looking for Kennedy Walsh."

"This is Kennedy." I stop walking, right by Matt's truck, and I lean against it to find the engine still warm. He must have just gotten home and little butterflies erupt in my stomach as I think about seeing him inside Storm House.

"This is Jesse from The Lower Deck. Daisy speaks highly of you and suggested I hire you to play at my establishment."

I smile at that. I don't know Daisy well, but she's a straight shooter, and I think men are rather intimidated by her. It was so nice of her to vouch for me.

"Yes, I would love to play."

"How would Tuesday and Saturday evenings work? Eight to ten."

I swallow hard, as I mentally go over Madelyn and my mother's schedule. Tuesdays might be a bit tough, but I'm sure I can work it out. "That sounds great. When should I start?"

"Next week. Come in early to fill out your paperwork."

I agree and end the call. I'll have to take Daisy out for a drink to thank her. But right now, I need to settle the butterflies in my stomach before I step into Storm House and see Matt. I force my legs to work, head up the stairs and knock on the front door. I wait and glance around. Maybe Matt isn't home, and he walked to wherever he was going. I try the door. It opens. Shoot, do I enter? Maybe it was left open for me. I push it open and step inside, hoping I don't get arrested for breaking and entering.

"Hello," I call out, working to sound light and cheery, not nervous—or excited—to see Matt. My voice is met with silence. I stand in the quiet for a little while longer, the scent of smelly hockey equipment filling my senses. Eww. I take in the numerous duffle bags tossed against the wall of the hall, each bag with the last name of the player on it. I hope it's not my responsibility to wash their gear. I walk slowly, searching for Matt's bag, and I don't know why. Maybe I want to see if he really does keep a pair of shorts inside.

What the hell am I doing? I shake my head, and start walking through the house, trying to gauge how long it's going to take me to straighten up and pull together a lasagna. For the most part, the place is clean. The housekeeper only quit the other day, so that's not surprising. I walk to the kitchen and open the fridge to find it fully stocked. I spot last week's untouched lasagna. Surely it hasn't been tampered with, right? Was Matt the reason the last girl quit, and possibly poisoned the food? I shut the fridge and start opening cupboards to find them completely stocked too. Am I in charge of buying groceries?

Do I clean the bedrooms?

I still don't know exactly what I signed on for. I know what I didn't sign on for, however, and that was sleeping with Matt. Nope, that's totally out of the question, and I hope I never have to walk into his bedroom, or see the bed that a million girls rolled through.

"Hi."

I spin at the sound of Matt's voice, and there's nothing I can do to stop the gasp when I spot him standing in the doorway, a towel knotted at his waist as he uses another small towel to scrub his hair dry.

"Sorry," he says quickly. "I didn't mean to scare you."

"I thought I was alone."

Do not look down, Kennedy. Do not check out his abs, or anything that lies below that towel.

The only way I can stop myself is by rushing back to the fridge and opening it. I enjoy the rush of cold air as the door blocks him from my view.

"I just got home from practice," he explains. "I was hoping to be showered and dressed before you got here. I heard a noise, and investigated."

"Just me." My God, I sound like I'd just swallowed the contents in a helium balloon and ate it afterward.

"I thought maybe someone had broken in."

"Does that happen often?" I ask, as I grab a couple big packages of ground beef and set them on the counter. I'm thankful that lasagna requires numerous items. That gives me a reason to hang out inside his fridge.

He quietly snorts a laugh. "More often than you'd think. Sometimes it's a rival team member looking to cause trouble. Sometimes it's a girl looking to surprise one of us."

I grab an armload of cheese and veggies and deposit them on the counter. "Sorry to disappoint."

"Who said I was disappointed?"

The deepening of his voice stops me and I can barely get air when I turn to him, that same genuine kindness and warmth in his eyes from the other night. There's something else there though, something that looks a lot like...want.

I can't go there.

He examines my face. "How is your eye? It doesn't look too bad."

"It's tender, and I covered it in makeup to hide the bruise. No need to draw attention and start rumors."

"Maybe you should see a doctor?"

"And maybe *you* should go upstairs and get dressed."

His head angles, and a small smile flirts with his lips. Christ, why didn't I just come right out and tell him that his near nakedness is messing with my brain...and body?

"Right, I'm on it."

"My eye is okay, Matt. It's just a bruise. I don't need to see a doctor." I smile at him, appreciating his concern.

He nods and turns and yes, I stare at his backside until he disappears from my line of sight. Once he's gone, I lean against the counter and take deep breaths until I'm almost woozy. Who am I kidding, seeing him standing there, his gorgeous, hard six-pack on display made me lightheaded. And don't even get me started on the way his towel tented, and yes, of course I stole a peek.

Needing to busy my hands before I follow him upstairs and help him out of his towel, I search for a frying pan and toss the meat in to brown it. I add a bunch of spices before I reach for my phone and turn on some music. I hum softly, and when footsteps behind me let me know Matt is back, I spin, but my forced smile falls as my gaze lands on one of Matt's teammates.

"Who are you?" he asks, his gaze blatantly moving up and down my body as he rakes his damp red hair back. He frowns, and I get it, he's trying to figure out why a girl like me—the antithesis to the cheerleaders—would be inside this house. He probably can't figure out which guy took me home, or why.

"I'm—"

"Move it, Cheddar."

The guy spins, and in walks Matt, looking so damn handsome in his tight-fitting T-shirt and low slung jeans.

"Did you just call him cheddar?" I ask.

Matt arches a brow, as he grins at me. God, does any man have a right to look that good, from a simple grin? "Yeah why?"

I glance at the guy...Cheddar. "Is that your name?"

The two burst out laughing and I stand there feeling like a fool as they slap one another on the back. "Oh, I get it. Your hair is orange. Wait, that's kind of mean."

"Nah, it's not mean," Cheddar adds. "It's a nickname, we all have one, and who doesn't like cheddar cheese, right?"

"I guess." What is Matt's nickname? Did they secretly give me one the other night?

"Do you like cheddar?" he asks, and I'm starting to worry he's not talking about the dairy product and who doesn't love cheddar. It's only my love language.

"Ah, yeah."

He smirks. "Glad to hear it."

"Kennedy is our new housekeeper," Matt tells Cheddar as he cracks his knuckles. "Be nice to her or I'll fuck you up."

Why is he telling him to be nice to me? Are they not nice to girls who aren't in their house for sex? Is there something about me that says I'm not worth being nice to? I know I'm not your typical beauty, and clothes sort of hang on my body, but shouldn't we all always be nice to each other?

"You be nice to her," Cheddar counters. "And you're the one who fucks things up." Cheddar's long lashes wink over green eyes. "If you know what I mean."

Matt groans as I say, "Yes, I know what you mean." It's a good reminder, though. There might be this strange attraction between Matt and me—or it could all be in my mind—but Matt is Matt, and I'm not sleeping with a self-serving, plea-sure-seeking guy like him. I am not setting myself up for that kind of failure, not again.

"Then you know to stay away from him."

"We're friends," Matt says.

"Friends," I agree.

"Okay, you two are friends." He jabs his thumb into his chest. "Me, on the other hand. There is absolutely no reason to stay away from Cheddar." He grins, and it's hungry and wolfish as he comes closer, and looks over my shoulder as I remain forward, staring at Matt. "Whatcha making?"

"Lasagna."

He puts his nose close to my hair. "Mmm, smells good."

Is he talking about the spices or my hair? Also, what is going on? Up until last night I wasn't on any guy's radar and now these two both seem very interested in me. Did they lose a bet or something?

"Can't wait to eat it," he says and once again, I'm a little concerned we're not talking about the lasagna.

"Don't you have class?" Matt says and Cheddar exhales slowly.

"Yeah."

"Beat it, then."

"You have class too, you know."

"Yeah, I'll be there. I need to get Kennedy a key and go over a few things."

Cheddar rolls his eyes. "Yeah, well. I'm not worried about you messing around with this one." He glances at me. "She's too smart for that."

I nod, and Cheddar pushes past Matt and heads upstairs. The shower turns on and Matt walks over to the fridge and pulls out a sports drink. He holds it out to me. "No thanks."

He shuts the fridge, twists off the top and takes a big drink. I try not to stare, or watch the way his throat works. I also try not to look at his big hands.

He finishes drinking and I begin, "About the other night." He stares at me, like he was waiting for me to bring up my daughter. "I don't usually talk about my personal life."

He sets his drink on the counter. "It's your business, Kennedy, not anyone else's."

"Yeah, you're right."

"She looks like you."

I smile. "You think?" I ask, even though I know she does.

"Yeah, she's real sweet."

I swallow. Is he complimenting me?

"Thank you."

He glances around. "Are you sure you have time to take on this job?"

Oh, God, he's not going to fire me before I get started, is he? "Oh, yes for sure."

"Okay, good and just so you know, our last housekeeper always made extra, and took it home with her. It's part of the bargain. The least we could do for having to pick up after us."

Great, he knows I'm broke-ass poor. "Okay." I'm not sure I believe him, but I appreciate the gesture. I just don't want his pity. I never wanted anyone's pity.

"Do you want me to show you around?" he asks.

"That's probably a good idea." We both reach for the pan at the same time to take it off the burner. I quickly pull away.

"Sorry," he says and holds his hands up, palms out.

"It's okay."

"Do we want to start upstairs?" For the briefest of seconds, I think he's talking about taking me to his bedroom and I can't stop my eyes from widening in shock. He chuckles. "I mean, in the bathrooms. You don't have to clean our rooms."

"Oh, good."

"You don't have to do anything you don't want to do, Kennedy."

Those blue eyes of his move over my face, a new kind of appreciation and admiration in them. Does he see me differently, now that he knows I'm a mother? Does it put his new housekeeper in the hands-off category? That's what I want, right?

So why then does the idea of that disappoint me?

● 4

MATT

I walk ahead of Kennedy as I lead her up the stairs, keeping a bit of distance between us. Hey, I'm not about to corrupt a girl who has a baby to care for. I've never slept with a mommy and I'm not about to begin now. Like I said before, I'm all wrong for her, and the fact that she has a child simply cements that. So now I have two reasons to keep a level of separation. One, she's our housekeeper, and finding someone to clean a frat house is no easy chore, and two, she's a girl with responsibilities, I'm a guy with none.

"Your daughter," I begin when I reach the hall. "How old is she?"

"A year and a half."

I nod and walk down the hall, waiting for more, or at least for her to tell me her name, but she doesn't. She's private and I respect that. "Her father must be so proud." Jesus, why am I fishing for information? Didn't I just lecture myself on the reasons to stay away. Still I can't help but wonder if she's married, or living with some guy. From the way she talked about needing work, I get the sense he's not in the picture. I'm not sure why I'm happy about that. I shouldn't be. I hate deadbeat dads. That's something I'd never want to be, which is why I'll never be the guy with kids. Imagine responsibility being thrust on a guy like me. Those who know me would die a sudden death, no doubt.

But would you, Matt? Would it be the worst thing in the world, and why are you living up to what others think of you?

"He's ah..."

As she hesitates, I spin and take in her big, vulnerable brown eyes. While she might come off as fragile, she's not. She's tough. Every inch of me knows she's the kind of girl who does what needs to be done, herself be damned, and that kind of bugs me and makes me want to help her out, cut her some slack, somehow.

"Sorry, not my business."

"He's not in the picture," she blurts out, and the two of us stand there staring at each other, silence filling the hall as some deeper understanding passes between us. I don't even need to ask if he's at least financially responsible. She wouldn't be working her ass off going to school and holding down a couple of jobs if he was. I don't know much about that since everything's been handed to me, but goddammit, it's all I can do not to hunt the bastard down and have a talk with him—with my fist.

"Okay," I tell her, breaking the moment. "There are two floors with bedrooms, but you don't have to touch those." I make a face, hoping it pulls a laugh from her. "No more touching boxer shorts."

She grins, and my heart skips a beat. "Thank God."

"That bad, huh?"

"You're really asking, Matt?" she says with a laugh that curls around me.

I like her.

I smile and touch my head. "A little dense. Too many hits on the ice."

She shakes her head. "You're anything but dense."

Her compliment puffs my chest out. "I do okay," I say. The truth is, while hockey is my focus, my grades are pretty damn good. Lots of professors cut players slack, but I don't want that. I want to be accountable, even if it's only to myself. I'm in animal science with my buddy Chase because it's what interests me. I grew up on a massive dairy farm, and while I was kept from the work, it didn't mean I wasn't interested in learning more about it, and hey, everyone needs something to fall back on if the NHL doesn't work out. After retirement, I won't have to work—I come from wealth —but I'm not the kind of guy who can sit around doing nothing.

I turn around and show her the bathrooms, and slow my steps as we walk by my bedroom, my door wide open. I glance in, and she does too.

"This is your room?"

"What gave it away?"

"All I had to do was look at it to know it was your room."

"How?"

"I've heard all about this room, Matt."

"You...heard about my room?" What the hell? I mean I know I have a revolving door, but how would she have heard about my room. She doesn't hang in the same circle as I do.

"Yes, I heard it's where fun goes to die." Her face is so straight, for a second I don't realize she's kidding. But then her lush lips quirk at the corners.

"Hey, not funny," I shoot back. "What do you know about fun, anyway?"

Her smile fades and shit, now I feel like a jerk. She has a child to take care of on top of school and work. Responsibility, rather than fun, is what she's made of. The complete opposite of me. "I didn't mean it like that."

She just shakes it off, and smiles and stands at the threshold. "If you really want to know what gave it away, it's the chair at your desk."

I frown, and zero in on my chair to find a pair of black boxer shorts hanging off it. Laughing, I step into my room, snatch them up and slam dunk them into my hamper.

"You could have been a basketball star," she teases, remaining at the door. I get it. She doesn't want to cross some imaginary line, and I fully respect that. "That's not what really gave it away?"

"No?"

She gestures with a nod to the picture on my bookshelf, and I smile. "Right. My youngest brother gave me that before I came here. We're close and he misses me. I miss him too."

She points to it. "Do you mind?"

"Not at all." She doesn't move, so I pick the picture up and bring it to her. "We took that last Christmas."

She smiles, a longing in her eyes. "You have a big beautiful family."

"Yup." I start pointing to the people in the picture, rattling off their names. "Grandpa is the reason I'm in hockey. He loves the game." I laugh. "Do not even try to talk to him when the Oilers are playing."

Thick dark lashes fall slowly over big brown eyes, and this might sound cliché but I momentarily lose myself in them. "Do you think you'll play for Edmonton?"

I blink to get my focus. "I'm drafted to Tampa, but if Grandpa has a say, I will someday."

"Does he?"

Her fast question takes me by surprise. Grandpa has a one-track mind, but he doesn't have that kind of influence over anyone but our family—especially me and my youngest brother.

"No." She hands the picture back and I set it on my book-shelf. "I don't know."

"What do you want to do, Matt? Is hockey your passion too?"

Wow, the last time anyone asked what I wanted to do was… never. "I want to play hockey. My favorite team is Edmonton. I grew up in Alberta, but hey, I'll be happy on any team." She smiles. "After you travel the world as a busker…." I begin, going back to our earlier conversation, but that's when it hits me. She has responsibilities, and can't just go wherever the wind takes her. "Um, what do you want to do?"

"I want to be a singer-songwriter. I don't need fame, but I would love to make a decent living at it."

I plop onto my bed, and she continues to stand at my door. "You're really good."

She angles her head and eyes me like I might have taken too many sticks to the head. She'd be right. "How do you know that?"

Now it's my turn to look at her like she might have a concussion. "Ah, campus pub. Wasn't it just the other night I got you fired?" I tease.

Her laugh is loud and musical, beautiful and interesting, just like her. "No one listens to me. You can't even hear me sing or play over the crowd, especially after a game."

"A game you never watched. Where's your team spirit?" She smiles at me, but that was a selfish thing to say. She has more important things to do. "If you think no one is listening, why do you do it then, Kennedy?"

"I need the experience for a credit in my program, and the money." I pause and wait for more of an explanation, because in my gut, I sense there is more. Her head lowers, and there's a very real seriousness about her when she says quietly, "And for me. I play for me too."

I lean toward her, my elbows on my knees, my heart pounding a little harder in my chest. "For the record. I listened, and I heard. Every single word."

She straightens a bit at my seriousness, her smile falling off. "Really?"

"Yes, so when I say you're good, you can trust my word on that. I'd love to hear you sing some of the songs you wrote."

She shrugs, her shoulders curling in, a new kind of self-consciousness about her, and I understand that. It's not easy to put yourself out there. "I'm not sure I'm ready for that."

"Someday, then." She nods, and I ask, "How did you get into music?" I stare at her, noting the dark smudges beneath her eyes. Did she get enough sleep last night? Was she up all night with her daughter? "You can have a seat if you want. I have a reputation, I know, but don't worry, I'm not going to try anything."

"Good, because I don't want that."

I kick my chair out, and she stares at it for a second. I'm guessing she's debating on whether she can trust me or not. A second later she must decide she can because she steps into my room and sits. She lets out a puff of air.

"Thanks. Madelyn has been teething and it's not been fun."

I nod in understanding, although I have no understanding at all. The only thing that keeps me up or wakes me up in the night is a hot girl ready to go for another round. Wow, I am kind of a dick.

She leans forward, her blouse falling open. I try not to look. I really do, but Jesus, while she's far too thin, her tits are round and plump, and calling my name.

"I must look like a mess." She brushes her hair from her forehead, but she's beautiful even with mussed up curls.

I clear my throat and marshal my cock into submission. "You don't."

She doesn't comment on that, instead she turns the subject back to music. "My mom is musical. She played everything, and when I was young, our house was filled with dancing and music."

She briefly closes her eyes, a smile touching her mouth, and I have no doubt she's reliving those happy days. But there's something else in her voice, and her body language that has me asking, "When you were young?"

Her lids fly open, and she jerks her gaze away. She doesn't want me to see what she's thinking, but I caught the hurt. "Yeah, you know…" She flops her hand over. "Life, work, responsibilities." She shrugs, and with a humorless laugh adds, "Sometimes that can make the music fade."

"Was your dad musical?" I'm pushing, I know, but I'm intrigued.

"No," she blurts out, her hard expression and the way she jumped to her feet putting an end to my questioning. Shit, I hit on a sore spot. I follow her up, and dip my head as I stand over her, our bodies close.

"I didn't mean to upset you."

She shakes her head and laughs. "It's okay. You didn't. I just don't want to come off sounding like a tragic country song." Her head lifts, those dark eyes back on mine. "I'm not," she says adamantly.

"I know." I shouldn't touch her, but I can't seem to stop myself. I reach out and lightly brush her hair from her shoulder. Her eyes briefly shut, the little intake of air, not missed by me. Fuck, I don't want to like touching her so much. I don't even want to like her. "Just promise me your music will never fade."

Her eyes partially open, and there's heat and want dancing there. It wraps around my dick and tugs. I'm a guy with no responsibilities, no substance, a guy who has never been said no to by a woman, and for the first time in my life, I'm the one saying no.

I back up an inch and she blinks her eyes back into focus. Her head jerks back like I just slapped her, and fuck, I don't want to hurt her feelings, but no, we can't do anything. I can't even touch her again.

"Why would you say that?" she asks.

"Because we all need your music, Kennedy." I honestly have no idea what I'm saying. But she's sweet and kind, and while life is rough for her, I'm pretty sure her music is her savior, and while I haven't known her long—I've been watching her from afar for quite some time now—the thoughts of life stripping music from her soul cuts into me like a blade.

She swallows hard. "Thank you." The door downstairs opens and slams shut, and she jumps back.

"I guess we should finish the tour."

"Yeah, and I need to get back to making you guys a lasagna that's poison free. I should get rid of the one in the fridge, right?"

"No one seems to be eating it."

"Do you often have women wanting to poison you?" she asks, going back to our playful banter.

"I'm sure the lasagna is fine."

We head toward the stairs and she glances at me over her shoulder, a cute smirk on her face. "I'll heat it up for you then."

"Hard pass," I say, and she laughs.

"I promise my lasagna will be poison free, and the best thing you've ever put in your mouth."

"Those are some confident words." I could make a joke about what things I like to put in my mouth, and normally I would. I'm kind of an ass like that, but Kennedy brings out a different side to me, and I sort of like it.

I follow her into the kitchen, and wave to Josh, who came in a minute ago and is now plunked on the sofa in the main gathering room.

She turns the stove back on, and shifts to face me. "What do they call you, Matt?"

"Matt," I say.

"No, your nickname. Cheddar said you all have one."

I shake my head. "Do you really want to know?"

"Is it bad?"

"No."

"Okay, then tell me."

"They call me Milk Man."

Her eyes go wide, and she glances down at her chest, which is so goddamn awesome, it's been hard to concentrate. I haven't been able to stop thinking about her breasts since she bent forward and gave me a sneak peek.

"Because you like—"

"No," I blurt out. "It's because I grew up on a dairy farm, and on the ice, I deliver."

"Oh, I get it." She grins. "That's cute." She nibbles her lip, more questions dancing in her gorgeous eyes.

"What?"

She has a mischievous, playful look on her face. "So you don't like—"

"I like them just fine. Okay, I like them lot." I turn and mumble under my breath as I head back to the steps, so I can lock myself in my room. Honestly, I'm glad I didn't grow up on a cattle farm. Then they might have called me the meat man, and wouldn't you know it, that would have been just about right for what I'm about to take into my hands when I get to my room.

5

KENNEDY

As my friend Amy, who I met at this playground when I first started bringing Madelyn here months ago, takes turns pushing Madelyn and her own daughter on the swings, I settle onto the bench, slide the tab open on my thermos cup and take a much-needed sip of coffee. I'll be glad when the teething stops and I can get a good night's sleep. At least it's Saturday and I didn't have to get up early for classes and tonight, I have my first a gig at The Lower Deck.

Madelyn laughs and the sound fills my heart. Honestly, I'm so lucky to have Amy. She's a few years older than me, and happily married. She and her husband Doug are always inviting me over, but I just never have the time. Not only that, I think they're trying to set me up with one of their friends, and I don't have the time for that either. No. Thank. You.

I'm sure the guy is nice and all, but I'm not ready for any kind of relationship. I need to get my own life in order before I can bring anyone into it, and I'm very protective of Madelyn.

She does not need another man ditching her when he's gotten what he wanted from me. Besides, going to their house, with any guy, my choice or theirs, conveys seriousness in our relationship, and that's not going to happen for a very long time, if ever.

I smile at my little girl. I'll never regretting having her, even though I know the struggles of being a single mom. At least I have my mother to help me. Mom had no one, and I think she did a pretty damn good job, if I do say so myself. That thought makes me chuckle. I tug out my notebook and pen and lift my face to the sun as I silently run lyrics through my brain.

Feet pound the path behind me, as joggers run on the track circling the park. If I turn will I see Matt? I often see him running on the weekends, but up until the other day, he didn't know who I was. Not that he'd ever glance at the playground area. Why would he? Everyone here has a child and that's definitely not on his radar any time soon.

I have the weekends off from cleaning and cooking and while I'm happy for the reprieve—Matt always seems to be around when I'm there, no matter the time of day. Is he location tracking me or something? I laugh at that. After finding out I'm a mom, he's been keeping his distance, and for that I'm grateful.

Yeah sure, Kennedy. You know you want to bone him.

What the ever-loving hell?

"What?" Amy calls out, and I stiffen. Shoot, did I say that out loud.

"Oh, just working on some lyrics."

Bone him? Those words aren't even in my vocabulary, so why am I thinking like that?

"Which you're going to play for me soon, right?"

"You bet," I say, like I always do. I'm not ready to share my music just yet. I want to make sure it's good enough before I open myself up like that. I glance around the track. Why the hell am I looking for Matt?

I shake my head. What is going on with me? He's the last guy I should be thinking, dreaming and fantasizing about at night when I'm in bed all alone. He's a damn man whore and everyone knows it. But he's so darn nice to look at.

My heart leaps into my throat as he passes in front of my line of sight, dressed in nothing but his running shorts. His gaze shifts, and I quickly avert mine. Shit, did he see me staring... searching? I glance at my ever-astute friend Amy, who is angling her head as her gaze races over my face.

"What?" I ask lightly, praying she didn't see my ridiculous behaviour and knowing I'm wrong.

There's deep curiosity in her eyes as her gaze goes from me to Matt's back, and then to me again. "Something...or rather, someone I should know about?"

"No," I say quickly, and pray to God the heat crawling into my neck doesn't reach my cheeks and give me away.

"Then why did your eyes bug out of your head when you spotted that hottie running over there?"

"What?" I ask again and glance around, feigning innocence, and okay, maybe hoping to catch another glimpse of Matt. But he's long gone. "I have no idea what you're talking about." I focus on Madelyn. "Are you having fun, Madelyn?"

Amy laughs. "Oh, nice try."

"Oh, wait, that guy?" I point toward the running track when Matt appears again.

One hand goes to her hip. "Yeah, that guy."

"Oh, he's nobody." I tap my pen on my notepad. "I mean, I just met him. He's the one who hired me to clean Storm House."

"You mean the guy who stood up for you at the campus pub?"

"Yeah, that's the guy."

"He's cute, huh?"

I shrug. "I suppose some girls might think so."

"Not you though, huh? You're immune to broad shoulders, cut abs, and a face that looks like it was sculpted by Michelangelo?"

"You got all that from him running by?"

"No."

I eye her, and take in her smirk. "No?"

"No, I got all that from looking at him standing behind you."

I spin, and my notepad, pen and backpack go flying. The second I set eyes on Matt, standing behind me, all damp from running and breathing hard, I lose my ability to think.

"Hi," he says.

My God, did he hear Amy?

"Hi," I say and back up a bit as his pheromones curl around me. "What are you doing here?"

Ohmigod, Kennedy, way to ask a stupid question.

He jerks his head toward the track, and I pinch myself, anything to keep my eyes from dropping to take in his body. How is it possible that his abs are even harder than they were the other day, when I found him watching me in the kitchen?

Do not think about Matt and hard.

Goddammit, I'm thinking about it.

"Running."

"What?"

He puts his big hand on the bench, and leans forward to stretch out his legs. "Running."

"Oh, right, yeah—"

"Hi, I'm Amy."

I let loose a breath as Amy comes to my rescue before I say anything else.

"Nice to meet you. I'm Matt."

"Yeah, you are."

"What?" A grin plays with his lips and while I'm forcing myself not to stare, I'm also plotting ways to kill Amy, partly for putting that grin there, and partly for her comment. *Yeah, you are.* Seriously, Amy?

"I was just telling Amy you were the guy who hired me." I point to the track. "We noticed you running."

"You noticed me running?"

Okay, I can't tell if he's messing with me or not.

"Yeah, well, I happened to glance that way and you happened to run right in front of where I was looking."

"I noticed you here too."

"Oh." Before I can say more, he turns towards the kids. "Hi Madelyn," he says and smiles. It's easy to tell he's comfortable around kids, and I assume it's because he has a couple of younger siblings. His gaze moves to Chloe. "That's Chloe, Amy's daughter."

"Hi Chloe," he says and she gives him a cheesy smile that makes us all laugh. Poor Chloe is going through a stage where she's trying to perfect her smile, but just can't quite get it.

"I'm here, now it's a party," Beckett says as he comes jogging over, and I just laugh at him. He nudges Matt. "Hey Kennedy," he says casually like I'm one of them, but I'm not. They're a tight circle and I orbit somewhere outside it. I pull some animal crackers from my bag. "Are we running or is it snack time?" Beckett asks. "Oh wait, when it's animal crackers it's always snack time," Beck jokes. I open the box and hold it out to him and he snatches up a few crackers.

Matt shoves him and he nearly chokes on the dry cracker. "Beck, those are for Madelyn and Chloe."

"Who?"

"The kids," he explains and points.

"Oh..." Beckett holds a half-eaten cookie out. "Want it back?"

I laugh at their antics. "No, and there's plenty." I hand a couple to the kids and I shake a few more out for Beckett. I pull out two juice packs and add straws.

"You wouldn't happen to have another one of those, would you?" Beck leans forward and tries to peek into my bag.

"Beck," Matt warns and hands him a water bottle. "Drink this."

"I don't want your—"

"Drink," Matt says and Beck shrugs and takes a long pull from the bottle. He hands it back and starts stretching out.

"I guess I should finish my run," Matt says, not at all looking like he's in a hurry to go anywhere.

"Yeah, it's about nap time for these two."

"You coming to the party at the house tonight, Kennedy?" Beckett asks, and the question totally takes me by surprise. I've never attended—never even been invited—to a hockey party before.

"No, I have a gig, and then there's Madelyn. I don't like to leave her with my mom any longer than I have to."

"Oh, I can take Madelyn tonight," Amy kindly blurts out. Ohmigod, what is she trying to do here? I get that she'd like to see me with someone, but Matt is not that someone.

"No, that's okay. I have studying to do anyway." I point to the paper on the ground. "My lyrics..." Way to find all the excuses, girl. But seriously, spending more time around these guys isn't in my best interests.

Hell it isn't!

Okay, that was my ovaries screaming, not my brain.

In the distance, I see someone wave to me, and as she gets closer, I realize it's Piper Thorne. She slows down when she sees Matt standing next to me, the two of us in conversation. I don't think Matt and Piper are friends. I met her my freshman year, and while we're very different, we hit it off.

But the fact that Matt and I are in the playground area of the park, our bodies close, would make anyone stand up and take notice.

I wave to Piper, expecting an interrogation later when I run into her on campus. Beck makes a sound, a half snort, half groan, as he glares at Piper.

"Do you two know each other?" I ask Beck.

"Something like that." He goes back to stretching. "You're coming tonight," Beck announces, more of a statement than a question, and it's clear Piper is not someone he wants to talk about so I leave it at that.

Amy speaks for me. "Of course she's coming tonight."

"Amy..." Exasperated I turn to my friend, and she smiles innocently. I don't need to turn back to know Matt has moved closer to me. I can feel his energy, it curls around me, warms my blood and makes me jittery.

His hand brushes my thigh as he circles the bench, coming around to my side and putting his foot on the wooden slats to tighten his laces. The view is perfection, and don't even get me started on how his movement showcases his taut physique.

I nearly bite off my tongue.

I toss a cookie into my mouth to keep myself from moaning and he gives me a really sweet smile as he pulls himself up to his full height.

"I'll see you later, Kennedy."

He takes off running, and I stand there. Does that mean he wants me to go to the party, or does he mean he'll see me at the house when I'm cleaning it? I can't even imagine the mess it's going to be in after a party. Why again did I agree to cook and clean for a frat house? My daughter giggles, and right there, my friends, is the answer to that question.

"See you later," I call out as the two guys take off, and I forcibly tear my gaze away from Matt's cute butt and go attend to my little girl.

"He's cute."

I glare at Amy. "Are we doing this again?" Amy laughs and I add, "He's an egotistical, self-centered jock, who sleeps his way around campus."

"Damn, I need to get myself on campus."

I put one hand on my hip and frown. "You're married."

"And you're not," she shoots back, looking rather pleased with herself because yeah, I walked right into that.

While I glare at her, her words do affect me. It's true, I've been lonely, and that's probably why Matt's attention, his conversation, and his slight touches keep sending my brain into a tither. Honestly, when I left his place the other day, I was ready to borrow my daughter's soother and curl up in the fetal position. I'd be lying if I said I didn't like his touch, but I can't...I just can't get involved.

Why can't you?

If you're careful, and don't fall for him, why can't you have a little fun.

"Because I have a daughter," I whisper to myself.

Amy puts her hands on my arms, and her eyes meet mine. As she looks at me, I'm sure she can see deep into my soul, read my internal struggles.

"A happy mother makes a happier daughter," she says.

I open my mouth, about to protest, but she continues with, "You deserve to have a life too, Kennedy."

"I will, after college, and after—"

"There will always be an after. How about just this week, you concentrate on the now."

"Amy—"

"I'll watch Madelyn tonight. Chloe will love the sleepover. You..." She taps my nose. "Go to the party, and ride that boy like your car broke down and it's your only form of transportation."

I gasp, as she grins at me. Deep between my legs though. Not laughing. Nope, my sex isn't laughing at all. It's jumping to attention and after a long dormant year, ready to get some...

"But I'm not going to that party," I protest.

Amy glares at me. "You're going to the party."

I open my mouth to counter, only to shut it again.

Oh, God, I'm going to go, aren't I?

● **6**

MATT

It's nine o'clock, and I'm sitting on my bed, tossing a ball against my wall and catching it. Riveting, I know, and so not like me. Normally I'd be downstairs, the first one to the keg, but I'm not and I have no idea what the hell is wrong with me. Maybe I have a little idea, and maybe her name is Kennedy.

I can't even count how many times I've lectured myself on staying away from her, and while I plan to do that, I can't stop thinking about her. Let's be real, if I planned to keep away from her, why the hell did I run straight for her when I caught her watching me at the park today? The play area has never been on my radar before, and today I couldn't help but scan it, and much to my delight found Kennedy hanging out there. If I knew what was good for her, I should have kept running. Selfish bastard that I am, I hunted her down like she was prey.

My door is flung open and in walks Beck. "What the fuck are you doing?" he asks when he finds me on my bed, dressed only in my boxers.

I sit up and slide my fingers through my hair to brush it back. "What?"

He stares at me for a second. "Are you sick?"

I toss my ball at him and he catches it. "No, why?"

He tosses the ball back. "You look like shit."

"Thanks." I drop the ball and push to my feet as loud shrill laughter reaches my ears. Odd how that sound is annoying me tonight. Usually I'd be right there, partying and laughing along with the loudest person in the room. Yeah, it's true. I usually am the loudest in the room. I can see why Beckett is confused.

He takes a small tentative step toward me, his eyes narrow, assessing me. "Wait, are you okay?" he asks, a little more serious this time.

I turn away from his inspection. "Yeah, just tired."

"You want to talk about...*her*?"

Fuck.

"No idea what you're talking about." I walk to my dresser and tug a clean T-shirt out. I pull it on and finally face him—I guess the cat's out of the bag, so to speak—and he leans against my doorjamb, his arms folded like he's not going anywhere until I spill. "She has a kid," is all I say, but my words hold so much weight the air in the room grows heavy, and pushes down on my shoulders. "I just can't...you know."

He goes quiet for a second, and glances at the floor. A beat passes before his eyes lift to mine again. "You're right. You can't get involved with her. Let's go drink some beer."

Okay, so the fact that Beck gets it, and he's not trying to talk me into banging her, lets me know just how wrong it is that I'm thinking about doing just that.

"Can't get involved with who?" Tank asks as he comes bursting into my room.

Fuck, I don't want to talk to him about Kennedy. Tank eyes me. "Wait, are you hitting on the new housekeeper?"

"No, it's not—"

"Dude, I heard she has a kid."

Wow, word spreads fast around this place. "So?"

"So," he says looking at me like I'm thick and I have no doubt I am. "A girl like that, she's gonna get her claws into you man. She's probably looking for a baby daddy. A guy on his way to the NHL..." He rubs his fingers together. "A guy who can buy her a home and take care of all her needs."

"Shut the fuck up, man," Beckett growls. "You have no idea what you're talking about. Besides, my man isn't into her, right Matt?"

"Right." Lies, all lies. "Now get the fuck out," I say to Tank.

He shrugs and Beckett turns sideways so he can step into the hall. "Don't listen to me then, Milk Man. But I know what I'm talking about. Happened to my cousin's friend."

"Ignore him." Beck eyes me carefully and adds, "She's not like that, and none of this matters because you're not getting involved."

"Right." I nod toward the hall, and push Tank's words out of my brain. "I'll be right down."

He pushes off the door frame, eyes me for a quick second, and when another shrill of laughter rises up the stairs, he turns and disappears. I walk to my window and glance out at the streetlights. Really, it's for the best if Kennedy doesn't come here after her set tonight. I turn and tug on my jeans before heading down the stairs leading to the main level, where people are just starting to show up. I stupidly glance around, like a kid searching for Santa on Christmas morning, but of course Kennedy isn't here. Her set at the bar wouldn't even be over yet.

The front door flies open and in struts a couple cheerleaders. They run up and throw their arms around me, and I make small talk, all the while looking over their heads at the open door. No, I don't expect Kennedy to walk through, but I can't seem to help myself from checking.

Caitlyn smiles at me, and runs her fingers down my chest. "Catch up with you later, Matt?"

"Yeah, sure," I say. This is where I need to be, and these are girls I need to be with. They know what they're getting and what they're not when they crawl into my bed. The less I think about Kennedy or spend time with her the better, and of course that begs the question as to why I'm walking down the front steps, away from Storm House and toward the city's waterfront.

The din of the noise spilling from the house grows faint as I quicken my pace, the cooler night air falling over me. I would have grabbed a sweater had I known I'd be outside and for all I know, Kennedy is done her set and is home with her little girl. Maybe I'll catch up with her on the path, though. That is if she didn't drive to the waterfront pub, which she probably did because it's a long hike from her place. Not only can it be dangerous for a girl to walk home alone in the city, she has that big heavy guitar she lugs around.

I pass by numerous other students out partying—Halifax is definitely a college town—and I'm practically jogging, a weird sense of panic inside me as The Lower Deck comes into view, and music spills from the door as patrons come and go.

I step inside and my gaze goes straight to the small stage, and a sense of relief comes over me. Inching away from the crowd to stand against the wall, out of the way, I listen to Kennedy sing as she strums along. Laughter breaks out at one of the tables, and while it catches my attention, and my anger, it doesn't throw Kennedy off one bit. She was right, though, when she said no one listens. I resist the urge to walk over to the guy laughing and tell him to have some fucking manners. I don't. I won't do anything to jeopardize this job for Kennedy.

She finishes her song, rests her guitar on her leg, and takes a sip of water. As the crowd continues to talk, I step up to the bar, grab a stool and gesture for a beer. I sip it quietly as Kennedy checks her phone. Her lips curl, and it makes me happy that something on the screen made her smile.

She plays another song, and I can't take my eyes off her as she blocks out the noise and sings. A few guys come stumbling in, falling over one another, and squeeze around a table that's already full. A few of the guys keep checking out Kennedy and while I have no right to get pissed off, it doesn't stop me. Again, though...hands to myself.

My beer is about half gone as she ends the song and slides the microphone stand back so she can squat down and put her guitar into the case.

"Show us your tits," someone screams out, and I stop breathing, my hands fisting at my sides. Kennedy freezes for a split second and I'm impressed at how quickly she pulls herself together and resumes what she's doing. Way to keep it together, Kennedy, although she should never have to stand there and smile as some douchebag demeans her. Seriously though, I'm disgusted by the behaviour of my fellow male students and if I see that guy outside, he's going to say hello to my fist.

Kennedy steps off the stage, and I sit and debate about following her out the door. Stalkerish just a little? Okay, yeah, stalkerish just a lot. I take one last sip of my beer and head outside. I glance into the night, and spot her on the other side of the street. There might not be much to her, but the girl can move fast when she wants to.

I dodge an oncoming car and run across the street, catching up with Kennedy on the path. "Hey," I call out, alerting her to my presence so I don't scare the crap out of her. I'm not interested in having a guitar smashed across my head, and this girl is a survivor so I wouldn't put it past her.

She turns, and her eyes go wide. "Matt." She looks around, like she's searching for my friends, and I suddenly feel foolish for hunting her down. "What are you doing here?"

I jerk my thumb over my shoulder. "I was just checking out your show." She stares at me, and my foolish level jumps to a new degree. Shit.

"You guys are having a party tonight." She shakes her head, a few strands of hair spilling from the clip she's using to hold it together in a big knot. "Aren't you supposed to be there?"

"No one will notice I'm not."

She continues to stare at me. A moment passes and she starts to laugh. "Yeah, they will. From what I hear, you're the life of the party."

I step closer and the second her warm, vanilla scent fills my senses, I wish I hadn't. "Oh, you've been asking around about me, have you?"

"Well no...uh..." She stumbles a bit, and adds, "It's just that you hear things on campus."

"I'll make it there, eventually." Needing to do something—anything—because if she keeps wetting her bottom lip like that, I'm going to tug it into my mouth and devour it, I glance around. "Where's your car?"

"Oh, uh." She stammers a bit again, and almost looks embarrassed when she tells me, "I walked here, actually. It's such a nice night, and I could use the exercise."

Is she kidding me? If you turn her sideways, she'd disappear. "Come on, I'll walk you home." Without waiting for her to protest, I take her guitar from her, and start moving. I take a few steps, and I glance over my shoulder to find her standing still, her head tilted like she can't figure out what's going on. "Coming?"

She blinks rapidly. "Yeah." She hurries to catch up to me, and reaches for her guitar, but I hold it tight. "You don't need to walk me home."

"Why, are you going somewhere else? Change your mind about the party?" Something comes over her face, something that looks like I hit the nail on the head. Holy shit, she's going to the party. SHE'S GOING TO THE FUCKING PARTY. I work hard to ignore the ball of excitement expanding in my chest, making it hard to fill my lungs with air. I should not be this happy about her coming to the party —one I didn't even invite her to.

Oh, fuck.

"I was thinking about it." She gives a noncommittal shrug. "I wasn't sure, though. I brought a change of clothes just in case." Her laugh is nervous. "Although I wasn't really sure what to wear." That's when I notice her backpack. I take it from her and shoulder it myself.

She's about to protest and I just shake my head no. Clearly this girl is not used to other people helping her out, and dammit, it makes me want to do it all the more. Yeah, maybe that's the reason I want, and like, to be around her. Maybe I just went to the bar to help a girl out when she needed it and wanting to be around her has nothing to do with the appendage between my legs. Deep down I know I really, really shouldn't be trying to mess around with a girl like Kennedy—for her sake. Also there's a good chance it's Beckett she likes. Not that I think she should or shouldn't be with him, but hey, it's not my choice.

"You're fine," I say, my gaze taking in her sweater and jeans. I don't want her changing into something that might raise Beckett's blood pressure, and other body parts. My buddy won't go after her because he knows I like her—even though I can't have her—right?

Could this be any more fucked up?

A few people walk by us on the sidewalk, and someone I don't even know holds his hand up and gives me a high five before he turns to check out who I'm with. He looks as surprised as everyone else.

"I don't know." Her steps slow as she glances down at her clothes, second guessing herself.

"Come for a drink. If you don't want to stay, don't stay." I'm trying to sound casual, and not jealous that she's going because Beckett asked her to.

"You think?"

"Sure." I'm not trying to talk her into it or out of it, I don't think. I just want her to do what she wants, although I would be lying if I said I didn't want to hang with her a bit longer. "I'm sure Madelyn is having a great time."

She smiles at me, and it's the same smile she gave her phone earlier. "She probably is."

"Was that Madelyn on the phone, earlier?"

"What?"

"When you finished your song, you checked your phone and smiled. You just had that same smile." Okay, now I really am coming off as stalkerish, and goddammit, am I really jealous that she reserves those sweet smiles for her daughter?

Christ, I need a check-up and possibly some counselling.

"Yes," she says. "Amy sent a picture of them watching a movie, it was so cute."

"Can I see?"

She reaches for her phone and hesitates. "You don't have to do that."

"Do what?"

"Pretend you're interested."

I pull my phone from my pocket, and search through my photos. "This is Liam. My youngest brother." I hold out a picture of my brother on my lap, and she takes it from me. "He was only two there. I was ten."

"Big age gap." She smiles at the photo. "So adorable."

"Maybe, but he's a big pain in the ass too." My words are filled with love and admiration, and no matter how much my siblings get on my nerves, I'll always love them, and appreciate what they do for me.

"I bet you were a good brother."

I shrug. "I was okay." I might not have been much use on the farm, but I did like playing with my kid brother, and teaching him hockey skills. Grandpa really liked that. "We're actually pretty close. I love the kid. I'm tight with all my siblings."

"That's great, Matt."

I lift my chin, so proud of my kid brother. "But Liam, he's going to be the next great NHL Hall of Famer."

She arches a brow. "I thought that was going to be you."

I chuckle. "Time will tell."

She hands back the phone. "You want that, though. You want to be in the NHL?"

"I do. I love the game. It's my life. I'm not really good at anything else," I admit, then quickly add, "I don't really have much time for anything else, either." Shit, wait, I don't mean to sound upset by that, or ungrateful for all the opportunities handed to me. I was just stating a fact. Hockey is my passion and it's the only thing I'm expected to excel at. I've never been expected to do anything else and I can't lose focus, can't let anything distract me from the NHL. Grandpa wouldn't allow anything short of death keep me from playing.

She eyes me, going quiet for a second as we approach Storm House. "I know all about time, Matt."

I nod. "Maybe we're not so different after all," I say, even though she has way more responsibilities than I do. I've never had anyone rely on me and I bet it's all kinds of scary.

I take another look at my brother and me in the picture before I tuck my phone away. "You're right. He's kind of adorable." I smack my lips and give her a playful wink. "Going to be a heartbreaker, I bet."

She laughs, and our bodies brush. I suck in a fast breath, the heat from her skin wrapping around my dick and tugging. The fact that she also drew in a breath is a good indication that she's not immune to me either.

She pulls herself together much faster than I do and asks, "A heartbreaker, huh? So it's not just hockey you're teaching him, I take it." She playfully nudges me with her shoulder, keeping things light between us as the air around us charges, grows volatile. I glance up, expecting to see lightning streak across the sky, or at least fireworks.

"Hey," I say, trying not to sound like I'm sporting a boner. "I don't go around breaking hearts. For the record, a girl knows what she's getting with me."

Her steps slow, as I become the full focus of her attention. "And what exactly is that, Matt?"

I stiffen a little at her question. It really shouldn't have taken me by surprise. I just told her girls knew what they were getting, but I guess I never defined it before. "A good time," I tell her, and I have no idea why voicing those shallow, hollow words leave a huge knot in my gut. I mean, I know that's what I am. A guy with no substance.

She nods, accepting that. "There's nothing wrong with that, you know. If that's all you can give, and she knows it…" She shrugs. "I think the fact that you put that right out there is admirable, Matt. No expectations, no hurts. That's honest and smart."

Okay, why do I feel like this conversation isn't just about me anymore? Did someone fool her, hurt her, and trick her into believing there was more between them? Is that what happened with Madelyn's father? I want to ask, and I'm about to, but stop when she puts her hand on my cheek.

"Just for the record, it was you I was talking about in that picture."

7

KENNEDY

With bravado sizzling through my veins, I square my shoulders and start walking with a new kind of confidence, leaving an open-mouthed, shocked Matt behind me, clutching my guitar even tighter. I guess he didn't think I'd so blatantly tell him he was adorable —although I'm sure he hears it a lot from the bevy of girls who shadow him after a game, or before a game...or across campus. I'm really not sure what came over me, but maybe it was the fact that Matt is so completely open and honest when it comes to relationships—or lack thereof—and if something happens between us, which I want it to, I have nothing to worry about.

I'm not looking for anything that resembles a commitment— I have no time for that—and I'm not in the market for heartache. Matt isn't looking for anything serious, either. I don't know why that is, and his reasons are his own, but one night together? One night to remember what it feels like to be touched, kissed, pleasured...why not, right? Why shouldn't

I take Amy's advice and simply forget about life and responsibilities for just one night?

With my ex, I went into the relationship with rose-colored glasses, giving him my virginity and my heart, and look how that ended. God, he was so charming, so convincing, promising me the world, only to abort when the condom broke. It's all fun and games until someone gets pregnant, right? But hey it takes two to tango. Matt doesn't let any girl get her hopes up, and that I respect greatly. Others might not, but me, it's exactly what I'm looking for.

He jogs to catch up to me, and I take in the profile of his handsome face as he rushes past me, running up the stairs of Storm House to open the door. I smile at him as I walk inside, and he gives me a strange look, like he suddenly doesn't know what's going on or who I am. I'm the same girl as I was when we met at the bar, but tonight, my shoulders feel a bit lighter. Tomorrow things will go back to normal, and that's how I want it. I do have responsibilities, after all, and I'll just have to deal with seeing him while cleaning the frat house, and that's easy. I'll just change my hours.

A few heads turn my way as I enter, and I get it. I've never been to a frat party before. I stand still and soak in the noise, the ambiance, and the shrills of laughter coming from the kitchen. This is what I've missed out on, and I honestly think one night here will be enough to last me a lifetime.

A fine shiver goes through me when Matt steps up behind me, his breath warm on my neck. "Do you want a drink?"

I nod, and spot Piper in the corner, having a conversation with Beckett. I can't tell what they're saying, but I don't think it's a love fest.

"Don't go anywhere, I'll grab you a drink, and then put your bag and guitar in my room for safe keeping. I'll be right back, okay?" Matt says. I nod again, and I stare after him as he disappears into the kitchen. I walk slowly, moving around the room, taking it all in. Lots of the girls are in clothes so skimpy and tight they'd be too big on my daughter, but others are dressed in jeans and sweaters like me. I'm not as out of place as I thought I'd be. I meander, running my finger along the back of the sofa, and stepping on potato chips that I'll have to vacuum up tomorrow. But that thought is for tomorrow. Before I realize it, Piper snatches my arm and pulls me to her.

"What's going on with you and Matt?" she asks quickly, and I lift my gaze to find a worried set of eyes latched on to me. They belong to Beckett.

"Hi Beckett," I say.

"Hey, Kennedy. Glad you came." Strange, he doesn't look glad, and he was the one who practically insisted I come tonight. Maybe he's just upset with something Piper said to him or maybe he didn't expect me to come. Did Matt give him grief for issuing the invitation? That doesn't make sense, though. Matt wouldn't have shown up at the club and walked me here if he didn't want me at the party.

"Are you two..." I wave my hand back and forth between the two of them and if looks could kill, I'd be gutted and slayed by now. My God, I can practically cut the tension between the two of them with a dull butter knife.

"No," Piper says. "I've known Beck for years. We grew up in the same town." She snarls at him before she tugs me closer. What the heck is their deal? "What is going on with you and Matt?"

I don't miss the way Beckett moves a bit closer to hear my answer. Before I can tell them nothing is going on—yet—someone squeals and tugs Piper away. She yelps in response, and in the blink of an eye she's lost in the crowd, leaving me alone with Beckett.

Beckett moves from one foot to the other. Is he nervous or something? "Did you want a drink?" He holds out a red Solo cup. "I can grab you a beer or whatever you'd like."

"Thanks, but Matt is grabbing me one."

"Oh. You saw Matt?"

"I actually ran into him outside The Lower Deck. He was there to hear me play." His brow knits together as he swirls the beer in his cup before taking a long pull.

"Want me to show you around?"

I chuckle. "I clean this place. I already know my way around."

"Oh, right." He laughs. "Your lasagna was amazeballs."

"I didn't make a lasagna."

His jaw drops open. "Fuck, you mean I ate—"

"I'm kidding." I grab his arm, and his eyes shut.

He wipes his brow in a show of relief. "Thank God."

I look over my shoulder, but Matt seems to have disappeared. Is he not coming back with my drink? Maybe some cheerleader already has him undressed and in his bed. I'm not jealous. Not one tiny bit. It's just that I sort of set my mind on being in his bed tonight. I want that to happen before I stupidly chicken out, because the longer he's MIA, the more and more I'm starting to worry that I made a mistake.

"Come on," Beckett says quickly, tossing his arm over my shoulder to lead me into a room where a bunch of people are playing beer pong. "You can be my partner."

"I don't have a beer." As soon as the words are out of my mouth, a beer is thrust into my hand. "Oh." I glance into the cup. Should I even drink this? I might not be a party girl, but I know better than to drink from a cup handed to me by someone I don't know.

I spot Matt standing in the doorway, his body stiff, hard, as his gaze goes back and forth between Beckett and me. It's hard to tell from where I'm standing but I think I spot anger, and maybe disappointment in his eyes. He pushes off the doorway, walks up to me, takes the red Solo cup from my hand and replaces it with the one he's been holding.

"You never know," he says, putting his mouth close to my ear and sending waves of heat straight to the juncture of my legs.

"Matt..."

He stares at me for a moment, like he's at war with himself, and then a resolute look smooths out his features. He gives me a curt nod, and disappears, leaving me with Beckett, and I blink, confused. What the hell is going on? He comes to the bar to listen to me sing, walks me here and then leaves me? Was I wrong, thinking that he might want to have sex with me? The tension that enveloped us when we were walking and talking, was I the only one feeling it?

I take as sip of the beer and my stomach churns as it hits, but it's not the alcohol making me question my decisions. I was straight up sober when I decided to come here, and now for Matt to walk around like I don't exist... Okay, maybe it's not that bad, he did make sure my drink was safe, but still, to hand it over and walk away?

"Come on, it's your turn," Beckett informs me, his smile faltering only for a second as he glances over my shoulder and I get the oddest sense that there was some secret exchange between the two guys.

With my brain racing, I turn back to Beckett, and want to ask if Matt is okay, but he puts a ball into my hand, moves me until I'm lined up with the table, and tells me to throw. I toss the ball, and get it in the cup. Everyone cheers and the guys on the other side of the table take a drink. The next thing I know, I'm drinking, and as the game goes on, I grow weary of this whole scene. I really don't want to be here anymore.

I excuse myself, making an excuse that I have to go to the bathroom, and leave the room. I cringe as I walk around, watching drunk people spill food and booze. I came here to enjoy myself, to be part of something, to feel like I belong, but I am completely alone in this crowd. I spot Daisy, who waves me over, and I hold my finger up, indicating that I need a second. I don't want to be rude, but honestly I just want to get out of here.

I find the front door, and just as I'm about to bolt, someone comes barreling in, nearly knocking me on my ass, and that's when I remember my guitar. Groaning, and dreading what I might find if I go to Matt's bedroom, I keep my head down and hurry up the stairs, trying to avoid conversation. I hurry down the hallway, my steps slowing as I approach Matt's cracked door and hear his voice.

Shoot, he's in there with someone, and I don't even want to examine the sour taste in my mouth, and the upset in my stomach. I'm about to turn, but when he continues talking, his words rough and tortured and making no sense—and no one is answering—I stop. Is he okay? Did he drink too much? Maybe I should go get one of his friends.

You're his friend, Kennedy. Sure, you just met, and you were hoping for friends with benefits, but you're his friend, nonetheless.

I take a tentative step closer, and peer in to find Matt staring out his window. I steal a glance around, but his room is empty. I push on the door slightly and it creaks. Matt spins, his eyes wide when they land on mine.

"What's going on? What are you doing up here?" I glance around again, but there are no half naked girls in his room. "Who were you talking to?"

"No one."

Did some girl run and hide in his closet or something? I turn to look, but his closet is open and empty. Concern grows in my stomach. Maybe he really has taken one too many hits on the ice.

"Matt..."

He rakes an agitated hand through his hair, and stares at me. Everything about him is serious, intense, and tension is so thick in the room, I'm sure I could scoop it up with a spoon.

"Kennedy..." His voice is rough, and broken, as he backs up, and starts pacing the length of his room. "You...me...Beckett."

"What about Beckett?"

"You like him, I get it. No, I want to get it, I want to like it, he's a nice guy, but fuck. I have no idea what's going on with me. I want you, okay? I know I'm no good for you. I'm an asshole with a reputation. But I want you."

I put my arms around myself, suddenly chilled. "I don't think you're an asshole."

He stops pacing, and my heart races as he turns to face me. "But you agree with the reputation?"

"You do have one, Matt."

"Yeah, okay, so you have a kid and I don't want to drag you into my bed." He briefly closes his eyes. "No, I do. I do want to drag you in my bed." He pauses and says, "You're cold." As if acting on instinct, he crosses the room and holds his arms out, a question in his eyes.

"Yes," I agree.

He starts rubbing my arms. "I just can't, and this tension, or at least I thought there was tension, but you want to be with Beckett."

"Matt—"

"I came up here so I didn't have to see the two of you together, but I'm a fucking mess. I was trying to talk myself into not going downstairs, tossing you over my shoulder caveman-style, and coming back up here and depositing you in my bed."

I smile. Wow, Matt's always in control of himself, on and off the ice. I've never seen him like this before. But I guess I don't really know him that well either, and we're not going to get to know each other—other than physically, that is.

"Hey, Milk Man." While I want this, in the back of my mind, Cheddar's words lightly jangle. *She's too smart for that.* I don't want tonight to be smart, or responsible, or anything but a good time. No emotions, just pleasure.

"Yeah?"

"For the record, I was walking tonight, not for exercise but because my car has been making a funny noise." I reach up and tug the elastic from my hair, letting it fall over my shoulders.

His eyes narrow, his confused gaze moving over my face, not at all understanding why I'm bringing up my car when he's spilling his guts.

He calms a bit. "Okay...Did you need me to give you a ride, deliver you to your door, or something?"

"Yes and no. I want you to give me a ride, but not home, and I want you to deliver." I point to his bed. "Right there."

He angles his head and follows my finger. "Kennedy? What the...are you serious?"

"Yes." I step closer, my body bumping his. "I want to ride you like you're my only form of transportation."

8

MATT

No, no, no this can't be happening. I'm supposed to stay away from her. I promised myself I would, and I might be a man of little substance, but promises mean something to me, even promises to myself. But fuck me sideways. How the hell can I walk away, or tell her to leave when she's looking up at me with those big needy eyes, asking for something I can—just shouldn't—give?

"Kennedy," I whisper, and search her flushed face. All I see there is want, need and a hope that I'm not sure I have the strength to walk away from. One, because everything about her weakens me, and two, she came to me for something—me —and I don't think this is something she does often. I definitely don't want to hurt her feelings by turning her away, even though she probably shouldn't be with me.

As if reading my worries, she says, "Just tonight. Nothing more. No tomorrows." I swallow as my dick tries to overrule my brain. "I know who you are Matt, and what you're all about and tonight, just for one night, I want to forget about life for a while...with you."

Everything in the way she adds, *with you*, fucks with me, and not just physically. She wants me, and I want her, and I might be a lot of things, but I'm not a guy who's going to turn away a girl who's gazing up at him with pleading eyes. And let's be real here, I'm not altruistic by any means. I'm a selfish bastard, and yeah, this isn't just for her. Who would it serve to lie and pretend otherwise?

"If...if that's something you might want," she murmurs, her voice a little less sure now, probably because I've been standing here staring at her in silence as my brain works to formulate a response.

"Kennedy," I say again, my brain shutting down as my dick thickens, and presses against my unforgiving zipper.

Dazed eyes glance down, staring at the collar of my shirt. "I know I'm not the kind of girl you usually—"

"Don't," I growl quickly and loudly. Her eyes refocus, settling on my face. "You're beautiful, Kennedy. Too good for me, but you already know that. Just...don't compare yourself to anyone else, or think you're not the one I want to take to my bed tonight."

"You want me, Matt?"

"Yeah, I fucking want you, and I'm going to prove this isn't the room where fun dies," I add, to lighten the tension settling in my throat. Her grin curls around me, tugs at my balls, and I back up an inch, wanting a better look at her. "I thought you said you knew a lot about me..." I wave my hand around. "And about my room."

"I did."

"Then why are you still dressed?" A chuckle rumbles in her throat, and I smile, loving the sound and wanting to hear more of it. I step up to her, cup her cheek and bend my head. Heaven. I'm sure I died and went to heaven the second my lips touch hers and a soft moan of want rumbles around our bodies. I slide my other hand around her back and drag her even closer to settle her against my erection, putting to rest any doubt that I want her.

She moves her hips slowly, a soft massage of my cock. "Matt...please."

I break the kiss and brush her hair from her face. "You want to ride me, Kennedy?" I ask.

An almost sheepish look comes over her. "Amy sort of put that idea in my head."

"I knew there was a reason I liked her, but I need to know that it's what you want, too."

There isn't an ounce of hesitation about her when she answers. "It's what I want."

I inch back, and already miss her warmth as I circle her body and walk to my door. It shuts with a click, and Kennedy spins, her body physically reacting as I slide the bolt home.

I crook my finger and she takes three small steps and closes the distance. I pull her against me, kiss her sweet mouth again, and run my hands along her back until I'm cupping her perfect ass. Her hands rest on my hips as I move against her, my cock is desperate to slide inside her hot body.

"Now, about getting you naked." I spin both of us, until she's pressed against the door, and I stand back. Her fingers go to the hem of her sweater, and in one swift move, she pulls it over her head and tosses it to the floor. She pushes the top button on her blouse through the hole, and her chest rises with a little hitch in her breath. My gaze lifts, takes in the hesitancy that wasn't there seconds ago.

"Kennedy, if you don't—"

"I do," she answers quickly. "I want this, Matt." She toys with the button. "It's just...it's been a while."

I nod in understanding, step closer and take her hands and put them at her sides. "You don't have to be nervous."

She nods. "What if I'm not, if it's not good...I know you've had..." Big worried eyes blink up at me, and my heart jumps.

I take her hand and place it on my throbbing cock. "Just you being here in my room does this to me. I'll probably blow the second you get naked." That brings a smile to her face. "For the record, I was hard the last time you were in my room too."

"You get hard easy, huh?"

"Probably," I admit. "But I'm not sure I've ever been this hard." She smiles, humoring me. Obviously, she thinks it's a line. I'm about to tell her that it's not when she goes back to unbuttoning her blouse, and I lose the ability to form a struc-tured sentence. My gaze drops and I stare, transfixed, like a thirteen-year-old boy about to glimpse his first tit. What the hell is wrong with me? I don't know, but I can't wait to see, touch and kiss every inch of her.

She releases the buttons much slower than I would have. Heck, I probably would have destroyed that blouse, and left a pile of buttons scattered across my floor. I take a breath and keep my composure, right until she pops the last button and her shirt spreads, exposing the soft swell of her breasts.

Want.

I groan, and put my hands on her ribs, sliding upward to brush my thumbs over her nipples, hating that a piece of lace is keeping me from her lush tits. In a swift move, she reaches behind her back and unhooks her bra.

It falls forward to reveal gorgeous, lush breasts with my name written all over them. I toss the bra away, and bend to take a sweet, puckered nipple into my mouth. Her pert little bud swells beneath my soft licks, and white-hot need grips my balls.

"God, yes," she cries out and arches forward to feed me her breasts. My hands span her tiny ribcage again as I feast on her like she could very well be my last meal. Hey, at least I'd die a happy man. I slide my knee between her legs, and she moves against me, grinding her hot pussy against my thigh in a way that makes me want to turn her around and fuck her up against my bedroom door. Fuck, my cock aches for it. But it's been a while for her and if she's only asking for one night, then I want to make it exceptionally good and memorable, leaving her wanting more. Wait, what am I even saying? I'm never with the same girl twice.

Why then, do I already know this isn't going to be enough?

I drop to my knees and press my mouth to her soft, silky stomach, breathing her sweet scent into my lungs. As my cock aches for freedom, I pop the button on her jeans and just as I'm about to unzip them, the room goes dark. I freeze, and glance up at Kennedy as my eyes struggle to adjust.

"Did we lose power?" Music blares from downstairs, and I can see light seeping in beneath the doorframe, so I'm guessing we didn't.

"I thought...I turned the lights out."

I hesitate, and put my hands on her hips. "I want to see you."

"Matt..."

I take a couple of breaths and try to see this from her point of view. Most of the girls I'm with flaunt their bodies in sexy underwear. Although, Kennedy is a different kind of girl altogether, shy, and conservative, and there isn't a damn thing wrong with that. I stand, and cup her face, able to make out her features as my eyes adjust.

"Talk to me."

She swallows. "My body..."

"Your body is beautiful, Kennedy. You don't have to hide it from me." I dip my head and give her a soft kiss. "While I'd like to see you, if you want the lights off, we can keep them off."

"Thank you." Jesus, she's thanking me. I should be the one thanking her. She gives an almost nervous laugh. "I just... childbirth. C-section."

Fuck me.

Does she think I'm that shallow, that I'm going to be turned off of her body because it's not tight and perfect and might have scars? "It's okay. You don't have to do anything you don't want to do." I press my lips to hers, wanting to kiss away her worries while she's here with me, and when she melts into me, I'm sure I've succeeded.

With my arms around her waist again, I follow the path of the moonlight shining into my room and lead her to my bed, hoping I don't trip on anything. I safely reach my bed, and drop to my knees once again to tug her pants off. I get her naked and stay on my knees, pressing my mouth to her sweet pussy and widening her lips with my tongue.

Her hands grip my hair. "Oh God, Matt, that feels so good."

I run my tongue along the length of her, and her clit swells as I give it a couple extra licks with the soft blade of my tongue. She moves her hips, banging her body against my face, and I grip her outer thighs with my hands, sliding upward and around her hips until I'm gripping her ass. I squeeze her cheeks and pull her harder against my face.

Her hands touch my shoulders and tug at my shirt, and I stand, leaving her quivering as I reach behind my back and tug it off. Even though it's dark in the room, her moan of appreciation falls over me, and I groan as her hands slide over my skin, a slow, but needy exploration.

"You are so hard."

I laugh. "Don't I know it."

She chuckles and reaches for the button on my jeans, and she quickly has my pants open. I push them down until they're around my knees, and her gaze drops.

"I was wondering what these would look like on their owner." Her warm chuckle vibrates around my cock. "For the record, I might have imagined seeing you like this a time or two," she teases, having seen my boxers on the floor of my truck and on the back of my chair. She runs soft fingers under the elastic, and pulls it back. It snaps back against my skin.

"Hey," I say. "Wait, do they live up to your imagination?" God, why do I sound so needy?

"Not really."

My body stiffens and it's hard to see her expression as she drops onto my bed, moving out of the moonlight streaming into my room. "I should get dressed then?"

Her warm chuckle fills the room. "No, you should get out of them. Your boxers really aren't anything to write home about, Matt."

I tug my boxers down, along with my jeans, and kick them off, my dick as hard as granite. I step closer and cup the back of her head as her warm breath falls over my cock.

"Better?"

"Now this." She smirks, taking my cock into her small palm. "This lives up to my imagination, and is definitely something to write home about."

"Should I put that in my next email update to my family?" That makes her laugh hard, and I have to admit, I like making her laugh. "Dear Family, my dick has impressed Kennedy so much that from here on out, it will be her only form of transportation." My brain shuts down as pre-cum spills from my crown and she leans forward to lick me clean. "Fuck me."

"I like the sound of that," she responds, and swallows me deep, sucking so hard and thoroughly, I wobble on my feet. I grip her hair, and hang on as my eyes slip shut, wanting to do nothing more than to treasure the moment, treasure her. She cups my aching balls and massages lightly, like my pleasure is important to her. I can't remember the last time a girl cradled my balls. I'm not even sure they like it, but Kennedy sure as hell seems to like everything about my body, and in a few seconds, I plan to show her that I like everything about hers, and that her insecurities are for nothing when she's with me.

Her throaty moan reverberates down the length of my dick, and I tug on her hair gently to ease her off. "Remember what I said about blowing it?"

"I thought that was what I was doing."

I grin, and shake my head. She's funny and I like it. "I mean, if you keep that up, I'm going to lose it, and I'm not ready for that."

"Oh, are there things you need to do first?"

"If you must know, yes." I press my lips to hers, and push her down onto her back as I kiss her. I fall over her and her hands slide around my shoulders, and goosebumps form on my skin as she touches me. My mouth leaves hers and with my knees on the floor, and her legs wrapped around my back, I press my lips to her neck, wanting my mouth on every inch of her body. The lights stay off, I get it, but dammit I'm having a hard time, wishing I could see her. Everything about this night is going to fuel my fantasies for days, and I guess I'll just have to use my other four senses when I jerk off to the memory of Kennedy.

I breathe her in, and she moves her hips, her body so goddamn needy it's making me insane. I slide down, taking her breast into my mouth again, and suck long and hard, savoring the essence of her. She moans and groans and moves beneath me, and I love how worked up she's getting. Truth be told, I love that it was me she wanted tonight, and while I had tried to be okay with the idea of her liking my buddy, it was going to be really hard not to want to punch him. But he's a good guy, and he was looking out for my interests by trying to keep her away from me. I get that now, but what I don't get is why the fuck I'm thinking about anything but the woman beneath me, gyrating against my cock.

I push off her body, and stand. She reaches for me and moans in protest. "I'm not going anywhere." I climb onto the bed beside her, and move her to the center of the mattress, where I can have my way with her.

I put my finger in her mouth and she sucks it. Once it's wet, I trail it downward and circle her nipples, getting them nice and wet. She rotates and I put my finger in her mouth again as I shift closer and rub my cock against her outer thighs.

"Matt," she cries out, but I'm not ready to fuck yet. Well, I am ready, but first I want her sweet release in my mouth. I walk my wet finger down her stomach, going over a little raised scar low on her belly. She sucks in a breath, but her scars don't bother me. I go lower, until my hand is between her legs.

"Widen for me," I whisper.

She spreads wide, welcoming me in and her sweet cunt is so damn wet, my finger easily slides in. "Fuck, babe," I groan. My finger is met with small, tight quivers, and her breathing changes. She's so close, so needy, and while I want to draw this out, Kennedy is in need of an orgasm.

I move between her legs again and take her clit into my mouth as I slide my finger in and out of her. She tosses her head from side to side, her climax growing, building steam, and I add a second finger, giving her more to grip on to.

"Matt," she cries between pants, and I change the pace and rhythm, fucking her faster, harder.

"Yessss..." Her sweet hiss strokes my balls, and I nearly come as I glance up to see her eyes roll back, her body a shuddering mess as an orgasm takes hold of her. Perfect. She's so goddamn perfect when she comes. Her body quivers, her muscles squeeze my fingers, like a woman who hasn't been pleasured in far too long. I lap at her, drinking her all in as I slowly bring her back down, wanting to do this over and over again for her—if she'll let me.

She rakes her fingers through my hair and pulls me toward her. My mouth is wet with her juices as I find her lips and kiss her, starved for so much more.

"So good," she murmurs, but we're not done yet.

I inch back, pull a condom from my nightstand, and I rip into it. On the bed, I balance on my knees, ready to sheathe myself and slide home. Before I can put the condom on, Kennedy closes her hand over mine.

"Stop."

What the fuck? Now she's having second thoughts?

9

KENNEDY

Matt freezes for a brief second, and before I can speak, he inches back. "Yeah, sure. Whatever you want, Kennedy."

It takes me a second to comprehend that he's about to climb off the bed—hey my brain is still enjoying its post-orgasm bliss—but the second understanding hits, I shake my head fast and put my hand on his chest to stop him. "No."

"I know," he assures. "It's okay, Kennedy. I get it. No means no and I told you you'd never have to do anything you didn't want to do."

My heart swells and I take a fast breath working to keep my emotions out of this, but my God, could he be any sweeter?

"Matt," I say and inch forward, to wrap my mouth around his cock. I take him to the back of my throat, and he groans, and rocks into me, going a little bit deeper.

"Kennedy...what...what are you..." His voice is hoarse, cracked, and...full of confusion.

I let his cock fall from my mouth and keep my hands wrapped around it. "I didn't want to stop this." I gesture toward his erection, before I take the condom from him and wave it. "I wanted you to stop this."

His entire body goes stiff, and his eyes widen. Whoa, I have no idea what's going on in his head—honestly, I'd be surprised if he had any blood left, considering the size of his cock—but he looks a bit horrified.

"You want to have sex without a condom?"

"No," I say quickly. I don't trust condoms, that's how I got pregnant, and that's why I'm now on the pill. Matt has a reputation, and there are other things to consider.

He shakes his head. "I don't have sex without condoms."

"I don't blame you. I stopped you because I wanted to put it on you."

"Oh." A wave of relief softens the sharp lines in his jaw as he exhales. "I thought—"

I cup his face. "You know what, Matt? I'm sorry. I didn't mean to shout no like that, and I really love how you didn't question me, or push me for more when you thought I wanted to stop." I lean forward and place a soft kiss on his mouth. "The world needs more guys like you."

"I don't know about that."

"I do."

He might be a player, but deep down, I think he's one of the good ones. I'm not sure why he doesn't believe that about himself, and tonight is definitely not the time to examine that further. I take the condom from the wrapper and place it on his crown. A hard quake goes through him as I roll it on, and I smile at his reaction.

"Oh fuck, that feels good."

I give his chest a shove and he falls backward, flat on his back, right where I want him. Repositioning, I toss my legs over him, and there's heat in his eyes as his warm hands stroke my outer thighs and hips.

"Is this the part where you ride me?" he teases.

I fall forward, my breasts squished against his chest as my lips find his. "Yes," I say.

Big hands span my waist and easily lift me. He positions me over his erect cock, and I moan as he begins to pull me down. His crown breaches my opening, and I gasp as he stretches and fills me. He slows the pace to give me a second to get accustomed to the feeling, and the second I begin to move my hips, trying to drop down, desperate for him to impale me, he tightens his hold to control the pace.

He inches his cock into me, painfully slow. "Easy," he whispers. "I don't want to hurt you."

Once again, my heart swells with his sweetness. He offers one glorious inch at a time, going still inside me as his crown presses against my cervix. My entire body quivers, and he lets go of my hips to take my breasts into his big, warm palms. I arch into his touch, his cock deep and full and still inside me. I gently move my hips, rotating around his cock, and smile, revelling in the way his eyes roll back in his head. I like seeing this guy come unhinged with me on top of him.

I press my hands to his chest and rock against him, and he grips my breasts tighter, not in control of himself. I lift a bit, and slide back down hard. I repeat the motion, and grind my clit on his pubic bone, a new kind of pleasure building inside me. God, his cock feels so good inside me, so thick and deep, and every time I lift and drop down again, the hit to my cervix reverberates through my entire body.

"Fuck, Kennedy," he groans.

He grips my hips, taking pressure off my thighs as he lifts me and pulls me back down again and again. We move together, oblivious to the party going on outside the door, and our bodies bang and rock together. My body burns, moisture breaking out on my skin, and I can't believe I'm close to having a second orgasm. Yeah, clearly, it's been too long since I've been touched, and I'm sure I've never been pleasured by such capable hands before.

He lifts me, and I expect a downward tug, but instead, he keeps me high, and I balance on my knees. I'm not sure what he's doing, but I'm game for anything. He lifts his hips, powering into me, and it drives the air from my lungs.

"Oh, yes," I cry out and slide a finger between my legs, to rub my clit. He glances down and with his encouraging groan of pleasure I let loose a keening cry, forgetting about everything but the delicious heat building inside me and spreading through my body. I'd like to say I'd forgotten how good sex was, but I'm not so sure it was ever this good with my ex. Then again, he was probably coming to me spent and tired. You know, because he had a wife at home in need of satisfaction too. Yeah, and I can see how me getting pregnant would put a damper on that.

But I don't want to think about that right now.

I dip my head, watching, loving the way my nether lips hug his pistoning cock as he drives in and out of my body. I am so wet, it's dripping down his cock and my thighs. His grip on my hips tightens, hard enough to leave tiny finger bruises tomorrow, as his face twists, like the pleasure is too much to bear. I can't believe I do this to him. I mean, I can't believe I'm here in the first place.

"Ride me, baby," he begs, as I begin to move, meeting him halfway. I meet his intense gaze and hold it as another blissful wave washes over me and takes me on a journey of sheer pleasure. My body breaks again, a full-on body orgasm wrecking me from the top of my head to the tip of my toes. I cry out and lean forward as my spasming muscles suck his cock in deeper.

"Jesus, yes," he grunts as I come all over his cock. He brushes my hair back, and inches up, pulling my mouth to his. He kisses me deeply as I keep coming, and his kisses slow, his cock stilling high inside me as his head drops back to the bed and he spurts out his release. His face twists again, and my body absorbs each pulse of his cock as he depletes himself.

We're both breathing hard, eating up the oxygen in the room as we ride the high. I fall over him, rest my cheek against his strong, pounding heart. His hands lightly travel from the small of my back to my hair. He gathers it in his hand and smooths it over my shoulder. It's so weird. His touch is so soft and gentle, tender even, which is such a contrast to this big, bad defenseman with a reputation. But nothing in the way he's touched me, kissed me, or pleasured me was selfish. Not at all. His touch exudes warmth, as he cares for my body.

A fine shiver races through me as my heart takes a few extra beats. *Do not go there, Kennedy. This is sex, and sex only.*

He rolls me to my side, quickly disposes of the condom and settles in next to me. His big arms circle me, his hug curling around my heart, as he pulls the blankets over me, tucking me in on the outside, a gesture so simple, yet so sweet. God, I am so pathetic and needy. I guess that's why it's so easy for me to read more into things when I know better. Lessons learned and all.

He runs his fingers through my hair. "You warm now?"

"Yes," I croak out, sounding like a damn frog, and he inches back to see me. "Dry throat," I say, and he nods. God, the last thing I need is for him to think I developed feelings after one round of orgasmic sex. I am far too smart for that.

"Mine is too. Hang on." He gently eases me off his chest and fluffs a pillow around my head. He tugs on his clothes, and I admire the silhouette of his body in the moonlight shining into the room. "I'll be right back." He quickly leaves his room, and I tug the blankets to my chin. Now that I'm alone in his room, I'm not sure what to do. Get dressed and get the heck out of here, or snuggle in with Matt when he returns? I certainly know which sounds better, and with Mom no doubt sleeping, and Madelyn having fun at a sleepover, I really have no reason to escape. Besides, tonight is all about me. In my heart, I know it's okay to have a me day, but as a mother, I can't quite shake the guilt.

Another thought hits me. Does Matt want to get back to the party? It's at his frat house, so he probably does.

The door creaks open, and he steps in, locking it behind him. I expected him to bring me a red Solo cup full of beer, but no, he has two water bottles and for that I'm thankful. I sit up, and the blankets fall, exposing my chest. Even though the lights aren't on, his eyes drop fast, and I quickly pull the blanket up.

"Get over here, Milk Man," I tease.

"Can I turn on the lamp?"

"Sure." He sets the bottles down, and I wince as he flicks the light on. I study his body as he tears his clothes off again, and jumps into bed with me. He hits the mattress so hard, it nearly knocks me to the floor. I laugh as he grabs me.

"Sorry about that."

He cracks the bottles and hands one to me and I take a big gulp. He does the same, finishing half the bottle off in one big slurp. I set the bottle down, and throw my feet over the side, hiding the scars on my stomach as I search for my clothes.

"Kennedy?" he says, his voice soft, confused, full of...vulnerability?

I glance at him over my shoulder, and wish I hadn't. My God, there's such a sweetness about him, a warmth and openness that peeks over the barriers protecting my heart.

"You should get back to your party." He goes completely silent, a hurt look in his eyes as he blinks.

"Is that what you want?"

Does what I want matter? Honestly, when has what I ever wanted mattered, and when was the last time anyone asked me that? I really don't know. "I just mean, it's your place, your party, your friends. They're probably looking for you." I try to make my voice light when I say, "You have fans to please." Yes, I'm talking about all the girls, and I'm sure he knows it. I just hope I don't sound jealous because I'm not.

Not much, anyway.

"Do you have to go, Kennedy?" His lids dip, low over his gorgeous eyes. "Is there somewhere else you want to be?"

"Well no, but you must want—"

Before I even realize what's happening, he's pulling me back and tucking me under him, pinning me in place with his big body. "You think you know what I want, do you? You spend one hour in my bed and have my life all figured out?" He's teasing, I get that, but there's something else, something more, something deep and dark and insecure that he hides from the world, and maybe himself.

I laugh. "I'm not sure how that's possible, when I don't even have my life figured out."

"What are you talking about? You're going to be a famous singer, remember?"

"Right now, I'm just trying to get through the teething years." Shit, why did I bring up Madelyn? Why would he want to hear about my struggles after a glorious round of sex?

"I remember those days," he says. I angle my head, not at all getting it, and he continues with, "I'm not saying I had it as tough as you, not even close, but my youngest brother's room was right across from mine, and ugh, he would cry all night. So, I get the crying but I didn't have to get up with him and then go to school and everything else you do in a day."

"She's worth it." I yawn, and he rolls off me and tucks me in next to him.

"You're a good mom." I smile, even though he doesn't really know if I am or not. "Now sleep," he commands in a soft voice.

"Sleep..." I moan, and my eyes fall shut. "The other awesome s-word."

He chuckles. "No interruptions until morning."

"Not even if I wake up in the middle of the night and want to have sex again?"

"Correction, no interruptions unless you want to have sex, which I hope you do."

I chuckle as I relax, and he lightly brushes my hair in a gentle manner that's so calming.

"Fine, but I can't stay until morning. I am not doing the walk of shame."

"There's no shame in what we just did, Kennedy." I take a big breath and as I release it, expelling every ounce of tension inside me, he goes very, very quiet. I'm about to turn to see if he's okay but stop when he asks. "Are you ashamed?"

"No, not at all." I flip over to see him. I smile at him and he smiles back. There's something very sensitive and deep about this man.

"Good. Does that mean we can do it again?" His grin is sexy and devilish and so damn tempting.

I lightly tap his cute nose. "You're not supposed to be sleeping with the housekeeper."

"Fine, you're fired." I'm about to sit up, shocked at his words, but he holds me down. "I'm kidding. The guys would kill me if I fucked things up with our awesome new housekeeper. They're still raving about your lasagna."

"Really?"

"Yeah…" He dips his head and presses his soft lips to mine. "That's only because they haven't tasted your lips."

I smile at his corniness. "Are you saying you're going to rave about my lips?"

"No, did you miss the part where I said they'd kill me if I fucked things up with the new housekeeper?" I laugh, loving his playful behaviour. "They're not going to, either, Kennedy."

My voice is low and tired when I ask, "Not going to what?"

"Taste your lips," he answers.

Wow, did I just hear possessiveness in his voice. I want to examine it, probably overthink it, but a few hours of uninterrupted sleep is too tempting.

"Okay," I say, my brain no longer functioning. "No tasting."

"Now sleep."

"Just for a bit," I whisper and snuggle in. I close my eyes. I cannot, will not stay the night. I can't mess up this job, get Matt in trouble with his frat brothers, or...fall for him.

My lids flicker open. Why on earth is it light out and where the heck is Matt?

MATT

I wake early as Kennedy moves in her sleep, stretching her arm out and smacking me in the face. I chuckle softly, and set her arm by her side, and pull the blankets up to keep her warm. She's always so damn cold. I steal a glance at the clock. It's early, and she didn't want to stay—heck, the last time I let a girl sleep over was never—but I didn't have the heart to wake her. She needs the sleep, and I just hope she's not pissed at me for not waking her.

I quietly slip from the bed and tug on my clothes as she makes a soft little moan and rolls over. My chest tightens a bit as I stare at her. She's a girl with lots of responsibilities—one who probably never asks for help—and I shouldn't be fucking around with her. I can't help it though, and there's a very big part of me that wants to help lighten her load. Although I doubt she'd ever allow it. What if she had no say in the matter?

I quietly crack my bedroom door. The house is quiet when I step into the hall and make a quick trip to the bathroom. I wash up and brush my teeth, and tiptoe downstairs, and take in the big mess—a mess I've never had to clean up before.

Before I tackle anything...coffee. I toss a pod into the machine and brew a cup. As I sip, I walk through the house. You know what? I think I might be getting tired of all this shit. I grab the trash can and walk around tossing cups and trash into it. I find a pair of panties on the sofa and toss them in too. I'm a little pissed that the place was left in this state for Kennedy to clean up.

I spend a good hour just picking up garbage, and I head outside to drop the bags into the trash bin. I step back inside, and I'm about to go to the kitchen for more coffee, but stop as Kennedy comes tiptoeing down the stairs. Backpack over her shoulder, guitar in hand, she has her head down and is moving quietly, and I don't want to frighten her, so I stand still, waiting for her to notice me. Is she sneaking out? Shit, she's probably mad I didn't wake her. One of the steps creaks and she cringes, her head lifting. Her eyes meet mine and go wide.

"Matt," she whispers. She looks around. "What...what uh, what are you doing? I thought..."

I could ask her the same, but I don't. "I woke up, thought I'd clean up a bit. Do you want coffee?"

"I..." She looks past me at the open door. "I should go."

"I can make it to go if you like."

She hesitates for a quick second. "Okay, that sounds great, actually."

I quietly close the door, and angle my head toward the kitchen. I toss another pod in the machine, and she takes a seat at the table.

"You were cleaning?"

"I didn't think it was fair to leave this mess for you," I explain. "I don't want you quitting after your first week." Her smile is soft and grateful.

"Thank you, but you didn't have to do that. You didn't even make any of the mess."

"Neither did you." I meet her eyes, take in the dark smudges. "Did you sleep okay?"

She stretches her arms out. "I don't remember the last time I slept that well. Thank you for letting me sleep in."

The coffee finishes dripping into the cup, and I pull it out, place it in front of her and grab the milk and sugar. "I thought you might be upset."

Her hand stops as she reaches for the milk. "It was really nice," she whispers.

I smile at her, and drop into the chair across from her. "When you first saw me, you said, I thought...What did you think?"

"Oh." She sighs and pours milk into her cup. "I just thought you were out running or something."

Christ is she used to guys running out on her? "I didn't want to leave my bed, not when you were in it, but I wanted to tidy up a bit."

She gives me a grateful smile before she takes a sip of coffee and my heart tightens.

"What are your plans for the day?"

"I'll probably take Madelyn to the park, and do some studying when she naps. You?"

"Practice, study, nap." She laughs, but it's clear we both lead very different lives. She takes another big sip of coffee.

"I should get going."

She stands and I stand with her. She gathers her things, walks to the door, with me following. She walks outside and so do I. She narrows her eyes, and shades the early morning sun with her palm. "What are you doing?"

"Taking you to get Madelyn."

"It's okay, I can walk."

"I can drive."

"You don't have to do that." Her backpack slips on her shoulder and I slide it off, tossing it over my own. "Amy just lives down the street from me."

I walk to my truck, and open the passenger side door. I wave my hand for her to climb in. "Come on, I'm giving you a ride." As soon as the words leave my mouth, her cheeks turn pink. Yeah, I'm thinking about the ride we had last night too. My fucking mind is blown. "I'm going that way, so you might as well tag along."

She laughs nervously as she comes toward me. "Oh, and why were you going that way?"

"To drive you," I say and take her guitar from her, closing her door after she gets in. I put her things in the back and circle the truck. She pulls her phone from her pocket to check messages as I slide into my seat, and start my vehicle, turning the heat up as she shivers beside me. I'd really like to warm her up by taking her back to bed.

I head toward her place, and she points to Amy's house. "Will they even be up? It's still early." She raises her brow. "What?"

"Did you really just ask that?"

"Okay, right. What was I thinking?"

"Just pull over here." She points to an empty parking spot on the street.

I ease the truck into a spot, and take off my seat belt. "Thanks." She reaches for her door, like she can't wait to escape.

"I can wait, drive you both home?"

"No," she says so quickly, my head rears back.

"Okay."

Her hand closes over my arm. "Matt," she begins. "I'm sorry. I just, I don't want..."

"You don't want Amy to know you spent the night with me."

"She knows, she was the one who suggested it," she admits with a laugh. "I don't want you to take this the wrong way, but I'm just very careful who I bring into Madelyn's life."

"I can understand that, Kennedy."

She nods, and there's a deep sadness in her eyes as she stares out the window. "She's had loss, you know."

"So have you."

Her gaze jerks to mine, surprise in her eyes. "What?"

"I don't know your circumstances. I don't need to know if you don't want to tell me. But it's clear whoever Madelyn's father is, he hurt the both of you."

Her shoulders sag. "He's not in our life anymore."

"I figured that." My hands tighten on the wheel. What kind of fucking guy walks away from his child? "I'm sorry."

"It's better this way," she says, trying to smile as she puts a twist on this. "I don't want a guy like him in Madelyn's life." I nod, in understanding.

"I believe you. I grew up with two parents, and I'm lucky because they're really great. Honestly, they always cut me slack so I could play hockey."

"That's great, Matt."

"Yeah."

"Why do you sound upset about it, then?"

Okay, she's intuitive, I knew that. "I'm not." I'm not about to get into woe is me with a girl who's having a hard time in life. Could I be any more of an asshole for just thinking it?

She eyes me, something akin to worry and disbelief swimming in her dark eyes. "I guess what I'm trying to say is I'm not one of those guys who believes a child needs both a mother and a father, when one of them isn't good to be around. Know what I mean?" Is that even coming out right?

"I do, and that's exactly how I feel. Growing up, it was just Mom and me. She gave me great opportunities, and I'm not lacking because I didn't have a male influence."

"You didn't know your dad?"

"No, I think she kept me from him on purpose." She gives a humorless laugh. "I followed Mom's example. I guess the apple doesn't fall far from the tree."

"In this case, it's not a bad thing. Your mother sounds like a wonderful woman, and you've followed in great footsteps."

Her smile wraps around my chest and constricts it. "Mom still helps me with Madelyn."

My heart warms at the love I hear in her voice as she talks about her mother, who clearly has a lot of belief in her daughter. "That's great, Kennedy."

She opens her door. "I better get going. I'm sure Amy must be pulling her hair out by now."

I put my hand on her arm. "Um, for the record, I really enjoyed last night."

A smile touches her lips. "For the record, I did too." She's about to get out and stops. "Hold it, who's keeping these records?" Her eyes widen as she feigns worry. "Oh, God, was I supposed to be doing that?"

Unable to help myself as she lightens the mood, I grip the back of her head and pull her mouth to mine. At first she's taken by surprise and goes stiff. It doesn't deter me. I kiss her gently, lightly brush my tongue across her lips and she moans and melts into me.

She pulls back and we're both breathless as she opens her door. It's probably a good thing she's escaping before we end up sprawled across the seats, finishing what I started. That would not be good, considering it's broad daylight and she has her daughter to collect. She gathers her things from the back, and my gaze follows her as she walks up the pathway to the front door. It opens and her friend Amy pops her head out and gives me a smile and two thumbs up. Kennedy shakes her head as I wave back and laugh. I think Amy is about to put my girlfriend under the microscope, wanting an in-depth play by play of last night.

Girlfriend?

Sure, she's a girl and my friend, and if I have to put a label on last night—and I don't really think that's necessary—but I'd call it a girl needing a little less reality, and a guy happy to give it to her. Yeah, I think that nicely sums it up. Why then, as I put my truck into gear, do I already miss her presence?

I crack the window, needing a bit of air as I drive back to the frat house. The place is still quiet—mostly—when I enter. Whispered words reach my ears as I walk into the kitchen and find two half-dressed girls standing there. Coffee in hand, they turn to me.

"Where were you last night?" Vanessa asks, her friend Tanisha raising her brow at me. "I looked everywhere for you."

I walk up to the sink, and run water and soap into it. "Sorry I missed you."

She goes quiet for a second. "Were you with that girl?"

"What girl?" I ask, my body tightening. I am not about to discuss Kennedy, or what we did with them.

"That singer. I saw you with her, then she was with Beckett, and that was the last I saw of her."

I mumble something about that not being her concern. Tanisha laughs. "My God, what would he be doing with her, Vanessa? Now Beckett I can understand. He'd screw anyone, even that weird guitar-girl."

"What the fuck." I'm about to lose my shit and show them where the front door is when Vanessa's mug hits the counter, and she walks up behind me. She puts her hands on my shoulders and starts rubbing. "God, you're so tense."

Normally I wouldn't mind being touched by one of the cheerleaders, now...I don't know, it sort of feels like cheating, of course I'm not, and I sure as hell don't appreciate them talking about Kennedy like that. I shrug her off and she makes a gasping sound.

"I'm good, Vanessa, and just so you know, guitar-girl's name is Kennedy, and if I ever hear you say anything rude about her..." I pause and point down the hall toward the front entrance. "You'll never walk through those doors again. Got it?"

They both stare wide-eyed. "What's gotten into you?" Vanessa finally asks.

What's gotten into me indeed? Or maybe it's what I've sunken into, and the answer to that is Kennedy and it's somehow messing with me.

"What's going on here?" Beckett asks, as he comes into the kitchen rubbing his bare chest. The girls flock to him.

"I think Matt woke up on the wrong side of the bed."

"Yeah, well both sides of my bed were empty," he says with a grin. "I need coffee."

He says something to the girls quietly and they both walk out of the kitchen. "You good, bro?"

"Yeah."

"You hook up with Kennedy?"

"Yeah."

"Can you say more than yeah?"

"Yeah."

He laughs and I hand him a mug of coffee. He glances around. "Did she clean before she left?"

"Something like that."

He eyes me for a moment, and I tug my phone from my pocket to see a message from my kid brother. "Weren't you supposed to *not* fuck with the new housekeeper?"

I drop down into the chair. "She's not going to quit." I don't think.

"You okay?"

"Yeah."

He chuckles. "Good. We have the visit to the children's hospital today."

"That's today? I thought that was next week."

"Nope, it's today, right after practice. You can make it, right?

"Of course." I'm not going to renege on my responsibilities. Besides, I like visiting the kids' hospital, and putting much-needed smiles on their faces.

I liked putting a smile on Kennedy's face too. But those thoughts are for another time, like when I'm alone in bed tonight, my hand on my dick. Unless of course, I can convince her to join me. Which I highly doubt. Besides, last night was a one-night thing. She never really answered me when I asked if we could do it again. I guess that means she doesn't want to, and I get it. She said she knew who I was and what I was about.

Does she though? Honestly, I'm not sure she can, when I myself don't really know who I am.

By the time I get home, after spending the rest of the morning gabbing with Amy as the kids played, Madelyn is tired again, and in need of a nap. Even though I slept well last night, I'd love to crawl into bed, and put last night on repeat in my brain, to try and figure out what possessed me to have sex with Matt. It's true, I am lonely, and I wanted to be touched, but maybe it really was a bad idea. I should have been stronger, and kept my distance. At least this morning wasn't awkward, and wow, I can't believe he was cleaning up to save me the trouble.

Now it's time to put him out of my mind, change up my hours when I clean, and tuck the memories of last night away. I'll pull them out when I'm lonely, and hope they leave me satisfied and not simply wanting more.

"Okay, chicken nugget," I say to a cranky Madelyn. "I know you had a lot of fun playing with Chloe, and it wore you out. Time for a nap." I drop my backpack and guitar on the table after entering the house and read the note on the table by the door. It makes me smile. I really don't know what my mother has against texting. I guess she's just old school. Her note lets me know she's going to be having dinner at Leo's place tonight, and not to wait up for her. That's code for she's probably staying overnight at his house. She never brings him here. Is she trying to protect me from the hurt of loss if things don't work out and they break up, much the same way I protect my daughter? I'm a grown woman for goodness sake. Still, I love that Mom cares so much about Madelyn and me.

I smile as I set the note down and shift Madelyn in my arms. It gives me great pleasure that Mom is spending time with a great guy like Leo, and that she's finding happiness in life again. She deserves it. I guess I deserved last night too, and really while I'm not sure it was my best decision, I'm not going to feel any kind of guilt over it.

"Juice," Madelyn whines. I slip off her coat and carry her to the kitchen where I grab the juice from the fridge and pour some into a sippy cup. Deciding I need a few snuggles before putting her to bed, I walk to the living room and settle in the rocking chair. She takes a few sips of her juice and I turn her to hold her over my shoulder. I hum lightly while rocking, and Madelyn's eyes aren't the only ones closing. I briefly shut mine and the next thing I know, a loud cry and an ungodly scream shocks me awake.

My lids fly open and I'm out of the chair in less than a second as Madelyn sits on the floor wailing. She puts her hand on the back of her head. I scoop her up, touching the big goose egg forming, and I can only surmise that she fell from my shoulder and hit her head on the coffee table. At least there's no blood, but what if there's internal bleeding? Every horrible scenario runs through my mind and it takes every ounce of my determination to keep my panic at bay.

"Madelyn, I'm so sorry." God, this was all my fault. I shouldn't have closed my eyes. I should have stayed awake. If I wasn't so tired from last night... Maybe this is some kind of punishment for shirking my responsibilities. Running on instinct, I put her coat back on, snatch up my purse and keys, and hurry to my car. I don't care if it's making funny sounds, I need to get her to urgent care and have that swelling looked at. She could very well have a concussion.

Her tears are falling hard as I get her into her car seat, and I cup her face and kiss her. "I'm so sorry, sweetheart. We're going to go get it checked out." I hurry to the driver's seat and my phone pings. Maybe it's Matt checking on me, but no we never exchanged texts, so it can't be him. Doesn't matter, I have no time to answer it now.

I drive as fast as I can to urgent care, and find a parking spot. I didn't even remember to bring her diaper bag or anything. Hopefully they'll take us in right away. In the waiting room, I hurry to reception, and it's hard to speak with Madelyn still crying.

I finally explain to the lady what's going on, and she sends me to another room for the nurse to give Madelyn an assessment. I rub Madelyn's back and follow the nurse.

"Kennedy?"

I spin at the sound of Matt's voice and stand there for a split second trying to figure out what's going on as my brain races to catch up. His gaze goes from me to Madelyn, and his blue eyes widen, equal amounts of shock and worry spilling across his face.

"Is Madelyn okay?"

"No," I blurt out quickly, my emotions finally getting the better of me. "She fell and has a big bump on her head. The nurse is going to assess her."

"Okay, come on." Without hesitation, he puts his arm around my back, and gives me a nudge to get me walking. I follow the receptionist, who has stopped at an open door.

"Have a seat in here," she says, and Matt follows me in.

I hug Madelyn to me, and swallow, desperate to get myself together for my daughter's sake. The nurse steps in and begins her assessment. She checks out Madelyn's eyes, pulse and asks me a few questions as I root through my purse looking for Madelyn's health card. With Madelyn squirming, it's hard to find anything.

"Let me help," Matt urges, and I'm not sure whether to hand over my purse or Madelyn. I finally give him my purse. "In my wallet." He nods, and pulls out my wallet, searching the cards until he finds the right one, and I am not sure why but his solidness, strength, and presence helps calm my frayed nerves. I've never really counted on anyone other than my mother, and I didn't want to disturb her today, so it's really nice to have another adult with me—one who is likely thinking with a calmer head than I am.

He hands over the card and I give him a grateful smile. Once the nurse enters the information into the computer, she pushes to her feet. "I'm going to take you right in."

I stand on shaky legs and glance at Matt. "That's bad, right?"

"No, she's a baby and a priority. The fact that she's not vomiting, or falling asleep, is a good thing. Trust me, I know a thing or two about concussions, and you did the right thing bringing her in."

He begins to follow me to the double swinging doors. "You don't have to..." I shake my head, having taken up enough of his time.

"I'm not leaving you." He pushes through the doors and holds them open for me. I don't have the time or energy to argue, and honestly, I don't want to admit how much I like that he's staying, or that I secretly wanted him to say he would. We're led to a small examination room, separated from the others by a curtain. There are two chairs and an examination table. I sit and Matt sits down next to me. He pulls a puppet from his pocket, and I stare at it, wondering if I'm the one who banged my head and now I'm currently hallucinating. Why on earth would Matt have a puppet, of a hockey player no less?

"Hey there, Madelyn," he says, and my daughter's cries soften. "My name is Gus the Goalie, and I'm so fast, I bet you can't even touch me."

Madelyn chuckles as Matt's puppet pretends to nibble on her foot. She reaches for the puppet and I stare as he tugs it from her reach, making her laugh harder.

"Told ya, I was too fast."

What the ever-loving hell is going on before my eyes? Although maybe I don't care or want to know, because the fact is he's calmed Madelyn and that is a miracle and a blessing.

The doctor walks in, and Matt takes the puppet off his hand and gives it to Madelyn to play with. As she remains completely fascinated by it, she's not at all bothered by the doctor or his examination, and I don't know how I'll ever make this up to Matt, but I sure as heck plan on it.

After the doctor checks the big bump on the back of her head, as well as the rest of her, he hands Madelyn a sticker but she's too fascinated by the puppet. "I don't think any X-rays are needed. She seems to be very happy now."

"Thanks to Matt."

"I guess her daddy knows what makes her happy."

"No, um..." I stop when the doctor turns his attention to some pamphlets, and pulls one out on concussions and what to look for. He hands it to me.

"Do I keep her awake?" I ask as I scan the pamphlet.

"If she's not exhibiting any signs of a concussion, it's okay to let her sleep. I would just check in on her every couple of hours."

"Okay, thank you so much." A huge wave of relief goes through me as I stand.

"You can also give her some ibuprofen for the pain if you think she needs it. If there's any change in how she's feeling, bring her back in immediately."

I thank him again, and walk out of the curtained room with Matt, and I'm not sure Madelyn is ever going to relinquish the puppet. She's rather fascinated by it. We walk through the long corridor and Matt pushes open the doors for me and we step out into the sunshine.

I walk and he follows me. "Did you drive here or do you need a lift?"

"I drove." I come to an abrupt stop and turn to him. "What are you doing here?"

"Oh," he says, like it's suddenly dawning on him that he was here for other reasons. "The guys and I volunteer in the children's ward."

"Of course, and that's why you have the puppet." I gently try to take it from Madelyn and she tugs it back, gurgling in protest. "Do you need this right now, or can I get it to you later?"

"I just finished up, so I don't need it. I'm really glad I ran into you. What are the odds?"

"Pretty low. This is the first time I've had to take her to urgent care and I hope it's the last. We were snuggling and I closed my eyes..." I briefly shut them again as guilt pummels me. A shiver goes through me as I think about how bad this could have been.

"You're cold." Matt puts his arm around me, and starts me walking. "I think you might still be in shock."

"You might be right."

He walks us to my car, and says, "I'll drive."

I gratefully hand the keys over, and get Madelyn buckled in. He starts the car and turns on the heater as the vehicle rumbles loudly.

He plays with the dial. "You don't have any heat."

"No, I've been meaning to get that fixed before winter." He pulls the keys from the ignition and hands them back to me.

"Come on, we're taking my truck. I'll come back later and get your car when you're home resting."

"No, Matt, I've taken up enough of your time."

"Kennedy, listen to me. This car is a death trap. I don't want you or Madelyn in it, okay?"

I nod, knowing he's right. "God, I did two things to jeopardize my daughter today." Tears build and there is nothing I can do to keep them from spilling.

"Madelyn is fine. I'm sure you're the one who isn't fine right now. So, I'm going to take you home, get you both tucked in and come back and get your car. Okay?"

"Okay." I nod and get out of the car. I tug Madelyn from the car seat and Matt unhooks it. He guides me to his vehicle and I'm surprised that he knows how to hook the chair up. Although he does come from a big family and has younger siblings.

Once we're in his truck and he has the heat on high, he casts me a glance. "What happened was an accident." I just nod as fresh tears threaten. "Did I ever tell you the story of when I nearly killed Liam, by mistake of course."

"What, no."

"I was eating grapes. He was about eight, and I thought it would be a fun game to try and toss them into his mouth. I kept getting him to stand back farther and farther, and in order to reach I threw one really hard. It totally got caught in his windpipe."

"Ohmigod, Matt. What happened?"

"I started yelling and Mom came and performed the Heimlich. She cleared it."

"Thank God."

"I know, right? Accidents happen all the time." His hand lands on my thigh, and he gives a little squeeze. "Madelyn is going to be okay."

I turn and look over my shoulder, and Madelyn is making all kinds of noises as she tries to rip the hockey stick from the puppet. I'll probably have to sew it on later. "Thank God Liam was okay."

"He texted me earlier. He and my grandfather are coming here next month when he's off school for reading week. Maybe you'll get to meet him."

"Yeah, maybe," I say but I doubt it. Unless I run into him at the frat house, and I'm sure his grandfather won't be staying there, especially over a party weekend. Exhaustion and a big adrenaline dump bring on a big yawn, and I let my lids fall for a second. Matt's truck slows and I open my eyes to find us in front of my place.

"Thank you so much, Matt."

He looks through the window. "Is your mother home?"

"No, she's out with her friend. She probably won't be home until tomorrow." I give him a tired smile. "Thanks again." I'm about to slide out when he takes his seatbelt off, and opens his door and gets out, instead of waving us off. I scramble from the vehicle and glance at him. "What are you doing?"

"Madelyn needs a nap, and needs to be checked on frequently. You're still in shock and clearly need to get some rest."

He circles the vehicle and opens the back door where Madelyn is sitting. He unhooks the car seat and pulls Madelyn and the seat out.

"Yes, I know but I still don't understand what you're doing."

"You need someone to take care of you and your daughter, and I'm it." He starts up the walkway to the front door. "You coming?"

I shake my head. What the ever-loving hell is happening in my life?

MATT

Kennedy stands on the stoop and stares at me like I might have a hockey stick growing out of my neck. I'm not trying to be bossy or an overbearing jerk. The furthest thing from it, really. She needs some help, and I see no reason why I can't be the guy to help her. As long as she lets me, that is. I'm not going to force the situation if she really wants to see the last of me.

"You really don't—"

Not wanting her to think I'm overstepping, and really wanting to be there for her and her daughter, I try to come at this from a different approach. "Would you like some help today, Kennedy? If you do, I'd like to help."

She stares at me for a second and I can almost see the slight drop of her shoulders as she resigns herself to the fact that she does need help.

"We're just going to nap."

"You need to check on Madelyn every so often while she sleeps, right?"

"Yes."

"Would it be okay with you if I helped you with that? She's already met me, so we're a bit past that, and she's clearly in love with my puppet."

She gives a nod. "Yes, thank you, Matt. I really appreciate the offer."

I hold my hand out and she stares at it. "Key."

"Right." She juts her hip out. "Can you get it in my purse?"

"Growing up, I was always taught never ever to go into a woman's purse." I unzip her purse and root inside. "Yet this is twice today I've been inside yours."

A strange sound squeaks in her throat, and I pull her keys out and glance at her. That hint of pink on her cheeks makes me realize what I just said. "Found them," is all I say. I'm not about to mention anything about last night in front of her sleepy daughter, who has started whimpering a bit again. I open the door and the warm scent of cinnamon hits me. Is someone baking?

"I'm going to take her straight to bed."

"Should I follow you, so I know where to check in on her?"

"Yes." We walk up the narrow flight of stairs in the old downtown home, and the floors creak beneath my feet. I try to remember the squeaky steps, so I don't wake Kennedy when checking on her daughter, and the fact that she trusts me enough to do that, says a lot. I guess she realizes I'm pretty good with kids, when there are no grapes involved.

I stand at the door as she puts Madelyn on the change table, changes her diaper and puts her into pajamas. She gently eases the puppet from her hand, and quickly replaces it with a stuffed elephant when Madelyn fusses. She hums softly to her daughter and rubs her back. Once Madelyn is settled, she tiptoes out of the room and closes the door, leaving it open an inch.

"My room is across the hall." I nod and she steps around me. "I'll leave the door open in case she wakes up."

I step into her room with her, and close the door tight. Her eyes go wide. "Matt."

"I shut it so we don't wake Madelyn."

"Doing what?"

"Talking."

"Oh."

"Wait, did you think—"

"No, no. I thought you meant talking."

I'm pretty sure that's not at all what she was thinking, but I keep it to myself. Does the fact that she was thinking about it, mean she might like to act on it? Not today, of course. We have her child to think about.

"I just wanted to say," I begin, my words whispered. "Shut your door, and get a good sleep. I'm going to have a friend get your car, and bring it back, and bring me my books. So, sleep as long as you like, and I'll keep checking in on Madelyn. I know a lot about concussions and if I think anything is out of the ordinary, I'll wake you."

She blinks up at me with eyes so sincere and thankful, my heart thumps a little harder in my chest. "Now get in bed."

She walks to her bed, pulls the covers back and climbs in. I pull the covers to her chin, tuck them around her and drop a soft kiss onto her forehead.

"Thanks, Matt."

"Sure." I give her one fast look, take in the way her appreciative eyes are following me, and I step from her room and close the door. I stand there for an extra moment, listening for sounds from both rooms. It wouldn't surprise me if Kennedy snuck back to her door and cracked it open a bit.

Once I'm satisfied that they're sleeping, I tiptoe back downstairs, working to avoid the creaks and stop at the foot of the stairs to glance around. The home is small, but cute, and very homey. Numerous pictures decorate the walls, and I can't help but take a look. I move through the small living room, grinning at a toothless Kennedy staring back at me in her kindergarten picture. Madelyn is her little mini-me.

I find the kitchen and get to work on putting on some coffee. They have an old-fashioned coffee maker with carafe, so it takes me a few minutes to find the grounds and load it. As it percolates, I grab my phone and call Beckett. He left the hospital before me, as he had some group project to work on, and I'm hoping he's done by now.

"Hey what's up?" he answers.

"Can you do me a favor, if you're not still busy?"

"Nope, not busy. What do you need?"

I explain everything that happened after he left the hospital and give him Kennedy's address, so he can go give her car a once over.

"Yeah, I'll be right there."

"Grab my books too. They're in my backpack."

"On it."

I hang up, and grab some milk from the fridge. It's weird being here while Kennedy is sleeping. Just opening her fridge feels invasive. I finish checking out the small house and all the pictures, and go to the front living room and scroll through my phone, watching some old games while I wait for Beckett. He shows up, drops me my books and I give him the keys to Kennedy's car. It's not a far walk and he doesn't seem to mind.

I go through my books and eventually my phone rings and I snatch it up before it wakes the girls. "Hey, what's happening?" I ask in whispered words.

"I'm at the service station. Kennedy can't drive this car. As soon as I started to drive, and heard all the clunking, I knew it was the tie rod end."

Beckett did mechanical work with his older brother growing up, so it's no wonder he was able to instantly identify the problem. "Shit."

"I can leave it here, but it will take a day or two, and uh...it's not cheap."

"Yeah, I know."

"Get it done?"

"Hell yeah, get it done."

"I'd do it for you, bud, but I don't have the place to work on it."

I nod, even though he can't see me. Beckett might have a reputation like me, but he's a good guy, who grew up with so little, so he's real self-reliant guy, a jack of all trades.

"I know you would and I appreciate it. Tell the garage to go ahead and fix it."

"I'm on it."

"Thanks, buddy." He hesitates, and I'm sure I know what he's thinking. "It's all good Beck."

"Okay."

"Catch up with you later."

We hang up and I pour another cup of coffee. I tiptoe back up the stairs and check on Madelyn. I listen to her soft breathing, and lightly touch her forehead. I find myself smiling as I watch her, remembering the days when Liam and Jaxon were babies.

I close the door as turn to leave and that's when it occurs to me that it's getting late in the day, and Kennedy still has to cook. She's probably not going to be too pleased with me taking her car to a garage, and she's going to demand she pay for it, which there's no way I'll allow since it was my decision to get it fixed, so maybe I can smooth things over if I cook a meal for her.

Either that, or poison her and her family.

Come on, dude, you can do this!

I head to the kitchen and start opening cupboards and the fridge. I stare into the abyss, not really having a clue. I could do take-out, but I think if I cook something, she'd appreciate it more. I bite the damn bullet and call my older sister Megan, who has kids of her own.

"Well, well, what's up little brother. Long time, no hear."

"Been busy. How's it going?"

"Jenny, leave him alone." I hear a bang in the background and a loud cry.

"Living the dream, little brother. Living the dream." I hear her husband Sean's voice in the background.

"Getting ready for Sunday dinner at Mom's?" I kind of miss those big Sunday dinners. I bet Kennedy and Madelyn would love sitting around the table and being loved by them all.

What the hell am I even saying?

"Yeah, just trying to comb the kids' hair and get them dressed. Are you okay?"

I realize I don't call often, and that's why she sounds concerned. "Yeah, I need a recipe. Something easy, and kid friendly."

A pause and then, "Who are you and what have you done with my brother?"

"Funny."

"I'm being serious." A loud bang reverberates through the phone, and nearly deafens me. "Sorry, just dropped a pan."

"Any ideas?"

"Who are you cooking for?"

I pace around the kitchen. "Just a friend who needs some help."

"What's her name?"

I groan. "Megan, can you help me or not?"

"Fine, I have an easy chicken casserole dish. I can text you—Devon, what did I tell you about. Ohmigod, Sean can you get him?"

"Give the kids a hug for me."

"I will right after I get them to sit still for five seconds."

Wow, when I hear the commotion at Megan's place, it makes me want to have a vasectomy. I'm not sure I can take that kind of chaos, now or ever. Honestly though, her kids are her life, and she adores them. My phone pings as her text comes through.

"Thanks, sis."

"You owe me all the details."

"Love you too."

I chuckle as I hang up and open the recipe. I find everything I need in her fridge and freezer, except for broccoli so I substitute it with cauliflower, and study the recipe carefully, reading it a few times before I even attempt the casserole.

I get to work, trying my best to be quiet, and finally get the chicken thawed and cooked. The kitchen looks like it was hit with an explosive by the time I'm done chopping vegetables and putting the casserole together. I stand back, hands on hips, and admire the finished product. I take a picture and shoot it off to my sister, who texts back that she's impressed. Hell, I'm impressed too. I wasn't sure I could pull it off.

I put the casserole in the oven, toss a few of the crushed-up cornflakes into my mouth and get to cleaning the kitchen.

She does not need to wake up to this kind of mess. Just as I finish cleaning and put the dish towel on the handle of the stove, footsteps reach my ears. I turn, and it's insane the way my heart jumps with happiness as she comes into the room. She waves her phone. "You texted me earlier today."

I nod, having forgotten that I sent her that text ages ago, when I'd finished visiting the kids in the children's hospital. "I was wondering how Madelyn made out with her sleepover."

"She did good." She glances around the kitchen suspicion in her eyes, like I've been up to something. The smell of course, gives it away. "How did you get my number?"

"You gave it to Daisy when she was setting that gig up for you at The Lower Deck."

"Oh, right."

"I wanted to ask about Madelyn, and you know, say...hey." *Wow, way to sound stupid, dude.* I don't want to come right out and tell her I couldn't stop thinking about her or our night. She'd no doubt show me the door.

"Hey," she says with a laugh and rubs her tired eyes. "Madelyn is still asleep. I just checked on her."

"She's okay. I checked on her a few times. I think she's just worn out from last night's playdate."

She laughs. "At least I'm no longer worn out from my play date last night." I swallow at the reminder and her cheeks turn that pretty shade of pink again. She steps into the room, and her body brushes mine as she bends forward to look in the oven's window. "Did you cook?"

"Yeah, I figured you guys would be hungry."

She spins and faces me, surprise in her dark eyes. "I can't believe you cooked."

"Yeah, I know. No one expects much from me." She angles her head, and I can almost hear her brain racing. "I just mean I'm not good at this. I'm not good at anything."

"You said that to me before."

Oh, she remembered that?

She reaches for a mug and pours a glass of water. "Why did you say you weren't good at anything else?"

I shrug, wishing I'd kept my stupid mouth shut. "I'd rather not tell you."

She stiffens a bit, and dammit, I offended her. "Yeah, of course. I totally understand." She takes a big drink and sets her glass in the sink.

"Kennedy," I begin quickly and touch her arm. She turns around. "I don't want to come off as a complainer, or an ungrateful bastard."

"Matt, it's okay."

As I stare at her, take in the warmth and compassion on her face, I realize she's not a girl to judge. "No one has ever expected anything from me, and I've lived up to that," I explain, telling her despite just saying I didn't want to. Her brow narrows and she remains quiet. Her knuckles lightly brush mine as she nods, sympathy blooming in her eyes as I continue. "Hockey is my life." I try to laugh it off. "It's all I was ever expected to be good at."

She takes my hand and leads me to the small table. I sit, and our fingers part, and I resist the urge to reach out to her again as she sets her hands on the table.

"I'm sure you worked long and hard at hockey. It's not easy to make it to your level, with the expectations of playing in the NHL."

"Don't get me wrong, I love hockey, but—"

She captures my hands. "I'm not getting you wrong, Matt. I'm only saying, you devoted a lot of time to get to where you are today and that's dedication and it's commendable."

"Thank you."

"I'm also sure you're good at anything you put your mind to. You just made a casserole, didn't you?" Her smile is sweet and supportive. "I think there's more to you than you even know."

My pulse thumps against my throat. I might not believe in me, and while I like that she believes in me, it's also very disconcerting. I don't want her to think I'm more when in fact, I might not be. Man, maybe I shouldn't have started anything with a girl like her.

I pull my hand back. "I should get going."

Her head rears back like I might have slapped her. "Oh, yeah, sure. Thank you so much for helping me today."

"Oh, your car. It's at the garage. The tie rod end was broken and it was dangerous to drive."

Horror moves over her face. "Matt—"

"It's okay. It's an easy fix. Won't cost hardly anything."

She pushes to her feet. "Are you sure?"

"Yeah, just a few bucks. You can do an extra hour at Storm House and that will cover it. I'll drop it off to you tomorrow if it's ready. Is that okay?"

"That's perfect." She gives me a warm smile, and my heart pinches too tight, warning me I need to get the hell out, now.

"Okay, I should go."

"Matt," she begins, and points to the stove. "Do you want to —" A loud wailing cry comes from upstairs before she can finish her sentence.

"You'd better…"

"Yeah."

I walk to the living room and snatch up my backpack. "See you around, Kennedy."

"Yeah, see you around," she responds, something very final in her words that I should be happy about, considering how different we are, but dammit, instead her words cut deep in a way that's completely unfamiliar to me.

Goddammit, this is so not good.

⓭

KENNEDY

I'm sitting in my bedroom, the window wide open as a beautiful late day breeze ruffles my curtains and washes over me. Dressed only in my yoga pants and a T-shirt, it chills my skin, but the fresh air is too nice to shut it out and Lord knows the snow will be here soon enough.

With Madelyn asleep in her room—she's been a nightmare to settle down today—and Mom fussing about downstairs, I'm working on my music and making notes on my music paper. I don't have to work at Storm House until tomorrow, and after a busy day of classes, I'm happy for the evening off, giving Mom a break from babysitting too. She worked all day at the diner, and deserves some time to herself.

I pick up my guitar and start playing the chords I've written, then begin to softly sing the words I composed to go with the chords. I sing quietly, not wanting to wake Madelyn up from her nap. A car pulls into our driveway, and I straighten, my heart jumping. I'd like to say I wasn't waiting for Matt to show up with my car, but that would be a lie, and it's not my car I've been waiting to see.

I stand quietly, and walk to my open window. He took off out of here yesterday so fast, you'd think I set his pants on fire. I was going to ask him to stay and eat with me, but after he opened up to me a bit, confessing something I'm guessing he regrets, he ran out like the devil himself was chasing him.

Mom's footsteps on the wooden floor below echo through the house, and the hinges on the front door creak as she pulls it open.

"Hi there, I'm here to return Kennedy's car and keys." I lean forward, glimpsing him as he dangles the keys toward Mom. Mom accepts them, and instead of letting him go, she engages him in conversation and I groan and push back from the window, not far enough that I can't hear, mind you.

"You're the young man who helped Kennedy out with Madelyn, and her car."

"Oh, she mentioned me?" For a guy who couldn't wait to get away from me, he does sound like he's fishing for information.

"Why of course. You're Matt. Hang on, let me get her."

I resist the urge to scream as Mom's steps come up the stairs. Like a kid caught with her hand in the cookie jar, I jump back on my bed and pick up my guitar. Mom pokes her head into my room. "Matt's here to return your car."

"Oh great, did you thank him for me?" She puts her fists on her hips, and gives me the look, the one that says she raised me better than that, and the truth is she did. I set the guitar down. "I should probably thank him myself."

My eyes lock on Matt's as I reach the bottom of the steps, and a part of me thinks I should have gone into nursing instead of music. That way there might be a defibrillator nearby to shock my racing heart and restore its natural heartbeat.

"I just wanted to drop the keys off," he says. "Your car is all fixed and safe."

"What do I owe you?"

He shrugs. "Nothing, just an hour's work at Storm House."

I know he must be lying. I didn't have a chance to check, but I'm pretty sure a tie rod end is more than an hour's minimum wage.

"Matt, I just finished making dinner," Mom calls out. "Meatloaf and mashed potatoes. Why don't you stay for a bite?"

He jerks his thumb out. "Oh, I don't want to intrude. I should probably get back to the house."

My mom waves her hand. "No intrusion at all, just a nice way for us to thank you for helping yesterday." Mom turns to me with her sugar sweet smile and eyes that warn I'd better use proper manners. I'm a grown ass adult with a child of my own, but with one look she can reduce me to my pre-teen self. She has good intentions, I realize, but I don't think this is a good idea. "Isn't that right, Kennedy?"

I put on a big smile. "Of course, Mother."

"I guess it's been a while since I had a home cooked meal. Last one was the lasagna Kennedy made and if she learned how to cook from you, I'm sure dinner will be delicious, but I don't want to—"

Mom turns. "It's settled then."

I roll my eyes and meet Matt's after Mom disappears. "You don't have to stay if you don't want."

"Meat, Kennedy." He stares at me wide eyed. "Meat."

"What?" I ask and crinkle my nose.

"Your mom had me at meatloaf, and the mashed potatoes are just a bonus. I'm from Alberta, remember, and this east coast town has far too much seafood," he says, his grin so adorable and earnest I can't help but laugh. "If you don't want me to stay, though. If you're busy?"

"No, come in. I just finished working on some music, and homemade meatloaf is the least we can do after all your help."

He nods, like he'll take that, but I have the weirdest feeling he wanted me to say something else, like I really wanted him to stay. If that was the case, what spooked him yesterday and had him running out of here? I'm not sure what is going on with him, but he's all kinds of contradictions.

"Maybe you'll play something for me after dinner."

"And maybe I won't." He grins and I gesture with my head. "Follow me," I say and we make our way to the kitchen, and I remember he already knows his way around our small place.

"Is there anything I can help you with, Ms. Walsh?" Matt asks. I wasn't even sure he knew my last name, but I guess Daisy must have given it to him, or he's done his research on me. I doubt it though. There is no way he went through my social media the same investigative way I went through his. I am so pathetic.

"Oh, honey, call me Barb," Mom says, and she gives him a big smile. "And if you want, you can help Kennedy set up and pour us an iced tea."

I go to the cabinet and pull out the placemats. As he sets them out, I give him the utensils and grab the iced tea, wishing it was something stronger. I might need to be a little tipsy to make it through this meal.

Mom hums as she finishes mashing the potatoes, and puts everything into bowls. Matt and I place them on the table and we all have a seat.

"Barb, this looks amazing."

"Dig in," she says and we all begin to fill our plates. Matt takes a bite of his mashed potatoes and closes his eyes and moans.

Really?

I resist the urge to tell him he sounds like he's having sex with the root vegetable. But I don't want to think about sex when Matt is sitting across the table from my mom. Better to think about him and sex when I'm in my bed alone.

"This is as good as Kennedy's lasagna," Matt says to Mom and while she's not one to need praise, she beams at Matt. Good God, is he so charming, that my mom is sort of swooning? Yeah, he is, and it's doing ridiculous things to me, too.

"Kennedy tells me you hired her after she lost her job at the pub."

He nods and jabs a few carrots. "It was good timing. Our last housekeeper had just quit without notice."

"Just like that? Why on earth would she just up and quit?" Mom gives a stern shake of her head. "That doesn't seem very professional."

"Not professional at all," I say, and pop a piece of meatloaf into my mouth. "Do you have any idea what happened, Matt?" I smirk at him. How is he going to explain this one?

He leans forward conspiratorially. "Between us, her lasagna was to *die* for, but it just didn't work out. Let's face it, the job blows."

Ohmigod! He did not just say that to my mother. Or am I just taking it the wrong way because I heard he had a thing with the cleaner, and well, we did things in his room.

"You're right, it does blow," Mom agrees and I resist the urge to crawl under the table as my mind drifts back to when I took his cock into my mouth. I get we're all adults, but I don't discuss sex in front of my mother. I'm also having a hard time believing my Mom is that naïve. Maybe she's playing along, to see where this goes. "All those frat boys around too. I'm sure that must have been hard."

Hard...Omg.

Matt smiles. "Don't worry, though. Kennedy is in good hands."

"Is she?"

"Yes," he assures her as the two look at each other, I can't help but think they both know exactly what they're saying to one another.

Matt smiles at me, and I just shake my head. "How is Madelyn?" he asks.

"She's good. Thanks for asking." It's actually really nice that he asked. I like his concern. "The swelling has gone down."

"Did you use an ice pack? That always helps me with the swelling."

Ohmigod, what the hell is he doing?

He glances at my mom. "I've taken a hit to the head a time or two."

"I bet you have."

We fall into easy conversation, Matt talking about his hockey, and classes and life growing up on a dairy farm, and soon enough our meal is finished, and Mom is standing to collect the dishes.

"I can do these, Barb," Matt offers. "It's the least I can do after such a delicious meal."

"Are you sure?"

"Yeah, no problem."

Mom dries her hands on a dish towel. "If you don't mind." She turns to me. "Leo and I are going to watch a movie tonight."

"Oh, okay," I say. Normally Mom doesn't go to Leo's on a Monday night.

She walks to the archway and glances back, a little twinkle in her eye. "Don't wait up for me."

I shake my head. What the hell is she trying to do? I get that she likes Matt, approves of him, but I am not in the market for a man, and if she thinks she's going to set me up with Matt because he was nice to me and my daughter, she has another thing coming. I don't have time for a relationship, nor do I want one.

Sex, on the other hand...

I shut down that internal voice.

"See you tomorrow," I say as she disappears.

"Have a wonderful night," she calls out from the hall.

I grab the dish soap and concentrate far too hard on squirting it on the dishes. Matt steps up beside me, his body close, his scent filling the air around me.

He snatches the dish towel from the stove. "Your mother isn't very subtle."

Great, even Matt knows my mother is trying to play matchmaker here. Mortified at my mother's blatantness, I shake my head, wanting to curl up into the fetal position and disappear. "She hates that I'm lonely."

His body brushes mine as the front door opens and closes, leaving us alone in the house, save for a sleeping Madelyn.

"You're lonely?"

I turn the water on and quickly explain. "No, I didn't mean it like that. I mean, she'd like to see me with a nice guy."

"And she thinks that's me?"

"Early onset of senility. Runs in the family, you know. You'd be wise to keep away from any of the Walsh women."

"I don't frighten that easy," he says.

"Really," I say, disbelief in my tone. His smile disappears, and his fingers tighten around the dish dryer. "You took off yesterday like something spooked you."

He looks down, his brows pulled together. "What we did the other night... I liked being with you, Kennedy."

"I liked being with you too," I admit. Where the heck is he going with this?

"Sex is it, though. I can't offer more."

"Did you think I was asking?"

"No." He gives a hard shake of his head. "I just want it to be clear, very clear."

"I told you, I know who you are and what you're all about." He steps a bit closer, one hand going around my waist to drag me to him. His head dips, his eyes on my mouth.

"Should we grab the ice?" I tease.

"Ice?" His voice is low and confused, as heat fills his gaze.

"For the swelling."

His eyes lift to mine, staring blankly, and I grin, waiting for the lightbulb to go off. Two beats later he snorts and laughs, and pulls me harder against his thickening cock.

"Maybe there are other ways we can take care of this swelling," he suggests, and practically jumps back, shock on his face, as Madelyn cries from upstairs.

I laugh at his surprise. "Can I take a rain check?" I ask.

"Yeah, sure. Sorry."

"Matt." I touch his arm. "There is nothing to be sorry about."

"I'm not used to..."

"Babies."

"Yeah, something like that," he mutters.

"They're very unpredictable. She's barely napped at all today. It's getting harder and harder to put her down for one. I'll be back in a minute." I hurry upstairs and open Madelyn's door. She stands and reaches for me as I cross the room. "Why hello there, chicken nugget." I pull her to me, and lightly touch the bump on the back of her head, happy that it's almost gone.

I hum to her quietly as I lay her on her change table, and she fusses as I try to change her diaper. My thought goes to the man downstairs and I realize I had no intention of bringing him into my daughter's life, but I guess life had other ideas. Doesn't it always?

"Guess who's here," I say to her as I get her changed and head back downstairs, taking much longer than I would have liked. "Do you remember Matt? He was the one who gave you the puppet at the hospital." For the life of me, I can't understand why I'm excited for her to see Matt again. Hell, I know why I'm excited. "Do you want to say hi to Matt?"

I step into the kitchen, only to discover...Matt's gone.

14

MATT

I quickly wash the dishes, and leave them on the tray to dry as I quietly walk into the hall. My heart pinches tight as I listen to Kennedy hum and talk quietly to her daughter upstairs. This house might be small, but it's quaint and full of love, and it's strange that I'm so comfortable here. My home is big, and noisy and always full of people, much like Storm House. This is kind of nice, and relaxing.

When I arrived, I had no intention of staying and really it wasn't the food that enticed me. I like spending time with Kennedy. She's funny and interesting, and...real. My buddy Brandon, who I met when I first arrived, told me the women in Nova Scotia were genuine and he was right. I grab my puppet from the back seat, and slip back into the house. I listen for Kennedy's voice at the bottom of the stairs. The sound of the fridge opening and closing in the kitchen draws my focus.

I head down the hall, and Kennedy spins when she sees me, surprise in her eyes. "Oh, I thought..." she begins as Madelyn reaches for the puppet in my hand.

"I was getting this." I drop into the chair next to Madelyn's highchair and hand her the puppet. "Did you think I left?"

"I didn't know what to think."

Shit, man. Someone really hurt her in the past. "I wanted to surprise little miss Madelyn."

Madelyn starts pulling at the hockey stick on the puppet. "I'm afraid she might destroy it."

"We have a bunch. She can have that one if you think it's safe."

"That's nice. You guys all use them at the hospital?"

I shrug as she puts a small plate of food into the microwave, everything about this so domesticated, so mundane ...so nice. "Yeah, it's nice to go cheer up the kids."

"That's a really great thing you all do."

"Maybe someday you'll come with me and sing some of your music to them."

She laughs at my insistence on hearing her music. "Wow, pushing it much?"

"I'll get to say I knew you when."

"When you're a big NHL star, I'll get to say the same."

I chuckle as the microwave beeps and she pulls the plate out, and puts her finger on the food to check the temperature. She sets the food in front of Madelyn, and gives her a small child's spoon. With the puppet in one hand and the spoon in the other, Madelyn digs right into her food.

"We're not keeping you from anything, are we?" Kennedy asks.

Why the heck does she always think there's somewhere else I'd rather be? "No, why? Is there somewhere you think I should be?"

"You don't have a game or practice, or homework?"

"I have a game next weekend. Friday night. You should come if you're free."

She laughs. "I'm never free, Matt." I'm about to apologize for saying something stupid, when she adds, "But maybe I'll get a sitter. I think it might be fun to watch a game."

My stomach jumps, far too happy at that. "Maybe we can get little miss Madelyn on the ice," I tell her. "There's a family skate on Saturday afternoon." Not that we're a family, and of course you don't have to be to go to the open skate. But now, after saying the word family, it's on my brain. I've never given much thought to it, really. I've only had one goal in life, hockey, and one person to take care of, me. I like being here for Kennedy though, and her daughter and the idea of skating together sounds like fun.

"Madelyn has never been on skates. Do you think she's too young?"

"I was on skates before I could walk," I tell her.

There's disbelief in her eyes as she helps Madelyn with her meat loaf. "Is that true?"

"Would I lie to you?"

"I guess you'd have no reason to lie about that."

"Like I said, Granddad is a huge hockey fan. He had all of us on skates early on. I was the only one who excelled at it, until Liam."

Madelyn lets out a squeal when the puppet falls to the floor and both Kennedy and I reach for it. Her hand closes over mine, and we laugh until our eyes meet and heat arcs between us.

"Got it," I say, and she lets my hand go and sits back in her chair, a pink hue on her face.

I hand the puppet back to Madelyn and she pushes it into her mashed potatoes. "Madelyn, no." Kennedy pulls the toy from the potatoes and some of them fall onto Madelyn's hair. "You're going to need a bath before our walk."

"Are you going to the park, again?"

"I'm not sure. I thought we'd just go for a stroll on the waterfront, maybe get this chicken nugget a Beaver Tail."

"I want a Beaver Tail," I blurt out, sounding like a four-year-old.

Kennedy laughs at me. "Okay, you can get one too."

I do a fist pump. "Nice."

"Okay, little miss," Kennedy begins, pulling Madelyn from the highchair. "Time to get you cleaned up." She positions her daughter on her hip. "We won't be long."

"I have my books in the car. I'll grab them, and do some work." She nods and before I head out, I rinse the potato off the puppet in case Madelyn wants to take it on the walk. I dart outside to grab my backpack. In the distance, I spot her friend Amy, who is waving, and as I wave back, I can just imagine the gossip tomorrow. Kennedy is a nice girl, and the last guy she should probably be associated with is me, but goddammit, I can't seem to help myself. Selfish, that's what I am. I can try to justify it by saying I'm helping Kennedy out, and was able to help her forget about real life and responsibilities for a little while, but a lot of what I'm doing has to do with what I want, and is that really fair to her or her daughter.

As that sober reality sinks in, I head back inside, and plop down on the sofa as she talks to her daughter. My phone pings and it's Liam, letting me know how excited he is that he'll be coming to visit next month. I text back and forth with him for a bit, and the next thing I know, Kennedy is coming down the stairs with her freshly bathed daughter in her arms.

I jump up, in more ways than one, and my heart pounds a little bit harder as Kennedy smiles at me. Jesus, I like her, but that's all this can be. I'm not thinking about more, am I? Christ, my focus is on my career, and hers is on her family and school. I can't—refuse—to think I want more, despite the fact that the mere sight of her throws me off my game.

I can't let anything throw me off my game.

"Hey," I say, taking note of her change of clothes. She's now in a pair of hip hugging jeans, and a sweater that showcases two delicious mounds my mouth would like to explore. I bite the inside of my mouth to get my shit together. Now is not the time to be thinking about such things.

"Maf. Maf. Maf," Madelyn chants, and Kennedy frowns as we stare at one another.

"What's Maf?" I ask, and Madelyn stretches toward me. Does she want me to hold her?

"I think...it's you." We both start laughing, and Madelyn sticks her hand out and starts waving her fingers toward the kitchen.

"Do you think she wants the puppet? I washed it in case she wanted to take it on the walk."

Kennedy blinks up at me, surprise in her eyes. It wraps around me and tugs at something deep. Cleaning the puppet was nothing, but to Kennedy it seems like the world, and makes me want to do more—everything—for her.

"That was sweet," she whispers quietly.

"Maybe that's what she's calling Maf."

She laughs, and it's light and musical and carefree. I want to make her laugh like that more often. "Of course it is. She's heard me call you Matt, and associates you with the puppet. She has a hard time with her T's, so she's saying Maf."

I chuckle. "I'll get it." I walk to the kitchen, snatch up the toy and find Kennedy on the porch putting Madelyn into a stroller. She locks up the house and the cooler night air falls over us as we make our way to the waterfront. It's Monday, and it's less busy than on the weekend, but I still see numerous people I know. As I wave and they walk by, their gazes go to Kennedy and then Madelyn. I'm sure they're wondering if the little girl is mine.

"You know a lot of people," Kennedy says as we step up to the kiosk to get a couple Beaver Tail pastries.

"Yeah. Being on the hockey team will do that," I say but I know what she's thinking—that I've been with a lot of girls. It's true. I can't deny it; nor can I forget that sex is the reason I'm here with Kennedy right now.

Why am I suddenly no longer okay with that?

"What's your favorite?" Kennedy asks, and I turn to her, staring blankly. She angles her head, her questioning eyes searching my face. "Are you okay?"

"Yeah, what did you ask?"

"What's your favorite kind of Beaver Tail?"

"Oh." I turn and check out the big board with all the fried dough flavors. "I like them all, but I think my favorite is the Banarama. How about you?"

"Trying to be healthy for Madelyn," she begins with a chuckle, because we both know there is nothing healthy about these pastries. "I'm going to get the apple pie."

"An apple a day," I say, and we step up to the counter, and I order. I reach for my wallet and she digs into her purse. "On me."

"You don't have to do that."

Money is an issue for her, I get that and I don't want to make her feel less, so I wink at her and whisper. "We can find ways for you to pay me back."

She leans into me, her sweet scent meandering through my blood and settling between my legs. But it's the pounding of my heart that's really catching my attention. "Oh, are we talking sexual favors for Beaver Tails?" she whispers.

She pulls back and my jaw drops, as I stare at her for a second before I start to laugh. She's so sweet, and reserved and sometimes the things that come out of her mouth shock me but they also thrill me. "I can't believe you said that."

"That's not an answer," she says, lifting her chin and inch.

"Would you hold it against me if I said yes?" I make a face, squishing my lips and give her a look that conveys worry mixed with hope, because yeah, I want her to hold it against me, and of course I'm talking about her body. I'm a selfish dick, remember?

Her grin is playful. "So your answer is yes?"

I try to figure out her game, and tentatively say, "Yes." The server steps up to the window, and because I'm still in shock, waiting for her answer, I stand there, as he tells us our order is up.

I finally find my voice. "Well...?"

"I guess you'll have to wait and see." She pushes the stroller to the other side of the kiosk to collect our food.

Fucking tease and I love it.

I follow her, and inconspicuously try to adjust my cock, and she's still grinning, fully aware of what she's doing to me. We carry our dessert to a close-by table. She pulls Madelyn from her stroller and sets her on her lap, and Madelyn is going crazy trying to get her hands on the pastry.

I laugh. "She's definitely a maritimer who loves her Beaver Tails," I laugh. I quickly learned that the people from the east coast provinces were called maritimers, because unlike my landlocked province, they're surrounded by water.

Madelyn manages to get a hold of the paper beneath the pastry and tugs. Her other hand goes straight into the apple and she grabs a fistful and eats it. "Madelyn," Kennedy scolds and I laugh.

"Hey, she has better manners than some of the guys at Storm House."

"Yeah, I know. I clean up after them, remember?"

"Right. Can she have a banana?"

"Sure."

I pluck a couple bananas off my dessert, and she says, "Maf," as I hand them to her. She gobbles one up, and with her hands full of sticky apple and banana, she reaches up and grabs a fistful of her mother's hair.

"This is why I always keep it tied back," she explains. Did she keep it down for me because I love running my fingers through it? She pulls an elastic band from her wrist and reaches up, but her fingers are sticky too. "Great, I made it worse."

"Let me help." I stand and start pulling her hair back. "Um, I think I might be making it worse."

"It can't get any worse, Maf," she says and I laugh. I haphazardly tie her hair back, and sit back down next to her. I bite back a grin at how messy I made the ponytail.

"That bad?" she laughs.

"No, you look gorgeous, as always."

She rolls her eyes at me, and rips off a piece of her dessert and takes a big bite. "Ohmigod, this is so good." She moans and the sound wraps around my cock and hugs tight.

"Try mine."

I hold it out for her, and Madelyn leans in and takes a big bite. We both laugh. "I'm so sorry," Kennedy apologizes.

"It's my fault. I should have anticipated that."

"Life with kids...there's no anticipating anything." She takes a bite of mine. "That's delicious. Try mine."

I glance at the gnarled mess, compliments of little miss Madelyn, and shake my head. "I think I'll pass."

She laughs. "I don't blame you." Her gaze lifts and her eyes go wide, her laugh dying an abrupt and painful death.

What the hell?

I lift my gaze to see what's upsetting her, but only see people milling about, talking and laughing as they stroll the waterfront. She shifts quickly, turning her focus directly on me, her chest rising and falling fast. I take another swift glance around as a couple walking a dog come close, and Kennedy curves her hand around the side of her face like she's trying not to be noticed.

"Kennedy?" I ask. I steal another quick glance at the couple, and don't miss the way the guy's gaze strays to Kennedy and then quickly shifts back to the woman he's with, his look of shock right on par with Kennedy's.

"Yeah," she replies quietly.

"Who...was that guy?" I ask, although I think I already know the answer.

She exhales slowly, a new kind of sadness about her. "That was my ex," she whispers, and shifts closer. I drop my pastry, my appetite gone. My God, from her reaction, I'm thinking she still loves him.

"Do you want to talk about it?" I ask and put my hand on her thigh, giving it a supportive squeeze.

She gives a fast and hard shake of her head, her ponytail swishing back and forth. "No."

"Okay," I say as my gut clenches, and I get it. I told her some personal things the other day, and she was a great listener, but I'm simply her fuck buddy, not her confidant.

Why the hell do I hate that so much?

15

KENNEDY

God, I can't believe we actually ran into Oliver and his wife—with her baby bump—and their dog. Talk about looking like the perfect family. They're not though. If they were, he wouldn't have been sleeping with me behind her back.

"Want to get out of here?" Matt asks, and I nod, not sure I can find my words. I hate that I'm upset. I'm over him, and I want to feel nothing, but that's hard to do when he just walked by me, as well as his sweet baby girl. Madelyn is better off not knowing him, or knowing how he rejected her. I don't need her growing up with deep rooted abandonment issues, like I have.

Matt stands and cleans up our mess as I get Madelyn back in her stroller. We're both silent, lost in our own thoughts as we walk, and while we're not verbally communicating, he puts his arm around me to give comfort, and I'm so happy he's with me right now. His presence is quiet, but comforting.

We reach my house, and I pull Madelyn from her seat. Normally I have to set her inside, and go back and get her stroller but Matt carries it up and sets it on the stoop. I have the oddest feeling he's going to run, and I should let him. I open the door, and he has a questioning look on his face.

"She'll be going to sleep soon. Want to come in and study with me?" I give him a small smile and work to lighten the mood by saying, "There's this payment for the Beaver Tail we have to discuss."

He grins, and nods. "When you put it like that." He reaches out and wipes something from my face. I raise a questioning brow and he explains, "Apple filling."

I give a humorless laugh. "I'm a mess, I can't believe you'd want to be seen with me."

"No, you're not, Kennedy," he says his voice low and husky, and honest. "You're kind of perfect."

I'm not great at accepting compliments, so I just laugh it off, but every moment I spend with him, he's proving to be very sweet and kind. I'm pretty sure there's more to Matt, but I know better than to think there can be more to us.

"Come on." We walk inside, and I get Madelyn a drink before turning on her favorite evening cartoon. Matt plunks in the chair beside the sofa and within minutes he's engrossed in the show.

"Do you want something to drink, Matt?"

"Shh," he teases. "I'm trying to get caught up."

I roll my eyes. "Can you watch her for a second? I'm going to run up and get my books."

"Sure," he agrees, and it's weird how much I trust him with my daughter, and it happened really quickly. I just need to be careful she doesn't get too used to Maf, get too comfortable with his presence. I grab my music sheets and pencil and head back down. Matt is laughing at something on the TV and Madelyn is staring at him, but it's what she does next that nearly tears my heart out of my chest.

She gets up, snatches up her favorite blanket and crawls onto Matt's lap. At first he seems a little shocked, but he's used to younger siblings so he tucks her in, wraps her in her blanket and the two of them continue to watch the show. I stand at the foot of the stairs and try to remember how to breathe. Yes, it's true and I really didn't want to admit it, but Madelyn does need a male influence in her life. It's good and healthy for her, but dammit, it's not going to be Matt.

"Hey," I murmur quietly and ease down onto the sofa. Matt casts a glance my way, and once again my heart stalls. Why does the picture before me look so cozy, warm and...right?

Madelyn leans forward, holds her hand out and wiggles her fingers in a wave. "Mom. Mom. Mom."

"Hey sweet girl," I say and she snuggles back in to Matt and turns to the TV. I don't blame her. I want to snuggle in too. I turn my attention to my music, although it's hard to concentrate on anything as my heart races in my chest. Tonight—this whole day, really—has been nothing but a roller coaster of emotions. When Madelyn's favorite show ends, and her eyes begin to droop, I drop my music sheets and stand.

I hold my hand out, and speak softly. "Time for me to take her up to bed."

"I can carry her if you want."

"If you don't mind."

He stands and shifts her until she has her head on his shoulder, and boom just like that, I'm pregnant. Not really, but holy hell, my ovaries are banging around like dice in a Yahtzee cup. Heat envelopes my body, and I wave my hand in front of my face as I follow them up the stairs.

He steps into her dark room, and I turn on the nightlight. "Just put her on the change table. I need to change her before bed."

"Okay," he agrees softly, his presence eating up the whole room and overwhelming me a bit. I draw in a breath, finding it harder and harder to get air as he sets her down, and backs out of the room. "Meet you downstairs?"

"I'll just be a minute," I tell him. His footsteps are quiet on the stairs, and I quickly get Madelyn changed and into her bed. I kiss my hand and place it on her forehead, and shut her door. Back downstairs, Matt has the TV off and his head lifts as I approach.

"She's good?"

"She is." I sigh, exhaustion overtaking me.

"Come here." He crooks his finger, and I walk over to him. He pulls me onto his lap, cups my cheeks and plants a warm, yet hungry kiss on my lips. I kiss him back, and we're both aroused and breathless as we break apart.

"What was that for?"

"I've been dying to do that since I arrived at your door."

"You waited a long time."

"I wasn't about to ravish you in front of your mother."

"Ravish? That just seemed like a kiss to me." I tap my chin. "Do you have something else on your mind, Matt? Something else you've been thinking about."

"As a matter of fact, I do."

"Oh?"

"You never did answer me?"

I cock my head, and try to figure out what he's talking about. "I don't remember the question."

"There was something about sexual favors for Beaver Tails."

I laugh loud, and cover my mouth to stifle it.

"Something about you holding it against me."

"You're right, I never did answer. I sort of left you hanging."

"You left me hanging and hard," he admits, and I sort of love it.

He rakes his hands through my hair. "My patience is at an end. I want an answer," he teases as his fingers get tangled in the dried apple and banana. I yelp and he jerks his hand back.

"Sorry."

"It's okay."

"This is a first," he snorts with a laugh.

"A first."

"Cock blocked by a Beaver Tail."

I laugh and point to the stairs. "I think I should probably jump in the shower."

"Okay."

I push from his lap, already missing his warmth, and I can feel his eyes on me as I take the steps upstairs. My heart is pounding as I enter the bathroom, and turn the spray to hot. I strip down and leave the door open an inch in case Madelyn cries out.

I pull the shower curtain back and climb in, a low moan in my throat as the hot water washes over my fatigued body. I reach for the shampoo, and my hand stops abruptly when the curtain inches open. My gaze flies to Matt, as he stands there, heat and hunger in his eyes, as his big hand grips the shower curtain. God, I want him to touch me.

"I decided I couldn't wait another second for your answer," he murmurs, his voice deep and thick with arousal. It travels through my body, and settles deep between my legs. I grow wet, and it's not from the spraying water. But that's when I realize I'm standing in front of him stark naked in a brightly lit room. Panicking, I turn a bit to hide the scars on my body, and he stiffens, fully aware of my insecurities.

"Kennedy," he says his voice dropping an octave, as I look at him over my shoulder. "You're beautiful. Every inch of your body is perfect and I don't care about scars. I know you do, but I want you to know I don't." I swallow, a bevy of emotions gripping my throat and making it hurt. "If you want me to go, I'll go, but I'd rather you..." His gaze drops and takes in my naked body. "...hold it against me."

I exhale slowly, as the heat in his eyes push back some of my insecurities. "The answer is yes. I'll hold it against you." A low growl rumbles in his throat and vibrates through me as I shift back, and make room for him. We hold each other's gaze for an extra moment before he starts to peel off his clothes and I stand still, admiring the show.

Once he's naked, he climbs in, his body so big and strong next to mine as he gathers me into his arms, his hard cock pressed against my stomach.

"You hold it against me, and I'll take really good care of you," he says, his head dipping, his delicious mouth so close to mine, my lips begin to tingle in anticipation. I sag against him, leaning into his strength, selfishly taking instead of giving, which is so not like me.

He turns to put me under the spray, and I lift my face, every inch of my body on fire with arousal. With one big hand, he squirts the shampoo into his other palm, and lathers my hair. I moan, and he puts his mouth close to my ear.

"I love when you make sounds like that."

"I love the way you touch me," I admit.

"Good, and I plan to pull plenty more of those moans from you."

I close my eyes, sure I've died and gone to heaven. The water rains down on me as he turns me, and pulls me against his body, so he can wash the sticky mess from my hair. His cock presses into my back, and I move my hips and moan the way he likes.

"Jesus," he grumbles, and I grin, loving how much he likes my body, even though I'm too thin, and scarred. Once he rinses out my hair, he lathers his hands again with my body wash, and begins with my throat. His big palms race over me, sliding over my breasts, stopping to pluck at my hard nipples and going lower. I suck in a fast breath as his fingers move over my caesarean scar, but he doesn't linger. For that I'm grateful, although I suspect that's not always going to be the way with him.

He cups my sex and moans against my neck. How is this so good with him? For a guy with a selfish reputation, he sure is giving during sex. One thick finger slides into my core, and I put my hands on the tile wall, and claw it.

"Matt...that is so good." I move against his cock, pushing his finger in deeper.

"Yeah, Kennedy, ride my finger."

I move my hips, gyrate and take everything I need from him. A second finger slides in and with each forward jerk of my hips, I stimulate my clit against his rough palm. God that is so good. I lift my face, and water runs down my back, between our bodies, and as he fucks me with his fingers, he pushes against my back. If I could, I'd reach around and try to help take the edge off for him, but our current position—his fingers pumping inside me—makes it hard.

His breathing is hot against my neck, labored, letting me know he's coming undone too. "Fuck my fingers, just like that," he growls against my ear, and I continue to rock, and massage his cock between our bodies. "You've got me so hard, babe."

"Let me take care of you."

"No," he says with such force it surprises me, and angles his fingers to hit the sensitive bundle of nerves inside my wet sex. I am so close to losing it when he whispers, "Right now I'm taking care of you, so deal."

"Deal?" I manage to get out with a laugh. I really love this side of him, and honestly I can't remember when someone put me first or took care of me.

"Yeah, deal. In fact, get used to it."

Oh, how I want to, but the one working brain cell still firing warns me this is just bedroom talk—or shower talk—and in the stark reality of day, I can't count on a guy who is only in this for the sex, and who am I to talk? I'm in it for the sex too, so now I'm going to shut down my rattled brain and enjoy this for what it is.

I inch my legs open a bit more, wanting this, but also wanting his cock inside me.

"That's it, open for me, and let me make you feel really good." His aroused voice is like a lick to my clit, and a new kind of desperation grips me as my orgasm builds around his pistoning fingers.

"I want your cock," I cry out. "I want to bend over for you and I want you to put your cock in me and fuck me just like this."

"Yeah, that's what you want?"

"I want to come all over your cock." His soft curses curl around me, and I love how my dirty talk affects him.

He doesn't pull his fingers out. He just keeps fucking me with them and his moans tell a story of their own. He loves pleasuring me, but he too is taking pleasure in this, and that takes my arousal to a whole new level. My ex always seemed to be in a hurry, chasing his own orgasms, and sometimes leaving me empty and hollow. At least now I know why he was in a rush—he had a wife to get home to.

But I don't want to think about that.

"Matt, please. Your cock." My God, I've never pleaded for anything before, never sounded so desperate, but I'm not ashamed of myself. Matt wants me to take everything I need.

He pulls his fingers from my pussy, and I lean forward, bracing my hands lower on the wall as I stick my ass out.

"You are fucking killing me, girl." He cups my ass and squeezes, his cock moving along the crevice as he rocks against me. I glance at him, and his eyes are dazed and hungry as he grips his cock and strokes himself, pulling hard at the crown.

"Put your cock in me," I beg.

He grips my hips, positions his thick cock at my entrance and in one fast thrust he's inside me, his deep, tortured moan echoing off the tile walls.

"You are so hot and tight," he groans, one hand going around my waist. He cups my breast, and lifts me until my back is pressed against his chest, and I love the position. He grunts in my ear as he pulls me down, seating his cock high inside me.

"Oh, yes," I cry as he hits my cervix hard, bringing on a full body shudder. I am so close, I'm going to explode, but I don't want to. Not yet. I want to enjoy his cock inside me, the friction he's creating as he moves his hips, his throbbing cock gliding over my sensitive skin.

He bends me forward again, placing my hands on the wall, and he groans. "The view from back here, Kennedy. I wish you could see my cock moving in and out of you."

"It feels so good."

"Yeah, it does."

We both fall quiet, our bodies moving together, each of us seeking pleasure as we fuck. My climax expands, until there's no taming it anymore. The second I come all over his cock, he presses against my back, his hands going to my tits.

"Fuck yeah," he growls, as my hot come lubricates my channel even more. I gasp for air, and scrape at the wall, as I come and come and come some more, my sex clenching hard around his cock. "I'm there, Kennedy."

He lets go high inside my body, and my release fades as his takes hold. With my eyes closed I concentrate on the points of pleasure, the way he spurts hot cum inside of me with each hard pulse. The warmth travels through me, touching the coolest parts of my soul and honest to God, I can't remember the last time I was this warm, inside and out.

I let my head hang as he depletes himself, and as soon as he's done, his arms wrap around my body tightly, and he pulls me back against him.

"Babe...I...Jesus...are you..."

I laugh, loving that he's been reduce to a hot mess, and not able to form any words. Does this happen to him often? "Are you okay?"

"No," he moans and swallows. His cock slides from my body, and he spins me. I take in his dazed eyes. "I'm not sure I've ever orgasmed that hard before."

A thrill goes through me. "It's not always like this for you?" Oh, God, way to sound like a needy girl in search of compliments.

He brushes my wet hair from my face as the water grows cooler. "No."

"Same," is all I say. As I stare up at him, my heart pounding in crazy ways that frighten me.

"Matt," I say, my breath stalling in my lungs.

His head angles in confusion and concern. "Yeah?"

"We didn't use a condom."

16

MATT

"**F**uck me." My heart races as I rub the back of my neck. "I'm sorry, Kennedy. This is my fault. I wasn't thinking." I shake my head, angry with myself. "I always wear a condom. I don't know what happened."

She's probably looking for a baby daddy.

As Tank's words bounce around in my addled brain, she steps a bit closer. "What happened is you had no blood left in your brain," she says, and suddenly, she doesn't seem as upset as she was when she first realized it. She can't want to get pregnant, right? Maybe it's because I told her I always use a condom, and now she knows I'm clean. Yeah, that has to be it, but there's obviously the pregnancy thing we have to worry about.

"I'm on the pill," she explains, being safe clearly on her mind too. "It helps regulate my periods, and I don't trust condoms anyway. I just like the double protection."

I exhale, and put my hands on her shoulders. I'm guessing a condom broke in her past and that's why she has a daughter.

She obviously doesn't want to talk about her ex, and I'm not going to push, even though I do want to know.

I nod. "I can understand that," I tell her, hating myself for letting Tank get in my head. Kennedy isn't the kind of girl to trap any guy. If she was, wouldn't her ex still be in her life?

I reach behind her and turn off the water as it grows colder, and she shivers. "Let's get you warmed up." I snatch a towel from the small closet and wrap her in it. She hugs it to her body and I grab another one, dry off and tie it around my waist

The door creaks as I open it and we both go still. No sound comes from Madelyn's room, so I capture Kennedy's hand after she gathers up our clothes, and walk down the hall to her room. I enter and flick on the light. I stand there and take in the warmth of the place, zeroing in on the pictures of her and her daughter on her dresser.

"Welcome to my childhood bedroom." She frowns as I take a better look around. "Not much has changed, except I took my boy band posters down when I moved back home."

I guess I'd didn't realize she used to live on her own. "You didn't always live here?"

"I moved out when I started at the academy. After I got pregnant, and couldn't work as much to pay rent, I had no choice. Someday I'd like to find a place for Madelyn and me."

"When you're a famous singer?"

Her look is almost shy, like she's not quite ready to believe in herself. "Yes, Matt, when I'm a famous singer."

"I believe in you. I know you'll do it. You should probably play me some of your music, so I can advise you which of your songs is the best one to launch your career."

"Oh, a music connoisseur now, are you?"

"I'm a man of many talents, Kennedy, surely you must know that by now."

"Oh, I know it," she says with a grin. "You're persistent too, and I also really like that you want to hear my music. My ex..." She shakes her head. "Maybe someday I'll play them for you."

"I'm looking forward to it," I tell her, and don't question her on her ex. I guess seeing him tonight has brought up some painful memories, and I really hate that. I'm not sure what happened, and maybe I'll never know, but when she's with me, I don't want her thinking about him. I want her happy.

I step up to her dresser. "Cute," I say and pick up a picture of Madelyn dressed up like a Dalmatian and Kennedy is Cruella.

She laughs. "I made those costumes. I always loved Halloween as a kid."

"Me too."

"Really?" I nod. "You're welcome to come out with Madelyn and me this year, if you have the time."

"Speaking of time," I say, not giving her an answer. Halloween is a long time off and she could be done with me by then. "How did you ever find the time to make costumes?"

"Do you know Piper Thorne?"

"Not really. All I know is that my buddy Beckett hates her."

"Oh, right. I think he snarled at her when we were in the park. What's their problem, anyway?"

"No clue. Beck doesn't say too much about it, but there's history there."

"Well, Piper helped me with these costumes. She wants to be in fashion."

"I actually thought she was doing a business degree, like Beck. I thought they had some of the same classes."

"Yeah, she is and they do."

As I set the picture down a quiver goes through her towel covered body. I note the goosebumps on her skin. "Let's get you tucked in." She takes two small steps to her dresser and pulls out a pair of pajama shorts and a T-shirt. Her towel falls to the floor, and my dick jumps up to take notice. I growl, and she glances at me over her shoulder, hiding herself from me, but at least she's grinning as I stand there and blatantly admire her naked body.

"Are you going camping?"

"What?" I ask, as my blood once again drains to body parts that require extra substance for rapid growth. She chuckles as she points down and I follow her gaze, to see my dick tenting the towel.

"You think you're funny, do you?"

She tugs on her clothes, rolls her hand in front of herself and takes a bow. "I'll be here all week."

I growl as my dick throbs for more. "Then I know where I'm going to be."

She holds my gaze. "You want to spend the week with me, Matt?"

I step up to her, roll her wet hair between my fingers. "Yeah, I kind of do." Concern moves over her face, and I realize things just took a turn in the room, the atmosphere a little more serious. "I can't seem to get enough of you," I say and press my lips to hers, bringing this back to sex. The truth is, I like being around her, and it's not just the sex. I can't explain it. I've never been with the same girl twice, and yet, after two times with her, I still want more.

"When you put it that way, I must confess, for the record," she says with a wink. "I can't quite get enough of you either." She grins. "I guess that's what happens after a long dry spell."

Her hands go around my body and she holds me to her. "You've not been with anyone since…"

"No," she says.

"Why me?" My heart thumps, and I wish I hadn't asked. I need to keep this casual.

At first she looks like she wants to say something serious, but then she grins, and steps back. I'm about to pull her to me, wanting her body next to mine again, but I stop as she puts her hands on my body and spins me. I turn, until I see myself in her mirror.

"That's why," she says. I try to laugh it off. But goddammit, there was a stupid part of me that hoped she saw me for more than just a body. But she doesn't—no girl does—and I'm not going to forget that.

I half expect her to ask why I wanted to have sex with her. She's definitely not the kind of girl I usually go for, and she has a child. She doesn't ask, though—maybe she really just doesn't care as long as she's getting my dick. She walks to her bed and pulls the blankets down. She slides in and I glance at my clothes on her desk chair. I guess this is where I make my exit. I step up to the clothes, and tug on my boxer. She clears her throat.

I turn to her. "Are you thirsty?"

"I am."

"I'll get you a drink of water."

She makes a move to get up. "I can do that."

I pull on my jeans, and tug on my T-shirt. "Be right back." In the hall, I walk quietly, carefully missing the creaky steps and head to the kitchen. I pour a big glass of water and take a drink, then refill it for Kennedy. I hurry back to her room and she's still snuggled in her bed, looking so damn adorable, I have no idea how I've gotten so lucky. Wait, yes I do. She likes my body. With that thought banging around inside my brain, I cross the room and perch on the side of the bed.

"I drank from it first," I tell her, and jokingly add, "Now you're going to have my germs."

She laughs. "I'm not afraid of your germs." I grin as she takes a big drink.

"I suppose after what we just did, and no condom, a few germs are the least of your worries."

"You're clean, you told me."

I nod, liking that she knows I wouldn't lie to her. Though she doesn't trust me enough to tell me private things, though. *Stop being such a goddamn whiny baby, dude.* I take the half empty glass from her and set it on the nightstand. "Next time we should probably use a condom, if it makes you feel better."

"That's pretty presumptuous." She slides to the other side of her bed.

"What?"

She puts her index finger on the mattress and draws circles. "You think we're doing this again."

"Aren't we?"

"Hell yeah, we are," she says and we both laugh. She crooks her finger, and I slide in. "You got one thing wrong though."

"Oh."

"I was thinking we'd do it without the condom, and I was thinking we could do it again, right now."

"Are you serious?" Christ, I sound like a juvenile.

She laughs. "As serious as that erection I saw tenting your towel."

"That's pretty fucking serious." I sink down and we share her pillow. I lightly run the pads of my fingers over her flushed cheeks. "No condom?"

"I think we're past that."

I roll on top of her. "I think you're right." I steal a glance around. "Sex in your childhood bedroom. What if your mother walks in on us? Will we get into trouble?" I grin, remembering the days I used to sneak through bedroom windows. While the excitement of getting caught added to the fun, I'm over it. I want to be with Kennedy, simply two adults enjoying each other.

"No, but if she does walk in, she's going to get one hell of an eyeful." She puts her hands around my neck and pulls my mouth to hers. "I really don't want to talk about my mother right now, and she's not home tonight because she clearly likes you."

"What's not to like?" I joke.

"I could do a list, but I have other things on my mind," she teases as she moves against my body."

"Hey," I say and kiss her mouth fiercely.

I break the kiss and she says, "Honestly though, she's been very good to Madelyn and me, although I think at some point she'd like to have her house back. We can be...a lot."

"She's trying to marry you off?"

She laughs. "Don't worry Matt. I won't let her get the wrong idea about you." She widens her legs until my cock is centered on her sex. "Also, we're still talking about my mother when I'd rather you put your cock inside me again."

"Is that what you want, babe?" Why do I always need to hear her say how much she wants me?

"Yes, I've had a hell of a week with work, school and cleaning this nasty frat house." She gives me a small grin. "Tonight, I want to forget all of that and just feel you inside me."

"I can do that."

"Yeah you're good at that." Her eyes fall shut as I tug on her T-shirt and she lifts her arms, helping me get it off. I go between her legs to get rid of her shorts, and once she's naked, I stand and make fast work of discarding my clothes. Once I'm back laying skin to skin on top of her, I kiss her mouth and slide down to devour her neck.

"Oh yeah, you're really good at this," she murmurs.

"Sex and hockey," I murmur between hot, open-mouthed kisses, trying to sound light—wanting to sound light. I'm hating this new kind of heaviness inside of me. "Two things I'm good at."

"Matt," she murmurs. "You're good at—" Her words, encouraging words no doubt that are just going to mean nothing in the big scheme of things, turn into a moan as I take one nipple into my mouth and suck hard. "Oh, that feels so good."

I cup her other breast, and pinch her nipple until she's squirming beneath me. I slide lower, wanting her sweet cunt filling my mouth, and when my lips glide across the puckered scar on her lower abdomen, she tenses.

"It's okay," I tell her. "I love every part of your body." It's not a lie. I move past her scar, as she's still uncomfortable with me acknowledging it, and I find the treasure I've been seeking. I lick her, and lift my head to check on her. Her body relaxes again and her hips come off the bed to meet my tongue. I stick it out, giving her exactly what she's seeking from me.

"You are so good at that," she cries out.

Yup, we already established I'm good at sex. I push those thoughts from my mind and go back to pleasuring her, wanting her to forget about real life for a while. She deserves that. I slide a finger into her, and my cock throbs. Christ, I've just been inside her and you'd think I'd be sated, but nope. Like I said, I can't get enough of her and I sort of like that she can't get enough of me, even though there's no chance of any kind of relationship. I guess we'll just have to keep fucking until we burn ourselves out.

I have to burn out. I don't have what it takes to step in and be her partner and Madelyn's male role model, right?

Why the hell not, Matt?

"Matt," she murmurs and I move up her body, wanting to see her face when she orgasms this time—no barrier between us. It's not a dangerous game because she's on the pill and she's clean. I've never taken any kind of risk before, but this is Kennedy and I trust her.

I cup her cheeks, and our eyes lock as I move my body, sliding my hard cock into her softness. "Matt," she murmurs, the pleasure in her eyes wrapping around my body and squeezing tight.

"Yeah, I know, Kennedy." I'm not sure what I know, only that there's something about being with her. Something different and powerful, like the moon's gravitational force creating a pull inside me. I'm that drawn to her.

This is still just sex, right?

If so, why the hell does it feel like so much more? Her hands slide around my neck, and she touches me; her caress is softer this time, no nails on my back, no rushed movements, just the two of us soaking in each other and not holding back as the waves crash over us.

Her eyes move over my face, dazed and half lidded, and I kiss her deeply, once again wanting to taste the depths of her as she comes around my cock. I grip her hips for leverage, and angle my body for deeper thrusts, and her eyes roll back.

"My God, Matt," she cries, and her chest rises and falls quickly. I glance down to see her gorgeous tits, her lush hard nipples and my orgasm takes hold. Kennedy breaks, and her hot cum sears my cock, the pleasure traveling all the way to my balls, squeezing out my release.

I come with her, filling her body with my seed, and it's so goddamn strange. I've always been so careful to use a condom, but I want my cum in her. I want to fill her and when it drips out, I want her to remember this night with a secret smile. Not that we're keeping this a secret. Okay, maybe we sort of are. I'm not supposed to be messing with her, and she shouldn't be messing with me, for numerous reasons.

I bury my face in her shoulder as I spurt the last of my cum into her, and I collapse on top of her tiny body, the two of us spent from our second round of sex. After a long moment, I lift my head, and her eyes are closed. I shift to the side and she makes a small noise, and I'm pretty sure she's half asleep.

I should go, leave her to get a good night sleep, as much as I don't want to. As much as I'd like to stay here until morning, it's probably not a good idea for Madelyn to see me in the morning, or Kennedy's neighbors, or the guys on my team.

Deciding to shoot her a text, which is probably a douche move, I stand, tug on my clothes and make a quick trip to the bathroom. Unable to leave her a hot sticky mess, I grab a cloth, run it under some warm water and quietly walk back to her room. She makes a small moan as I gently sit on the mattress, and wipe between her legs. Once she's clean, I tuck her in, and make my way to the door, sure she's fast asleep, until...

"He was married."

I take a breath and go still as her words ring through my brain. She's telling me something very important, something she holds close. She's trusting me in a new way and honest to

Christ, I don't want to read more into this, but it means a fucking lot to me that she's opening up her heart and not just her body.

My hand falls from the doorknob, and I turn around to find her sitting up a bit, her back propped on her pillow as she blinks at me.

My gaze rakes over her face, and my heart pinches tight as I see the hurt and disappointment. "Kennedy?"

17

KENNEDY

"He was married," I say quietly and pat the bed. He drops the washcloth as he takes a step toward me and I lift the sheets for him to get in. He gently eases himself down, fixing the sheets around us. Beneath the bedding, our hands seek out one another, and we link our fingers. His strength and presence gives me the strangest kind of courage, and while I never thought I'd tell another soul about what happened with Oliver, I find myself opening up. "He had a wife, and a dog, and now it looks like he has another baby on the way."

"Jesus." He scrubs his face and exhales as he tries to process. It's a lot to throw at him, especially after a beautiful night of sex.

A cold chill goes through me. "Can you pass me my clothes?" He hands me my pajama shorts and T-shirt and I climb into them. Somehow, they make me feel less vulnerable as I open up to Matt.

After a long moment, he says, "You didn't know." It's a statement, not a question, and I like that he just automatically knows I'm not the type of girl to get involved with a married man. I'm not.

"No. We never went back to his place because he said he had a roommate. I didn't question it. I can't deny that I used to think it was odd that this very educated, up and coming lawyer, still had a roommate."

"A lawyer, huh? Was that even true?"

I laugh, even though it's not at all funny. "I saw the business cards, but not the office. I'm guessing he kept me away because...you know...I was the side piece."

He squeezes my hand. "Don't say that."

"How would you say it?"

"You were his girlfriend, and he was an asshole. Simple as that."

I like that he's trying to convince me that I was more than a side piece. But I know what I am and what I'm not, and I'm not going to make the same mistakes again—especially not with Matt.

"How did you meet?"

"It was my freshman year. I was playing at a pub, and I noticed this guy in a business suit watching me. I always assumed he was winding down after a hard day at work. Everything about him was so put together, like he really had his life figured out. I was young and stupid, and sadly, I guess I was attracted to a guy who knew who he was and what he wanted in life. It was a hard hit when I realized that wasn't me, or Madelyn. Like I said, young and stupid."

"No, you weren't." I turn to him and give him a look that says I beg to differ. "Okay, you were young, but you didn't know he was married. He was clearly very good at hiding the fact that he had a whole other life."

"Yeah, I guess he was. He kept showing up on Thursday nights, and he would just sit quietly and have a beer while I played. After about a month, he talked to me. I thought he was shy and I found it endearing." I snort and it's followed by a humorless laugh. "I guess he was debating on whether to remain monogamous or not."

"Not," he growls.

"Yeah not. Now, I don't talk to guys who try to pick me up when I'm playing."

"I noticed that you try not to pay them any attention."

"I don't want to make another mistake. Not that Madelyn is a mistake. I'm not saying that."

"I know how much you love her."

"When that guy jumped on stage with a beer that night," I shake my head. "I just try to keep my head down, and my focus—"

"I'm glad it happened."

My eyes go wide and I turn to see him. "What?"

"That came out wrong." He shakes his head. "Let me try again. I hate that he touched you, and that you got fired. I just like that we met that night. That's all I'm trying to say."

"What a way to meet. Thank you, though. For helping me."

Matt pulls his hand from mine, and my throat tightens. Am I telling him too much, scaring him off? This is, after all, supposed to be about sex, but honestly, when we saw Oliver earlier, he really seemed interested in my past. I wasn't ready to tell him then. I am now, but does he want to hear it?

"Come here," he coaxes and puts his arm around me, shifting lower on the bed so my head is on his chest, his strong heartbeat pounding against my cheek.

I settle in and he lightly runs his fingers through my still damp hair. Everything in his touch is gentle, caring and so damn nice. "I was in love."

"Earlier, I thought you might still love him."

"Really, wow no. I could never love a man who cheated and could so easily turn his back on his own daughter."

"He knew about her then?"

"Yes, I told him. We weren't married or engaged, and when I got pregnant, I had visions of grandeur." A cynical laugh bubbles in my throat. "I figured we'd move in together, raise Madelyn, get a dog and be the perfect family."

"Except he already had the perfect family."

"A family, but not perfect, or he wouldn't have been sleeping with me."

"That's true." He touches my shoulder, pulls me tighter against him. "He just walked away after you told him?"

"Yeah, he freaked and told me he was married and couldn't do this, then he walked."

"Did he tell his wife about you?"

"Not that I know of and I seriously doubt it."

"She deserves to know."

"I couldn't do it, Matt. I couldn't break up a family whether they were happy or not, and at the end of the day, while I realize Madelyn needs a male influence in her life, she doesn't need his kind of influence."

He exhales and his chest rattles, like he's trying to control his rage. I lift my head, take in the anger in his eyes. "She deserved to know what was going on behind her back."

"I agree with you," I say. "I'm just not the one who was going to tell her. That's on him."

"You were too good for him, Kennedy."

My heart swells, feeling lighter somehow after opening up.

"Thank you for telling me all this," he whispers.

I turn my head and through his shirt, I press my lips to his stomach. "I wanted you to know."

"Why?"

"I...don't know." I shrug and think about it. "To be honest, it felt good to tell you, and I like that you don't judge me."

"Have others judged you?"

"No one really knows the whole story. My mother only knows bits and pieces. It's embarrassing."

"Kennedy," he says softly, and tugs me to him. "You have nothing to be embarrassed about. This is all on that asshole."

"Maybe, but now I go into things with open eyes and a closed heart. It's for the best," I say, as sleep pulls at me. Matt goes completely still and very quiet. "Matt?"

"Thanks for telling me something so personal. I know it wasn't easy to rehash all that."

It might not have been easy but I think it was cathartic. I open my mouth to tell him that and he says, "Sleep." I close my mouth and he runs his hand over my arm, keeping me against him as I let my lids fall shut. I can't remember the last time I felt so safe or so cherished. I take one last deep breath and the next thing I know, the sun is shining in my room, and the other side of my bed is empty. The emptiness that engulfs me nearly steals the air from my lungs, and I take a deep gulping breath.

No way am I going to allow it to overwhelm me. No way am I going to make past mistakes and think there is more going on here than there is. I can't think about myself, not when I have a daughter to care for. Wait, Madelyn should have been up by now. Panic grips my throat, and I toss the blankets off. She fell asleep ages ago, but I'm still worried sick that there's a delayed reaction from the concussion. I hurry to her room, and her bed is empty. I'm about to bolt, assuming she somehow climbed out of her crib. It's because of my overprotective nature that I've been slow to transition her to a bed, and I'm sure I'll have a million heart attacks when I finally do.

Maybe Mom came home early and took her down for breakfast. I'm about to bolt downstairs, when the sound of Matt's low voice rises up the steps and wraps around me. My heart thuds a little too hard as I walk to the top of the stairs and listen to Madelyn's giggles. I smile, and my chest shudders as emotions grip me. My brain on the other hand is telling me to abort. To walk away from Matt not just for my own sake, but for my daughter's. I can't let either one of us fall for him.

I head downstairs and find Madelyn in her highchair, her hair messy, her face full of blueberry yogurt as Matt does some kind of dance with the puppet. She's laughing her head off so loudly, they don't hear me, and my gaze goes to Matt. I didn't expect for him to stay over, nor did I expect him to be here this morning, and let me sleep in while he took care of my daughter.

He's dressed in the same clothes as yesterday, his hair sticking up all over the place, and a bit of scruff on his face. He's usually pretty clean shaven and I like this mussed up side of him. Who am I kidding, I like all the sides of him.

As if sensing me there, his head lifts and my heart swells so much at the warm sweet look he gives me, I'm sure it's going to burst from my chest.

Oh boy.

"Good morning," he says softly, his words wrapping around me like a comfortable blanket and making me forget this isn't a real, loving relationship we're in. Not that I would even know what that looks like. I'd been fooled once.

"I can't believe I didn't hear her."

"I can." He laughs, a devilish smirk on his face—one that's supposed to remind me of the two times we had sex last night and how it knocked me for a loop. Okay, he knocked me off my feet—the very first time he jumped to my rescue at the pub. "I got up the second she made a peep. I hope you don't mind."

"Mind, heck no. I can't remember the last time I heard her laugh so much."

"It's the charm," he admits with a grin.

"I think it's the puppet."

I laugh and he stares at me with those big soulful eyes and I feel like I just kicked a puppy. Not that I would ever kick a puppy, but you know what I mean. "I'm kidding. You're charming."

He grins and before I even realize what I'm doing, I cross the kitchen, bend and press my lips to his. Madelyn bangs her hand on the highchair table and I jump back, shaking my head.

"Sorry, I don't know why I did that."

He exhales and his eyes briefly close as he shakes his head. "It's the charm. It's my curse, Kennedy."

I laugh, loving that he's making light of it, because it could have gotten heavy very quickly. I don't want that. I don't want either of us to be uncomfortable at what this is and what it isn't. Note to self: no more morning kisses in the kitchen. Although I don't expect he'll be staying over again anytime soon.

"Don't you have a class to get to?" I ask.

"Don't you?"

"Yes, but I have to clean up Madelyn, grab a shower myself, get her food packed and get her to daycare, before I can get to class."

"What can I do to help?"

"It's okay. I got this. It's no different from any other morning."

"Yes, it is," he says and stands, coming close to me. My heart jumps, and my insides fire with need. "This morning I'm here."

I want to tell him I'm not about to get used to that, but I don't. "It's okay. I've got this." Damn if he doesn't look a little disappointed by that.

"How does the rest of your day look?"

"Classes, clean Storm House and cook up a casserole, them more classes. Pick Madelyn up and tonight I have a gig. How about you?"

Before he can answer, the front door creaks open and I instinctively jump back, breaking our contact. I don't miss the way Matt's eyes narrow in on me, like he's worried I'm ashamed of what we've done, and that I might not want to be seen with him, and I honestly don't know why I'm panicking. My mother doesn't care. She probably wants this.

Oh, maybe you're panicking because you're getting close and it's damn scary.

"As soon as she sees I'm here, she'll know."

"I know..." I glance down and frown. "I just—"

"Good morning," Mom calls out, loud enough to wake a herd of elephants in the Savannas. I get it, Mom, you're announcing your presence in case we're indecent.

"In here," I yell, and mom cautiously peeks around the corner. A wide smile spreads across her face when she sees Matt. "I'm not interrupting anything, am I?"

My God, subtle she is not.

"We're good. Just getting up and getting Madelyn ready."

"I'm here just in time to help," she announces, and scoops Madelyn up.

"You're here tonight, right?" I ask, hating that I have to ask her to care for Madelyn so often. "Remember the new gig at The Lower Deck. Tuesdays and Saturdays."

Mom frowns. "Shoot, I completely forgot. I won't be able to watch her tonight. I took an extra shift at the restaurant."

I nod quickly. I don't want mom ever to feel bad. "No worries," I say, even though I am worried. "I'll figure something out."

Matt's knuckles brush mine and I turn to him as he says, "I can watch her."

My first reaction is to tell him, "No." As soon as I do, Matt's face falls and he backs up another inch.

"Yeah, no, for sure."

"Matt," I begin quickly.

"I totally understand."

He doesn't understand. Not really and what the heck am I supposed to say? Oh, it's possible I'm falling for you, and my daughter might be too, so it's best we don't spend any more time with you. "You have other things to do. We don't want to be a burden," I explain.

"I wouldn't have offered if I had other things to do. I don't have practice or a game, and I do have some homework to catch up on. I can easily do it here. Heck, it's quieter here than at Storm House."

"It's settled then," Mom says. She puts Madelyn back in her highchair, efficiently claps her hands like it's time to move on, and she walks to the coffee pot to make coffee. I shake my head and meet Matt's eyes. He gets it. Mom is trying to set us up. I roll my eyes at him to make light of it.

"What time?" he asks quietly and while Mom has her back to us, he reaches out and lightly brushes his fingers over my wrist. The reaction it pulls from me is explosive, and I'm glad no one can see me but him.

"I start at seven, so I should leave here thirty minutes beforehand to get ready."

"I'll be here forty-five minutes beforehand."

I laugh. "Okay." Honestly, it's a bit of a relief not to have to scramble to find someone to watch her. I can always ask Amy, but she just had her on the weekend, and I hate to ask anyone too often.

"I'd better get going and get ready for class," Matt says. I nod, and he backs up, stooping down for a second to talk to Madelyn. "I guess I'll see you tonight, kiddo. We'll have pizza and beer, and stay up late watching late night talk shows." He lifts his head, a grin on his face, and I just shake my head at him.

"I'll be home a little after ten. Far too early for you to corrupt my daughter with late night talk shows."

He arches a brow, and I'm honestly having a hard time not hugging him. "You're okay with the pizza and beer, then?"

"What am I getting myself into?" I ask. Truthfully though, sometimes Matt does act like a kid and I actually like that about him. What I realize though, is he's not a kid and he's got a lot more going on than he lets anyone know.

"See you later, Barb."

"Have a great day, Matt."

"Maf," Madelyn calls out and we all laugh. My heart is floating somewhere in the vicinity of my throat as Matt leaves the kitchen, and I stare long after the front door shuts behind him. Mom clears her throat and I brace myself for the lecture.

"He's a nice boy," she says. I don't say anything and she continues with, "Madelyn seems to like him."

"We're just friends, Mom. He feels responsible for getting me fired and is helping me out." Oh, he's helping me out by giving me numerous orgasms too. I think it's best to keep that part to myself. Although, I'm sure it must be true. He asked me why him. I told him but I didn't ask him the same. I know there's more to him, but I also know there's not more to us. I'd have to be a fool to think I was the kind of girl he went for—heck, I've seen the girls on his arm—and I didn't want to hear he was just helping a girl out.

I probably wasn't as honest with him as I should have been when I answered his question— why him—though. Sure, he's hot and well built, and a face sculpted by the gods, but I wasn't just going to have sex or trust any guy around my daughter because of the way he looked. There's something sweet, and soft and sincere about Matt. I guess that's the reason I finally gave my body to him.

"Oh," Mom begins. "I'll be late at the restaurant tonight and since Leo's place is closer, I think I'll just crash there."

I spin. "Mom, no. This is your home."

She touches my cheek, and her warm smile and soft scent take me back to my younger years. When I would fall and hurt myself and she'd cradle me and tell me everything was going to be okay. She was mother and father to me, and that is not easy. I know it firsthand. Only my mom didn't have a mother like I have, someone to lean on and I've been leaning on her way too hard lately. She needs a life of her own. Maybe I could find an inexpensive place, and take on a roommate or two. Students are always moving in and out. While that sounds good in theory, most students don't want a baby hanging around.

I scoop Madelyn up, and after a quick bath, I set her in her crib to play and get myself ready. Thirty minutes later we're out the door, and I drop her off at daycare. The next thing I know, I'm in class, and I can't miss the way people are suddenly looking at me. Do I have something on my face? I brush my cheek, and sink a little lower in my seat. I don't mind being in the spotlight when I'm on stage. In real life, I prefer to keep to myself. I'm guessing everyone knows I'm sleeping with Matt and they're all probably trying to figure out why he's indulging me.

The rest of the morning goes by slowly and right before lunch, as I'm sitting in the sunlight, munching on a sandwich, my phone pings. I tug it from my pocket, and a stupid smile that I have no control over tugs at my lips. I guess Matt must be waiting for me at Storm House.

Matt: Where are you?

Me: Outside of Admin building. Eating.

Matt: I thought we could eat together.

Me: I didn't know.

. . .

Matt: Pack up your lunch and get over here.

With butterflies taking flight inside me, I wrap the plastic around the rest of my sandwich and jump to my feet. Jeez, with a smile I can't seem to wipe off my face, I'm sure I look like the village idiot. That has to be why people are staring. I've been grinning since I first got naked with Matt the night of the party.

Is that what he's up to now? Waiting for me so we can both get naked for an afternoon quickie. I'm not opposed to the idea, but it will mean I'll have to burn through Storm House to clean it, and get a meal prepared in under an hour. Is the quickie worth it?

Hell yeah.

As I cut across campus, there's a part of me that says I'm being silly, impulsive and ridiculously indulgent. I can't disagree with that logical side, but the needy side of me well, needs this. Craves it.

I reach Storm House and glance over my shoulder. My God, why do I feel like a kid with her hand in the cookie jar? I'm supposed to be here today. Having sex with Matt. I'm probably not suppose to be doing that. I reach for my key and the door opens and the second my gaze lands on Matt, freshly showered in clean jeans and T-shirt, his feet bare, I'm sure I'm going to melt into a puddle at his feet. He is seriously the hottest guy on the planet.

"Hi," he says and before I can get a word out, he pulls me to him and plants his mouth on mine. I whimper against him, and slide my arms around his shoulders, breathing in his fresh, soapy scent. I'm not sure what scent it is, but it's now become my favorite.

"Hi," I say back, our lips lingering, our foreheads pressed together.

"What took you so long?"

I laugh and he hauls me inside, taking my backpack from me and setting it on the table near the door. "I was eating lunch."

"Are you full?"

"No," I say. "I only had half a sandwich." I'm not about to tell him half a sandwich pretty much fills me, because I suspect he's up to something. Did he cook again? No, that would be ridiculous. This is about sex.

"Good." He takes my hand and leads me into the kitchen. My jaw gapes open as I take in the sushi laid out on the table. Something sparks inside my brain, and I lift my head to glance around. "Why is this place so clean?"

"I tidied up a bit." He shrugs, his expression a bit sheepish, maybe even unsure and...vulnerable. "So we could have a bit of time together."

"You wanted to eat together?" I shake my head.

"You like sushi, right?"

"I do. How did you know?"

He rolls one shoulder and glances at all the take-out containers. "I saw you at a sushi restaurant once. I assumed you liked it."

"That must have been a long time ago."

"What can I say, I have a good memory."

He remembered seeing me at the sushi restaurant? Up until the night at the bar, I didn't think he even knew I existed. Me, well, I definitely knew he existed. You'd have to be buried under a rock, not to have heard his name on campus.

Still hardly able to believe what's going on here, I mutter, "I thought we were having sex."

Why the hell is he suddenly frowning? "If that's what you want," he says. "I just thought, you know, it's lunch and we need to eat and you like sushi..."

"I do. It's my favorite food and are you really asking me to pick between every kind of sushi roll known to mankind and sex?" I laugh, but my insides are a bit wobbly. He didn't ask me to hurry over for sex, but instead to feed me? I don't know whether to laugh or cry.

"I just thought...it was stupid."

"Hell no, it wasn't." I step up to the table, wanting to lighten things up. He went out of his way to do something extremely nice, and I'm being ridiculous. And why am I being ridiculous? Oh, because my heart is a hot pumping mess, and no one has ever been so sweet to me before.

"For the record if you had to pick, which would it be?"

I laugh. "Well, up until you, I would have said sushi."

A big silly grin curls his lips. He opens his mouth like he wants to say something and the front door opens and what sounds like a herd of elephants come running in. I hear a lot of cursing and banging around in the other room, then the door opens and closes again, leaving us in silence.

He shakes his head, unimpressed. "I really need my own place."

"I know the feeling." I open one of the packages, take out a roll and hold it out to him. "You first."

His smile reappears and my insides squeeze tight enough to choke the oxygen from my lungs. He opens his mouth and I feed him the roll. "So good," he murmurs, and picks one up. He holds it out and I let him feed me. My eyes roll back in my head. I can't remember the last time I had sushi.

"Can we sit and eat?" I ask. "It's going to take forever feeding each other like this, and I want to chow down. It's going to get messy, so you might want to look away."

He laughs. "No way. I want to see this." He pulls a chair out and gestures for me to sit.

I eye him suspiciously before sitting. "Are you going to judge me?"

"No judgement from me, Kennedy." He holds both hands up, palms out. "Hey," he begins, his voice an octave lower. "You've seen me eat something I love, and I was all in, eating away like I'd been living on rations for the last year."

I bite my lip, understanding exactly what he's talking about by the mischief in his eyes. He takes another roll and feeds it to me. It's like a party on my tongue. "But seriously, you're the best thing I've ever tasted," he adds, not at all embarrassed as he sits across from me, and puts a couple rolls on a plate.

The roll gets stuck in my throat. God, it's ridiculous how my body reacts and how much I love the dirty things he says to me. I finally manage to swallow. "You can't say things like that when I have food in my mouth. I almost died."

He laughs at my exaggeration, and I stare at him. When the hell was the last time I simply laughed and had fun? A girl could definitely get used to this.

"On the farm when I was growing up, we had a dog who used to eat everything. I mean everything, and he especially loved my socks."

"Ew."

"Hey, it could have been worse."

"Yeah, it could have been your underwear."

"We're back to talking about my underwear?" He puts a few rolls on his plate and I load mine up as well, my entire body relaxing, as I enjoy our camaraderie, and easy conversation. I am absolutely loving everything about today. "Wait!" he practically yells, and my head lifts. "Oh my God, you can't stop thinking about them, can you?"

I crinkle up my nose. "What? No."

"No, you can't stop thinking about them, you mean?" He reaches for the soy sauce. "I knew it. You have an underwear fetish."

"No, I don't. I meant to say yes."

"Yes, you can't stop thinking about them?"

He starts laughing and I shake my head at his playfulness and the way he's twisting my words, and having a great time with me. "This isn't coming out right."

"Just admit, you have a thing for my boxers."

"I do not," I say, lifting my chin an inch. "For the record, I have a thing for what they're covering."

He stops laughing and sobers quickly. "Oh, yeah, I like that fetish much better."

I grin. "Good, now tell me about this sock-eating dog you had."

"Well, Chester wasn't the brightest dog, but he was the loyalist." He angles his head. "Is that a word.",

"It is, but not in the way you mean. I get it, though." I bite into a California roll, chewing slowly, so he will continue with his story.

"He got this one sock stuck, and I couldn't get it out. I ended up having to do the Heimlich maneuver." He pumps his hands in front of himself, imitating the movement.

"You lie!"

"No, it's true, I learned the Heimlich after Mom saved Liam. You know, the grape incident."

"No, I mean you're lying about giving your dog the Heimlich."

"What, no, I don't lie, and you can give dogs the Heimlich. I saved old Chester that day. He went on to eat many other socks."

I stare at him for a long second as he digs into the food. Is he for real? You know, authentic, kind, funny and...every type of awesome. I think he might be, which begs the question, if he's so great, why does he run away from relationships.

Be careful, Kennedy. You made this mistake one time before...

"What?" he asks when he finds me staring.

While I might have made mistakes in the past, I can't seem to keep my heart out of this one, and that's a big freaking problem. "You're something else, Matt."

His soft smile curls around my heart when he reaches out, lightly runs the rough pad of his thumb over my wrist, and responds with, "Yeah, you're something else too, Kennedy."

19

MATT

"I'm not so sure about this," Kennedy says to Amy, as they scoop the girls out of the back seat of Amy's SUV.

Since the rink is close to my place, I drove straight here to meet them, and take one look at Kennedy and Madelyn as Madelyn calls out, "Maf," and my insides melt a bit. God, I am in so much trouble. Why the hell did I bring two sweet girls like them into my messed-up life? I really am an asshole.

But what if I could do better? What if I had some substance to me, and there really is more to me than hockey?

"I think it will be fun, and if you want, you can wear a helmet. I brought mine and Doug's." Amy reaches into the back seat and holds up Doug's helmet, showing it to Kennedy. "He has a big melon head, but it will do in a pinch."

I laugh and it eases some of my jitters. Why do I have jitters, you ask? Oh, just being around Kennedy and her daughter does that to me.

"Did you just say your husband has a melon head?" I ask.

"Yeah, you'll see it when you meet him tonight. He had golf today so he couldn't make this, but he's looking forward to meeting you, Matt."

I arch a brow and glance at Amy. "When I meet him tonight?"

She waves her hand and shakes her head to brush me off, so I let it go. Without even thinking about it, I bend and scoop up Madelyn.

"Are you ready to become the next great female hockey player?" I ask her and adjust the hat on her head. She makes a fist and waves her fingers, Madelyn style. "I think that's a yes," I tell Kennedy who is standing deathly still watching us. Shoot, was I not supposed to pick Madelyn up?

I hand her over and Kennedy takes her without saying anything. Maybe her silence is her way of setting boundaries. I really don't know and if she's worried about us bonding, I'm afraid we're past that. Madelyn and I became besties and we had an awesome time when I watched her last week. Kennedy and I had the best time after she finished her set at The Lower Deck and we crawled into her bed together.

"I'm going to break my neck," Kennedy groans, and I take in the fluffy red sweater she's wearing, and those familiar body-hugging jeans I'd love to get her out of.

I nudge her. "Nah, I got you." She smiles up at me, and my heart warms at the trust shining in her eyes. I take her hand in mine, and her eyes widen as her smile flatlines, and I'm guessing she's shocked that I'm holding her hand in public. For a second I expect her to jerk hers back—I'm not sure she likes to be seen with me—but she doesn't and Amy smirks at the two of us as we all head inside.

We rent skates and get the girls all bundled up and in their helmets. The ice is pretty busy by the time we're ready, and I'm used to being on it with the team, not a bunch of families. I hold both Kennedy and Madelyn's hand, helping them on the ice, and they both wobble.

"Maybe you should wear that helmet," I tease. "Have you never been on skates?"

"Of course." She whacks me and nearly falls. "I need a moment to get my balance. It's not like riding a bike." I wrap one arm around her and hold tight until she gets her skating legs.

She balances herself as Amy takes to the ice, spinning around us and showing off her moves as I try to steady Kennedy. As Amy laughs and helps Chloe, Kennedy takes a moment to find her balance and once she does, she's pretty good.

"Look at me now," she brags and skates around us.

I smile as she holds her arms out and tries to show off. "Not bad at all."

I squat down in front of Madelyn and take both of her hands and help her. She giggles as I stand and she lets me pull her along. "She's a natural," I say to Kennedy who is standing over us watching. Kennedy gives me a big smile, and I'm happy she's enjoying herself. I thought she'd have fun out here.

We skate and laugh, and Madelyn falls on her butt a couple times, but she doesn't seem to mind too much—she's padded. Chloe and Madelyn giggle and shuffle, and Kennedy and Amy pull their phones out to take pictures.

"You guys get in the photo," I say and take Kennedy's phone from her. I take bunch of pictures and we all make our way around the rink again. The smell of chocolate reaches my nostrils, and I gesture toward the small canteen. "Hot chocolate?" I ask.

Kennedy's jaw gapes open, and I laugh when she asks, "Did you just meet me?"

The answer is yes—because the truth is I haven't known her for very long, and I still have a lot to learn. It's insane how excited I am about that. How long will the two of us keep seeing each other? Until she's no longer lonely and has had enough of me? Until another guy comes into her life and can give her more than just sex?

Fuck, I hate the idea of that.

So, what are you going to do about it, asshole?

We all skate off the ice, and Madelyn and Chloe wobble in their big snowsuits as we head to get a hot chocolate. I order three adult and two child size drinks and grab a bag of potato chips. We all sit on the bleachers, enjoying our hot chocolate and watching the families skate. I don't miss the melancholy look on Kennedy's face as she leans forward, watching the fathers play with their children. She wants that, and she was right when she said her daughter needed a male influence in her life. I'm just glad she's being careful and picky.

Chloe spills the bag of chips and starts fussing and crying and trying to pick them up off the dirty floor. "Looks like someone is in need of a nap," Amy says and starts taking Chloe's skates off.

Kennedy nods in agreement. "Madelyn does too. We should probably go."

"Okay," I say and take my skates off. Once we're all back in our street shoes, I return the skates, and the mid-afternoon sun shines down on us as we head outside. I carry the helmets to the SUV and when we reach it, my throat grows tight. Fuck. She's not even gone, yet there's a hollowed out feeling in my gut, knowing I'm going to spend the rest of my day without them.

"Does five sound okay?" Amy asks me, as she kicks her foot under the back hatch and it opens. I toss the helmets in and Amy throws in the big diaper bag she has with her. I narrow my eyes, confused and she continues with, "I know that's a bit early for dinner. But Kennedy plays tonight at seven, and that will give us some time to have some burgers, hang out, have a drink. Also, I'm keeping Madelyn for the night, so if you two want to hang out after her set..."

"Amy, I don't think—" Kennedy begins and I cut her off.

"You're about as subtle as Kennedy's mother," I laugh.

Amy laughs with me as Kennedy stares at us both with big, worried doe eyes. "You don't have to come if—"

I lean in and kiss her. Our lips linger for a moment, and a part of me worries that she's worried I might want more, and I can't risk her ending this—I am so fucked—so I whisper, "Food, Kennedy. When have you ever heard me turn down food?"

She laughs, and Madelyn throws her hand out, hits me in the eye, then grips my hair and tugs.

"Madelyn," Kennedy scolds. She pries her daughter's fingers from my hair. "Sorry, she's tired and cranky. I need to put her down for a nap."

I put my mouth close to her ear. "If I tug your hair, will you put me down for a nap?" A blush crawls into her cheeks.

"God, I wish I didn't have such great hearing," Amy mutters, and we all laugh.

"Yeah, I will." She winks at me. "But first I have to make a dish for the barbecue."

"No, you don't," Amy calls out from inside the vehicle.

I stare at Kennedy, perplexed. "How did she hear that?"

"I think she's a superhero in disguise, but if you want to come help me with the dish before we nap, I'd like that," Kennedy says, and I open the back door for her to get Madelyn into her seat.

After Kennedy buckles her in and shuts the door, I ask quietly, "Do you want me to follow you, or do you want me to lead?"

"I think she likes it when her man takes control," Amy screams out.

"Ohmigod," Kennedy groans, and covers her face with her hand. "Amy, I'm going to kill you." Amy simply laughs from the front seat. Kennedy shake her head, clearly embarrassed. "Just follow us."

"Okay, I'll follow in the rear," I say.

"That's what she said," Amy shouts out and on that note, Kennedy opens her door and climbs in. She just shakes her head at me as she closes her door and turns to Amy, ready to give her a mouthful, and now holy hell, all I can think in response to a mouthful is: that's what she said.

I laugh at my immature behaviour as I walk away and jump into my truck. I'm about to pull out of my spot when Vanessa and Tanisha jump behind my truck. What the hell are they doing? I could have killed them. I stop and Vanessa comes to the driver's side. I roll my window down.

"Where are you off to in such a hurry?" she asks, tapping a long manicured nail on my door. In the past I would have loved those nails, loved them on my back, but how impractical are they with a baby around? Short nails, yeah, that's where it's at. Up ahead, Amy stops at the lights, and I'm sure I see Kennedy watching us from the passenger side mirror.

"I have things to do," I say.

"Things like Kennedy?"

What the fuck?

Growing restless, I ask, "What do you want, Vanessa?"

She puts her hand on my shoulder and I flinch. "Are you coming to the party tonight?"

"Probably not."

She snorts. "Careful, Matty," she says.

"Careful of what?" I ask, wishing I hadn't.

She looks at me like I'm dense. "You'll be Kennedy's next baby daddy."

She saunters off, shaking her ass a little too hard, and Tanisha follows her, giggling along. I put my truck into gear. Christ, the last thing Kennedy wants right now is to have another child. She's fighting to finish college and seeking a singing career, wanting to give her daughter a good life. Tank and Vanessa have no idea what they're talking about. She wouldn't want me as a baby daddy anyway. She already told me she knew who I was and what I was about.

Yeah, I fucking hate that.

Not that I want to be anyone's baby daddy, but it would be nice if she thought I could be. I shake my head. What the hell am I even saying? I follow Amy's vehicle through traffic and pull in behind her in their driveway. Shaking off my encounter with Vanessa, and hoping Kennedy hadn't seen it, I get out of the truck. I'm not trying to hide anything. I just don't want her thinking I'm setting something up for later tonight.

I pull Madelyn's diaper bag from the back of the SUV after Amy pops the hatch, and Kennedy releases the car seat and puts it on the stroller wheels.

"All set?" I ask. "I can drive you guys back."

"It's easier just to wheel this thing down the street. Meet me there."

I'm about to bend and kiss her, and realize there are people on the street and she probably doesn't want that. I straighten, and wave to Amy. "Thanks for the invite, Amy."

"You guys don't have to bring anything," she says, and I note the way she has her hand on her stomach. Did the hot chocolate disagree with her? Or maybe all the spinning on the ice turned her stomach. Her grin is devilish. "You should use your free time in other ways."

Kennedy shoots back, "We're bringing something."

"Is she okay?" I ask Kennedy after Amy disappears into her house. "She's holding her stomach."

"That's what she gets for showing off," she says, with a tip of her nose.

"Wow, look at you. I didn't think you had a mean bone in your body."

"I don't, and honestly it's been what?" She glances at her phone. "A few days since I had a mean bone, or any bone in my body." Heat jumps into my cheeks and I think, for the first time in my life, I'm blushing. She grins, knowing exactly what she's doing to me.

"You've been thinking about that, huh?" I croak out.

"Long and hard," she answers.

Unable to help myself, because I'm clearly as juvenile as Amy, I respond with, "That's what she said."

This time her cheeks flame and we both burst out laughing. "Go, now." She points to my truck, and I jump into the driver's seat. I back out of the driveway and I reach her place before she does. I sit on the stoop and my gaze is laser focused on them as they come toward me. For the briefest of seconds, I let my mind wander. What would it be like if this was mine, Kennedy's and Madelyn's little place? I'm enjoying the little scenario quite a bit, and the thoughts of waiting for them after a long day of work holds a great amount of appeal.

I wave to her as she comes close, and she grins. "New to the neighborhood?" I tease.

"Fairly," she says playing along.

"Why don't you come on in, so we can get to know one another better?"

"I don't go into strange men's houses."

"You think I'm strange?"

She laughs at that and starts up the driveway. "I think you're a lot of things."

"All good, I assume."

"Well…" she cringes, and I help her with the stroller when she reaches me. We leave it on the stoop and I lift Madelyn out in her car seat.

"Come inside, little red, and let me show you something very good."

She laughs, and opens the door and the minute I walk across the threshold, a sense of warmth, of home and hearth washes over me.

"Just put her on the table," Kennedy says. I walk down the hall and put a very tired Madelyn on the kitchen table, and Kennedy unbuckles her.

"Let me just get her down for a nap, and then we'll whip something up and have a nap of our own."

My cock jumps, liking that idea. As Kennedy disappears upstairs, I place Madelyn's seat on the floor, and sit down to check messages on my phone. A stack of papers catches my attention, and I lean forward, nosey guy that I am, and read over the ads.

Kennedy is looking for a place of her own?

20

KENNEDY

I have no idea how Amy wrangled us into going to dinner at her place, and I'm not sure why Matt ever agreed. Okay, food is involved, but he can eat anywhere. Deep inside though, I like the idea of spending more time with him before I have to work tonight. My only problem is that I don't want him, or Amy, to think there is more to this than there really is. I always had it in the back of my mind, if I invited a guy to Amy's place, it meant we were serious. While I can admit to feeling something more for Matt, I don't think we can label what's going on here as serious.

"Sweet dreams, sweetie," I say to Madelyn as I tuck her in and stifle my own yawn. I'm going to need a nap myself. When Matt suggested it, I'm not sure sleeping is what he had in mind. I close her door and tip toe downstairs. My steps still in the kitchen and Matt lifts his head, an almost confused look on his face.

"You're thinking about moving out?"

"What?" I glance at the realtor cuts I printed out and left on the table.

His look is a bit sheepish as I meet his gaze again. "Sorry, I wasn't snooping. I set the car seat down and these were under it."

"It's okay," I say and step into the kitchen. I gather the listings up, tap them on the table to straighten the sheets and set them aside. "I was looking. I thought it might be time." I'd actually like a place so Mom can have her home and life back. Okay, I'd also be lying if I said I didn't want a place where Matt and I could go without worrying about my mother showing up or one of his frat buddies busting in, but that's getting ahead of myself. I have no idea how long this thing between us is going to last. I'm sure he's going to soon get tired of me. He's a guy who goes from girl to girl.

He's been hanging around a lot, Kennedy.

I don't want to give that too much thought, or hope. Wait, what exactly am I hoping for? I like him a lot, but I can't be thinking long term. That would be impossible, I'm sure. I turn the question on him, and teasingly ask, "How about you? You mentioned wanting your own place the other day. Are you getting tired of Storm House with all the parties?"

"Actually yeah, I am." He takes a deep, almost agonized breath and blows it out slowly. "I was thinking about moving out for my final year."

Okay, now that answer takes me by surprise. He's loved by all at Storm House and is the life of the party every weekend. "Really?"

"Lots of guys leave third or fourth year," he explains.

"I can understand that." I walk to the fridge, pull it open and glance at the contents. As my brain fires with that new information, I ask, "What do you think we should make for the BBQ?"

"I could run down the road and get something premade?" I glance at him over my shoulder and he's standing there looking good enough to eat, jerking his thumb over his broad shoulder. Honest to God, I could spend the rest of the day just looking at him.

"While that is sweet, I prefer to make something. Now what do I have to work with?"

He comes up behind me, leans over my body and whispers, "From where I'm standing it seems like you had a lot to work with." He puts his arms around my ribs and I expect him to grab my breasts but he doesn't, he just hugs me and the intimacy in the way he's holding me against his pounding heart messes with me in all kinds of weird and wonderful ways.

"How about a broccoli salad?" I suggest. I reach for the broccoli, and I push back to stand and he straightens with me, keeping his arms around my ribcage.

"Broccoli salad? I don't know where you come from, but in Alberta, trees do not belong in a salad, or anywhere else but the compost bin."

I spin and laugh at the way his lips are turned down in distaste. "You've never had it?"

"No, and I don't want to."

"I thought you were a little more adventurous than this."

"I'm adventurous sure, but I do not go on adventures with broccoli."

I laugh at that, and shove the broccoli into his chest. He takes it and sets it on the counter like it's diseased and might kill him. My God, the man is cute and makes me laugh. "Trust me on this."

He arches one brow, looking ridiculously adorable. "That's a big ask, Kennedy."

"I've trusted you with things." His grin is suddenly wicked, like he's remembering the way I put my body in his capable hands. "Yes, or no?" I put my hand on my hip, and wait for an answer. Truthfully, we've both been trusting each other with numerous things. I'm pretty sure broccoli isn't the hill he's going to die on.

He looks at the broccoli like it's a can of worms and crinkles his nose. "You really think I'll like it?"

"I do."

Hope jumps into his eyes. "Are you putting it over a big steak?"

"No, that's disgusting."

"How dare you."

"Yes or no?"

His shoulder sag, giving in to me. "Okay, fine. I trust you. But if I don't like it, you'll have to make it up to me."

I pull the mayonnaise from the fridge. "Really now. Why would I agree to that?"

"Because I asked, and I said pretty please."

I set the jar on the counter. "I didn't hear a pretty please."

He gathers me into his arms, and dips his head. His lips are so close to mine, a hairsbreadth away, and I wait for the kiss to come.

"Pretty please," he murmurs into my mouth, his warm, sweet breath fanning across my face and teasing the arousal building inside me.

My eyes fall shut. "Why is it I can't say no to you?" He kisses me, a light caress that shudders through me, and makes me want to skip the salad and run straight upstairs for our nap. "If you don't like it—which I know you will—how should I make it up to you?"

"Leave that to me."

I open one eye and take in his smirk. I'm not sure what he's up to, but I already know I'm going to like it. "Why do I think you're going to like it and pretend not to."

He playfully wags his eyebrows. "Now why would I do that?"

"I guess it depends on what me making it up to you means?" He whistles innocently, and I laugh. "One delicious broccoli salad coming up," I whisper, not wanting to break away from his warm hold.

"What can I do to help?"

"You can sit there and look pretty," I joke, but his smile falls. Shoot, I didn't mean to offend him, and why did that offend him? He knows he's good looking. He often jokes about it. But is that his way of hiding something? Like the fact that he'd like to be something other than a pretty face, and an excellent hockey player? He is more than that. Surely to God he knows that. I'm about to tell him when his phone pings.

"You going to get that?"

He pulls it from his pocket. "It's my brother Liam. I can message him back later. What can I do to help?"

"Can you cut up the broccoli into small pieces."

He salutes me. "I'm on it, Chef." He puts the broccoli on the cutting board. "Where was the broccoli when I made that casserole the other day?"

"Where on earth did you get that recipe?"

"My sister. I called her. She was run off her feet with her kids, and sent me the link. I had to use cauliflower. It was either that or some dried out mushrooms I found in the back of the fridge."

"Good call on the cauliflower."

"You never did tell me if it was any good." I start whistling innocently. "Oh my God, you hated it." He shakes his head and looks so lost and forlorn my heart squeezes tight. "I'm really not good at anything but hockey." He says it lightly but there's so much going on that I can't see.

I go up on my tip toes and kiss him. "I'm kidding. It was actually delicious. You're a great cook. Mom loved it and so did Madelyn, and you, sweet Matt, are good at a lot of things."

"You think?" he asks, his eyes wide, like a child looking for praise.

I stifle a yawn, exhaustion pulling at me. "Sure I do. You're good with—"

This time his phone rings, and he tugs it from his pocket. "Liam again."

"You better get it. He seems anxious."

He nods, and slides his finger across the phone. As he steps into the other room, I turn the music on low, to give him privacy.

He comes back and has a frown on his face. "Everything okay?"

"Yeah, he just wanted to check on hotels. They're booking their travel today."

"You must be excited to see them."

"I really am." He smiles and the tension leaves his body. "What was I doing?" he asks, a bit distracted.

"Broccoli."

"Right."

"Once you're done cutting the broccoli, we need to cut cheese, onions, and cook up some bacon, and I'll make the sauce."

"Bacon!" His jaw drops. "Why didn't you open with that?"

I laugh and we both get to work and it doesn't take long to get the salad thrown together. He still looks unsure as he glances at it in the big bowl.

"It will be good, I promise."

"If you say so."

I put the bowl in the fridge and stifle another yawn. "Come on," he says and captures my hand, his big palms swallowing mine whole. With unhurried steps, we go upstairs and into my room. Matt closes the door, and proceeds to strip off to his boxers. He climbs between the sheets, and gestures for me to join him.

"Okay," I say. I guess today there is no prolonged foreplay against the door, or in the shower. I strip off to my bra and underwear and climb in next to his big warm body. He turns me so I'm the little spoon to his big spoon, and I relax against him. When was the last time I felt so safe with someone?

He lightly touches my hair, his breath trickling over my neck, as he holds me tight and whispers, "Sweet dreams."

Holy, we really are having a nap. I thought nap was code for hot afternoon sex, and while that would have been nice, this is very nice too. I let my lids fall shut, my breathing slow as I absorb his warmth. Funny, when he invited me for lunch, I thought it was about sex too.

Isn't everything about us supposed to revolve around sex?

I'm pretty sure it is, and I'll think about that later, but right now, having a siesta with Matt, sounds like the most perfect afternoon in the world. The next thing I know, I'm waking up to Madelyn fussing in the other room. I open my eyes, and as reality comes racing back, I turn and once again, find the other side of the bed empty.

I sit up and I'm about to kick the blankets off, stopping as Matt's voice filters into my room. Is he explaining the rules of hockey to Madelyn? I laugh, and slide from the bed, tugging on an oversized sweater before crossing the room. My heart leaps into my throat as I see the two of them sitting in the rocking chair, Matt with the puppet going over some of Scotia Storm's plays.

"Aren't those a well-kept secret?" I ask quietly, and the second his head lifts, and I catch the smile on his face, I fall that much deeper in love with him.

Oh, boy.

"Sorry, didn't mean to wake you."

"Mom. Mom. Mom," Madelyn calls out giving me a backward wave. What would it be like if the three of us were a real family?

"You didn't and I needed to be up. We have to get to Amy's."

"Now I wish you hadn't woken up." I angle my head at his comment, one question dancing in my eyes, which he easily reads. "That way I would have gotten out of eating broccoli salad."

"Are you a child?" I joke.

"Nothing wrong with being a child. Right, Madelyn?" She giggles, and he adds, "Although being an adult, I get to decide what I want to eat and what I don't want to eat."

"You're eating the broccoli," I say, pinching my lips.

"Fine," he grumbles and I cross the small room to scoop up Madelyn. "I'll need to get her changed and dressed. Then we'll be ready to go."

"Are you forgetting something?"

I set Madelyn on her change table. "I don't think so."

"Pants," he grins with a laugh and points to my bare legs.

"You don't like this look?" I wave my hand down my body and stick one leg out. "I thought I was starting a new fashion trend."

"I like the look, but I like it when it's just the two of us. I don't need any of the guys on the team getting a look at those legs."

He's joking but wow, I'm pretty sure I see possessiveness in his gaze as he looks at me. Did I mention that I love the possessive way he looks at me? But once again, I wonder if we could even have a future if we both wanted one?

"Can you grab me her pink jumpsuit second drawer down?" I change Madelyn's diaper as he digs out the outfit, and after I get her in it, I head to my room to find pants. I'm used to having her in one arm and doing everything with the other, but when Matt sees me struggling, he takes her from me, like it's the most natural thing in the world for him to be cradling my daughter. I swear to God my ovaries just clenched at the adorable sight, and a quake goes through my entire body.

"You're always cold," he says mistaking my body's reaction. "Hey maybe you can come live with me in Tampa. Nice hot weather there."

He stands there waiting for me, his look casual and relaxed, like he didn't just talk about us living somewhere warm together. Clearly he was joking and I shouldn't read too much into it. Not wanting my overactive mind to run away on me, I find a pair of clean jeans and tug them on. I tie my hair back, and glance at myself in the mirror.

"I'll be heading to the pub to play after the BBQ," I explain, wanting him to know why I'm not wearing makeup or doing anything special with my hair.

"You look beautiful."

I smile at him and we head to the kitchen to grab the salad, and put Madelyn in her stroller when we get outside. Birds chirp as the last September air grows chillier in the evenings.

"Don't drop that," I say to Matt, as he carries the salad beside me.

He just gives me a cute grin as we approach Amy's door. She opens it and a smile dimples her cheeks as she takes the salad. "Mmm, my favorite." I arch a brow at Matt, and I'm about to grab Madelyn from her stroller, but he gets to her first. He scoops her out, and I don't miss the grin on Amy's face.

"Doug and Chloe are out back at the BBQ," she says to Matt. "Straight down the hall through those doors. Kennedy and I will just get this salad in the fridge." I brace myself, prepared for an inquisition as Matt heads down the hall. The second he disappears, she turns to me. "He's kind of great with Madelyn."

"I know."

"He seems like a really nice guy, Kennedy."

"I know."

She eyes me. "Ohmigod, you like him. Like you really, really like him."

I let loose a slow breath. "I know."

I pace back and forth, checking the arrival boards at the airport, waiting for Granddad and Liam's plane to land. I've been looking forward to their visit and can hardly believe it's already mid-October. Where the hell did the time go? I guess I've been so busy with Kennedy and Madelyn, hockey and school, time flew by without me even realizing it. You know what they say, time flies when you're having fun, and we have been having fun.

I've been doing so much with her. Things I never dreamt I would be doing. I can't help the big goofy smile spreading across my face as I think about the Halloween costumes we've both been working on. We're going as Popeye, Olive and Sweet Pea. I can't even imagine what the guys will think. Actually, I can and I don't give two fucks.

Hell, Kennedy even got me to eat broccoli salad when we went to Amy's barbecue and dammit, I liked it. She forced the truth out of me, and while the plan was that she'd make it up to me if I hated it, she rewarded me later in the bedroom, and I really need to stop thinking about that before my granddad and brother arrive.

I'd almost asked Kennedy if she wanted to come to the airport with me. In the end, I decided against it. It's best I greet them alone—grandad will have a million hockey questions that will bore Kennedy—and they'll meet tonight after the game, anyway. Speaking of my games. Kennedy's been coming to watch when she has the time, and it's crazy how much I love glancing up to see her cheering me on. I also love how she's become friends with Daisy and Sawyer. They love her as much as I do.

I mean, they *like* her as much as I do.

I pace some more after the board switches from on-time to arrived, and I head to the doors by the escalator to wait for them. People, some smiling, some grumpy, come through the doors, and my brother comes barrelling down the stairs in between the two rolling escalators. A smile lights up his face as he waves to me. I search for Grandad but obviously, Liam took off ahead of him and I'm sure Grandad isn't going to take the long-ass flight of stairs down.

"Hey little brother." I laugh, pull him into my arms and rub my knuckles on his head. He laughs and pretends to punch me in the stomach, and just like that, it's like old times. I really missed him, and yes, maybe as of late we haven't chatted as often, and maybe I haven't been there for him as much—I've been busy with other things—but I do love the kid.

"How's school?" I let him go and look him over. Jesus, he's almost as tall as me.

"School sucks."

I shake my head. "You need to keep your grades up if you want to play hockey."

"Hockey is my life." He says with a smile. It's my life too. It used to be my entire life. Now though, I have a little more going on and maybe that's a better balance.

"Do you have a hug for your grandfather?"

I lift my head at the sound of Grandad's voice. "Granddad," I say and throw my arms around him. "Sorry, just lecturing Liam on keeping his grades up so he can play hockey."

"That's what I like to hear," he says, and I nod. Of course, he does. His world is dairy farming and hockey and now that the farm is in my parents' hands, his world has pretty much narrowed to hockey.

Behind us, a loud ringing sound indicates the luggage is coming. I jerk my head toward the moving conveyor belt. "Let's get your luggage and get out of here."

"I can't wait for your game tonight," Liam says and I throw my arm around him. I smile at him. I do love his childlike enthusiasm. We gather up the luggage and head into the big parking garage. I put their things in the back and Liam jumps in the back seat, granddad taking the front. I drive out of the lot, pay for parking and head back to the city. "How is everything at home?" I ask.

"If you called more often, you'd know. Liam says he hardly ever hears from you anymore."

What the hell?

Granddad gives me a scowl, and I catch Liam's eyes in the rear-view mirror. We exchange a look that says I should be prepared for a lecture, and that he's sorry he ever said anything. Shit, I know I haven't called home much, but life is busy.

"I'm sorry—"

"It's okay, son," Granddad says, cutting me off. "I understand hockey takes up all your time." I nod and my grip tightens on the steering wheel. "Hockey does take up all your time, right?"

"Yeah, and school. I've been swamped." My stomach cramps and I sink a little into myself. I want to tell him about Kennedy, although I'm not sure right now is the time. He's tired, and clearly grumpy. Maybe after a nap at the hotel, he'll be in a better mood.

"Okay, good. You can't get into the NHL without putting the work into it, you know? It's what you've always been good at, Matt, and practice and focus will only make you greater."

My shoulders sag, and I'm once again that little boy who couldn't do anything right—anything but hockey, that is. "I know."

My phone pings and I ignore it, even though it's Kennedy—I can tell by the special ring tone. She pings again, and I hope everything is okay. I can't check because I'm driving and I'm not about to ask granddad to check for me.

"Something urgent?" granddad asks.

"No, nothing urgent." I turn the conversation to Liam, asking about school and hockey again. He rambles on for a bit, and I take in his big goofy smile, and the Morgan family charm that we inherited from dad and granddad—apparently, they were real ladies' men—radiates off him.

"How many girlfriends do you have?" I tease.

Grandad makes a disgruntled sound, and I turn to him as he stares straight ahead. I meet Liam's gaze again and that's when I notice the sadness about him. Jesus Christ, are they doing the same thing to him that they did to me? Forcing hockey down his throat at the expense of his childhood.

"I've been busy," he says, and the emptiness in his voice guts me. My heart pounds a little harder in my chest. I don't want Liam to miss his childhood. I choose my words carefully and keep a playful manner to them, wanting to get my point across to both Liam and my grandfather. "All work and no play—"

"Makes a great hockey player," my granddad finishes.

Jesus.

I used to be okay when it was just me—then again, maybe I was never okay with it—but to see the pressure on my brother, and that it's already starting to take a toll, doesn't sit well with me. Any words that come out of my mouth will be wasted or shot down in front of my grandfather, and he's not a man you can easily stand up to. Maybe when I get Liam alone I'll talk to him, see if hockey is really what he wants. Fuck, though. I guess I haven't been a great role model.

"Can you turn that up?" Liam asks when a song he likes comes on the radio, and I do. With the break in conversation, I concentrate on driving, and what I'm going to say to Liam when I have him alone. I was really looking forward to this visit, but now I have a knot in my stomach the size of a hockey puck, and there's no denying the tension in the vehicle. Granddad isn't happy about something. Hopefully after seeing me play tonight—and seeing that I'm on track for the NHL—it will put him in a better mood.

I turn the song down when it ends, and I turn the questions to Granddad, asking about home again, and what's new. He fills me in on the farm, my parents, and my sister's kids, and of course he talks about how my sister has them into ice skating already. He's still talking about how we might have more NHL players in the family as I pull up in front of his hotel.

"Sorry you can't stay with me," I say.

"Oh, no worries, son. You need to be at the house with other players."

"I was actually thinking of getting my own place."

Oh shit.

He frowns and his bushy brows burrow together. "You can't be worrying about taking care of your own place, Matt. You need to stay with the team."

"Yeah, okay," is all I say. How he can reduce me to an obedient child with a simple look is beyond me. My stomach feels hollow as I put the truck into park, and hop out to help them with the luggage. "Do you need a lift to the game?"

"No, Liam and I will be just fine. I'm looking forward to seeing my grandson play and win tonight."

No pressure there.

"Okay, game starts at seven. I have special seats for you, and afterward we can grab a bite to eat. I invited a friend along."

"Oh," he says as he lifts the handle on his luggage, Liam not paying attention as he messes around on his phone.

"Yeah, a friend. She uh, cooks and cleans at Storm House." That was a pretty lame thing to say. What do I say though?

We've not labeled anything between us. Do I call her my girl-friend...or simply, the girl I've been sleeping with? I have a feeling either of those things would send my grandfather into a fatal spinout.

"Will she be cooking or cleaning for us after the game?"

"No."

"Then why did you invite her?"

"I like her," I confess, just not admitting exactly how much I like her, or that we're currently making Halloween costumes together and I've never been happier as he stares at me for a second. "You'll like her too."

"Very well. Let's go Liam. I'll see you tonight at the game, Matt."

With that, he disappears behind the glass doors of the hotel's entrance, and I stand there for an extra second, simply trying to get my wind. The valet looks at me, and I pull myself together, and put my hand up, palm out to let him know I'm good. I should go back to Storm House and get ready for the game tonight, but the need to see Kennedy pulls at me. Her place is just two blocks from the hotel, and she's home working on our costumes. I pull out of the hotel entranceway and go straight to her place, waving to a buddy of mine when I see him step out of the small downtown grocery store. I'm sure Liam will be in there later stocking up on junk food for the night.

I pull into Kennedy's driveway, walk up the steps and knock. Her mother's voice calls out from inside, and the door opens. "Matt, what are you doing here? I thought you were picking up your grandfather and brother."

"I already did," I answer, and put on my best smile, even though my insides feel a little raked raw. I hated the look on Granddad's face when I mentioned Kennedy, I hated the way Liam deflated when I asked about girlfriends and Granddad shut me down. You know what I hate the most? That I've not really been there for Liam the last few years, and I've not been a great role model when it comes to life. Hockey yes, but life no.

"Kennedy is in the kitchen. Head on in."

I step inside, and an instant comfort comes over me. Barb goes upstairs. She's always great at giving us privacy, although this time maybe she feels the anxiety pouring off me.

"Thanks, Barb."

I head to the kitchen and Kennedy is sitting at the table, sewing our costumes. Her head lifts when I enter. The smile that lights up her face seeps under my skin and curls around my heart. Yeah, I really like her.

"I thought you were Piper. She's going to stop by sometime later today to give me a hand with the intricate details..." Her words fall off and she frowns as she stands. "Are you okay?" She comes straight to me, and puts her arms around my body. I hug her, and breathe in her scent, letting it soothe the unease inside me.

"I am now," I say.

She inches back and her gaze moves over my face. "Did something happen?"

I want to tell her everything, from how I feel to how I'm failing my brother, but she's meeting my family later and I don't want her nervous or anxious. Granddad had better not make her feel anything other than accepted. He's a mannerly gentleman, so I'm not too worried about it, and if he doesn't...shit might hit the fan.

I kiss her, with need and hunger, and when we break apart, my lips still hover close to hers as I whisper, "I just worry about Liam,'" I admit.

"Why?"

I shrug and run my hands up and down her arms. "I want to be a good example for him."

"Are you kidding me, Matt? You said he's going to be the next great NHL player and look at the example you're setting. You work hard and are committed to every practice and game. How much more of an example could you be?"

Oh, by being a better fucking human being. A guy with substance, who does other things—good things—outside of the rink. A guy who cares about more than hockey. A guy who can, maybe someday, be a good husband and dad. A guy who wants others to know that he could be those things.

Does Kennedy?

She angles her head, like she's waiting for me to say more, and when I don't, she presses a soft kiss to my lips and doesn't press, even though I know she'd like to get to the bottom of the matter, find out what's really on my mind, because she cares about me, she cares about my well-being—I care about hers too—and goddammit, as she looks at me, it's all I can do not to blurt out that I love her.

I fucking love her and in my heart, I believe she knows there's more to me.

"Kennedy." I brush her hair from her face and her eyes are wide as she stares back.

"Yeah."

I swallow. Hard. "See you tonight."

You goddamn chicken shit.

●22

KENNEDY

I sit between Daisy and Sawyer and cheer on the Scotia Storms. I had no idea how much fun hockey could be, and this is the third game I've been to over the last few weeks, and one of those was Daisy's game. I owe Amy big time for taking Madelyn each time, but now that I've been to a few games, I'm totally addicted.

Matt gets the puck, and I jump up, unable to help myself. The girls beside me, who've become my friends, both laugh as I make a fool of myself. Matt shoots the puck and Chase starts taking it down the ice, and that's when Sawyer jumps up. Now, as her man makes a play—it's my turn to laugh at her.

Is Matt my man?

"Okay, be quiet," she says.

Daisy raises her brow. "For a girl who hated hockey..."

Sawyer rolls her eyes and gives us a dismissive wave. "I know, I know. Give me a break."

I stare at Matt and as if sensing me looking, he casts a fast glance my way. My God, we've been spending all our time together, growing closer and closer, and I can't deny that I want more. Matt has proven time and time again to be a stand-up guy. Heck, just a few weeks ago when we went skating, I saw those girls all over him. I briefly wondered if they'd be hooking up later that night after Storm House's party, but no, he came to see me sing, and then we spent the rest of the night in his bedroom, alone.

When he's not studying, practicing or playing, we're doing things together—mostly family things. Except for the afternoons we steal together when I'm cleaning and cooking at Storm House, or the nights Mom stays out and we have her whole house to ourselves.

I've been searching for places to rent. I prefer a house over an apartment, and I have a lead on a few places. Matt has been helping me with the search, and there's one place I really like, but it's too expensive and I don't want to take on a roommate —been there done that. While I've envisioned Matt and I sharing a place, and a bed, I'm not about to bring that up.

A cheer goes through the crowd as Chase scores and I jump up, my thoughts zinging back to the game at hand. Matt glances my way again, and that now familiar flood of want and need overwhelms my body—and my heart.

For a long time now, we've both been adamant that this is just sex. I know we've been playing house, so to speak, and to be honest, I've been afraid to even allude to the fact that I wanted more, that we might already be more. Is this still about the sex for him? He's not saying much anymore and I'm not so sure he still believes that. How can a man who is so good with my daughter, and with me, who is always stepping up and being the man I know he is, not want what's right in front of him?

But is it selfish of me to ask him to step into an already made family? Madelyn isn't his, and I don't know if a guy who's never had any kind of responsibility outside of hockey wants us in his life. When I'm with him, I sense a hesitancy in him, and I'm not exactly sure what it is that he's afraid of. But there's something.

I glance around the busy rink. His grandfather and brother are here somewhere. Matt picked them up at the airport, and he's been busy with them all day, and I'm looking forward to meeting them. The team always goes to the campus pub after a game—Jimmy has finally let me back in after Matt talked to him, but his brother Liam is too young, so we're going to grab some nachos at The Lower Deck.

It's weird. I'm not sure if he's 'introducing' me to his family, or he just invited me along because we spend every spare moment together. I guess I'll wait and see how he introduces me.

"Who wants a drink?" Daisy asks, and both Sawyer and I nod.

"Good, get me one when you go," she teases and we both laugh at her humor. She stands when intermission hits and the team heads back to their locker rooms for a brief break.

Once Sawyer and I are alone, she turns to me, no doubt wanting to talk about her upcoming winter wedding. She's been planning it for a while now, and it's exciting to be involved. Apparently, she and Chase met in a snowstorm last February and she wants to get married in the winter. That is so not my idea of a wedding, but to each their own.

We spend a few minutes chatting about the venue and dresses before she takes my hand in hers. "I was wondering if you could do me a favor," she says, a worried but excited look on her face as she nibbles on her lip.

I brace myself, because this doesn't look good. Not good at all. "What?" I ask.

"Actually, it's two favors."

Daisy comes back with three drinks, and hands them over. "Did you ask?"

"I'm about to," Sawyer laughs.

Daisy wiggles, clearly knowing what's about to go down by the big grin on her face.

"Do you think you'd be able to sing and play guitar at the wedding? I know you're busy and it's a lot to ask, and I wasn't sure I should and—"

"It would be my honor, Sawyer," I announce, and a smile lights up her pretty face.

"Really?"

"Yes, really, and I've sort of been working on this love song that I could run by you."

Her jaw drops. "Are you kidding me. Our very own song?"

"Yes," I tell her and it's partially true. It will be their song at the wedding, but I've been drawing inspiration from my relationship with Matt. I have never been so inspired in my entire life and I'm pretty sure the song is going to get me honors in class. "What's the second thing?"

"We were wondering if Madelyn could be our flower girl."

My heart nearly bursts from my chest, and tears fill my eyes. "That would be so lovely."

Sawyer hugs me and I love being a part of this little group of women who all support one another. I'm part of the group even though I have Madelyn. To these women she's not a hindrance, or a drawback. I lost a lot of my former friends when I got pregnant and couldn't go to the parties.

We spend the entire intermission chatting about the wedding and I am thrilled to learn Piper is making her dress. When the guys return to the ice, we sip our drinks and cheer them on. My stomach is in a huge knot by the end of the game, not because we lost—we didn't—but because I'm about to meet his family.

We all file out of the rink and once outside I glance around, looking for an elderly gentleman and a fourteen-year-old boy who might be Matt's family. About twenty minutes later, Matt comes outside with them by his side, and he searches the crowd looking for me as I step up to them. A big, almost nervous smile, curls his lips. He puts his hand on my arm, but doesn't lean in for a kiss like he normally would. Okay, so he doesn't like public displays of affection in front of his family.

He doesn't want them to know what's between you two, Kennedy.

"Kennedy," he says. "This is my grandfather, Gary Morgan, and my brother Liam. Granddad and Liam this is Kennedy, the girl I told you about."

"The one that cooks and cleans for Storm House?" Gary asks.

My heart sinks into my shoes. Really, that's how Matt described me to his grandfather? I hold my hand out, hoping no one notices the shakiness as hurt squeezes my throat to the point of pain. His grandfather gives it a good hard shake as he offers me a pleasant smile. I turn my attention to Liam, who is grinning. Clearly the kid knows what Matt and I have been doing, even if Matt doesn't want them to know the truth.

Maybe you really are no one, Kennedy. Maybe you're just a bedmate.

Why then, would he invite me to this post hockey game dinner?

"Hey Liam," I say, shaking his hand and putting my palm over my stomach as it swirls with unease. "Matt tells me you're an amazing hockey player."

"Top player in his age group. They'll soon be moving him up," Gary chortles and beams at Liam. It's easy to tell how proud he is of his grandsons, and that's a good thing, right?

Liam throws his arm around his brother, and I can't believe how tall he is at fourteen. "I'm not as good at Matt. Great game tonight, bro."

"You're better than I was at your age," Matt says, and gestures toward the street. I smile at the love and encouragement between brothers. "Should we get going?"

He turns and I walk beside him. He doesn't take my hand but his does brush against mine as we walk. I catch his glance and he offers me an almost apologetic look. Is he apologizing for the way his grandfather brought up that I was the cook and cleaner? If that's all he knew about me, what did Matt expect?

I angle my head and study Matt's gait as he walks. He's different tonight, like something is bothering him. Clearly we need to talk, because the truth of the matter is, I've fallen for him, head over heels—I can no longer keep my feelings for him locked away. He's gotten into my heart, into my daughter and mother's hearts, as well. If I'm only his cook and cleaner, and if I let him into our lives when I'm nothing to him, I...I don't know what I'll do. How could I not open up to him though? He presents one Matt to the world and a different Matt to me. A Matt who is genuinely kind and caring, and so giving and thoughtful. I swallow against a pained throat, hoping I haven't simply been reading more into things, and seeing what I wanted to see.

Been there, done that.

"You did great tonight," I say, hoping my voice isn't as shaky as the rest of me.

His smile is soft, but there's a sadness there too. "Glad you came."

"Who knew hockey was so addictive?"

Who knew Matt was so addictive?

We reach the restaurant and I give the hostess our names, even though she knows me from my singing gigs. We're led to a table and Matt sits on the same side as me, his leg brushing against mine under the table. I glance at him and have no idea what to think. He's all kinds of contradictions tonight. Cool one second and intimately touching me in secret the next.

"Kennedy sings here," Matt tells his grandfather.

Gary's bushy eyebrows raise. "You're a singer?"

I nod, and while I'm proud of what I do, I say, "I'm in college right now, getting a music degree."

"Someday she'll be a famous singer, though," Matt says, his leg bumping mine.

Gary nods slowly, and a silence hangs in the air. He breaks it and says, "I guess a career in music will take you on the road then."

"I don't know about that." I shrug. "I don't want to be on the road. I have a daughter."

Matt tenses beside me, but his grandfather doesn't show any reaction to that announcement. I glance at Matt, and he averts his gaze. Was I not supposed to mention Madelyn?

"That must be hard juggling school, work and a daughter," Gary says.

"It is." I glance at Matt again, and my stomach churns at the odd way he's shifting nervously in his seat. I glance at the door, wishing I'd declined this invitation. I rub my uneasy gut again, my appetite dwindling fast. "I have help. My mother is here, and that's another reason I don't want to be on the road. Mom and Madelyn are very close and I want my daughter to grow up knowing her family."

"Yes, I can definitely understand that," Matt's grandfather agrees, setting his menu down. "We're hoping Matt eventually plays for Edmonton, to be closer to family. No matter which team he plays for though, he'll be on the road. Isn't that right, Matt?"

Gary stares directly at Matt and Matt clears his throat. "Yeah, during the season for sure, but I'll have a home base somewhere."

"In Alberta, we expect," Gary says, and Matt just nods.

"Kennedy plays guitar, too. She's very talented," Matt says, turning the conversation back to me, and I can't help but think this is some kind of interview. Does Matt need his grandfather's approval, or something?

"Really?" Liam leans closer. "I always wanted to play guitar."

"Why don't you?" I ask, taking in big eyes that are so similar to his brothers. "If you like and there's time, I can show you a few chords to get you started."

His smile falls fast, and he toys with the napkin on the table. "I just...I don't have time for that with hockey, practice, and everything."

I stare at him for a second, a new kind of tenseness around the table. I glance at Gary, who is studying the menu again, and turn to Matt, who has a frown on his face—the same frown he wore earlier today when he showed up at the house out of the blue. What the heck is going on here?

I glance at Liam. "You know what they say. All work and no play—"

"Makes for a great hockey player," Gary pipes in, and I stiffen as he eyes me, like he's daring me to challenge him. Since I'm not about to get into a debate with Matt's grandfather, it's not my place, I sit back a little as everyone goes silent, and pick up my menu.

The waitress comes and I'm grateful for the reprieve. We take turns giving our orders and after we hand the menus back, Matt pushes to his feet. "I'll be right back." He gestures to the long hall leading to the washrooms. "Have to make a quick trip."

His grandfather stands. "I have to as well."

While girls go to the washroom together all the time, it seems odd that Gary would jump up and go with Matt. I sense the guys are all close, but I also sense a bit of tension. Maybe that's why Matt was a bit worked up today when he stopped by earlier. He said he felt he was letting Liam down, but there's more going on here. Maybe later, when we're alone he'll open up to me.

Liam and I fall silent as the guys leave and once they're out of earshot, Liam turns his attention to me. "Are you Matt's girlfriend?"

Blunt and to the point. I like that, but how do I answer? I take the safe route, considering how Matt introduced me and say, "I'm his friend, yes." He eyes me and I'm pretty sure he's astute enough to read between the lines. "Do you have a girlfriend, Liam?"

He snorts, and there's this real sense of sadness about him. "Hockey," is all he says. "It takes all my time."

I fall silent when the server comes back with our drinks. She sets them in front of us and I pick up the conversation where we dropped it after she leaves. "Hockey is one thing, but surely you have friends you hang out with, and girls you like." Heck, he's a handsome teenager. I'm sure he has the girls falling all over him.

He glances over his shoulder, and when the coast is clear, he leans toward me. "I kind of like Luna. We're in English together, and she's a figure skater."

"Oh yeah?" He's trying so hard not to show his emotions, but he can't hide his big grin. "Are you going to ask her out?"

He shakes his head. "I don't know. I'm not sure she likes me, and—"

Just then Matt and Gary come back to the table, and Liam falls silent. I catch his eye and he gives a slight shake to his head and I get it. The conversation is over. Gary turns the conversation to hockey and Matt falls quiet as our food comes. I pick at mine, not having much of an appetite, and

Liam devours everything in front of him. I notice Matt's appetite isn't quite what it normally is. Did his grandfather say something unsettling when they went to the washroom? I can't help but think he did, and that it had everything to do with me.

We finish the meal and head outside. My stomach cramps again, and I put my hand over it.

"You okay?" Matt asks quietly.

I nod. "I think I need an antacid. I have some at home."

"Come on, I'll drop you off."

While I would prefer to walk and get my thoughts in order, I know Matt will put up a fuss and I just want this night over, no more tension. We make our way to Storm House, and I slide into the back seat of his truck, giving his grandfather the front. Matt is quiet as he drives and he drops me off at my place first. I say goodbye, and the place is quiet when I enter. Maybe I'll go pick Madelyn up at Amy's. First things first though. Antacids.

I head straight for the medicine cabinet and find it empty. I consider walking to the grocery store, which is just a block away, when my phone pings. Hoping it's Matt and he can stop by after he drops his grandfather off, I snatch my phone from my pocket and my jaw drops open when I see the message from Amy. Doug is working a night shift, and she needs me to run an errand for her if I have the time. I do have the time— especially since she has my daughter and it's too difficult to juggle two kids at the store.

I head back outside, and after locking up, hurry down the sidewalk. After the darkness, the florescent lights of the quiet grocery store hurt my eyes. I head straight to the back and grab what I need for Amy and myself. The second I turn around, I come face to face with Matt's grandfather. His stern gaze drops to the packages in my hand. My gaze follows. My heart jump into my mouth and steals my voice. Oh, God, does he think...

As soon as he opens his mouth, the pieces of the puzzle known as Matt all fall into place...

23

MATT

"I like her," Liam says as he plunks down on the sofa and kicks off his shoes. "She's really nice."

I glance around the large suite Granddad rented, and plop down into one of the side chairs. I smile at my kid brother as he pulls his phone from his pocket and glances at me over the top. "I think she's nice too," I tell him. I also think she's kind, sweet, smart, gorgeous, ambitious, and probably far too good for me.

He begins to scroll, and I reach for my own phone, anxious to see Kennedy tonight, but I can't just abandon my granddad and brother while they're in town. They're only here for a few days, but I really need to see Kennedy. I'm pretty sure it upset her when Granddad called her the cleaner and cook. Can I blame her? Hell no. She's more than that to me, and it's about goddamn time I told her.

Told the world!

"I don't think Granddad likes her very much," Liam says quietly as he scrolls. He glances at me again, gauging me with concerned eyes that match my own, and as my insides grow cold, I nod and grunt in agreement. I have no doubt Granddad dislikes her, despite how amazing she really is. Then again, would my grandfather like any woman in my life...in Liam's life? He thinks they're a distraction we don't need, and how fucking fair is that? He doesn't know Kennedy, and doesn't know what kind of woman she is.

Christ, at the restaurant when Granddad and I went to the washroom, he wanted to know the truth about Kennedy. Earlier in the day, I'd told him I liked her. Tonight, I told him that she was a kind and supportive woman, a woman who holds the responsibility of the world on her shoulders and that I wanted to be there for her. But until I talked to Kennedy, I didn't want to put a label on it and call her my girlfriend, or partner or whatever one calls the person he's in love with. Granddad didn't say too much, other than the fact that she had a child, and that I needed to put my energy into hockey. He asked if I'd come this far only to lose it all, and also pointed out that I wasn't cut out to take on the role of stepfather, and that I needed to be careful who I got involved with.

Who I got involved with?

Why the hell would he say something like that to me?

Oh, because no one thinks you're capable of anything else, and that every girl who wants you must want something from you.

I shake my head. No, that's wrong. I'm sure Kennedy sees me as more and I don't like my grandfather alluding to the fact that she wanted me because someday I'll be a huge hockey success. I love the game, but I'm so fucking tired of it being my life.

Christ, the only thing I'm supposed to worry about here at the academy is hockey. I'm the one who cares about my grades. Granddad would be happy for me to just get by because he doesn't want it to interfere with the sport. The man takes care of all my expenses—I'm surprised he didn't try to buy my grades too.

Honestly, at the end of the day, deep inside I know I am living up to everyone's expectations of myself, and I'm damn tired of it. Now Liam is doing the same thing. He should be out having fun with friends, and he should have a girlfriend. Just like I should be making plans with Kennedy. We've looked at houses together, houses for her and Madelyn, and you know what? I want to be part of their future plans. Down the road, I want to have a family with her. I'm about to tell Liam all that when my phone pings and my heart soars as a message from Kennedy comes in.

Kennedy: We need to talk.

Me: Yeah, we do.

Kennedy: Can you come by?

I glance up as the hotel door opens, and nearly drop the phone as my grandfather's stern eyes settle on me. I stand, every muscle in my body tenses. What the hell is going on? Is he hurt? Did he take a fall? Did he get robbed? Hell, this is a safe neighbourhood, but he went to the store and he's back here empty handed.

"Granddad?"

His focus turns to Liam. "Liam, can you go into the other room and close the door."

Liam's head lifts his wide eyes go from Granddad to me, back to Granddad. "Is everything okay?"

"Please, Liam. Your brother and I have to talk."

Granddad goes silent as Liam stands and walks into the other room. His door clicks shut and from the look on my grandfather's face, I know something bad is going down.

"Sit, Matt."

Since my legs will no longer hold me, I drop into the chair and he slowly crosses the room and sits across from me. "This girl. What do you really know about her?"

Okay, what the hell happened during the ten minutes he left to go to the nearby grocery store to get a bottle of rum.

"I know a lot. She's a student, has a daughter, and—"

"She's pregnant."

My throat dries as I sit up a little straighter in my chair, the room closing in on me. "What are you talking about?"

"I ran into her at the market. She's pregnant."

My mind races. She was rubbing her stomach an awful lot tonight, and she blamed it on indigestion. I remember the stories my mother told, how she ate antacids by the bucket when she was pregnant. But this is a mistake. Granddad has to be wrong. We've been using protection. No way is she pregnant.

"You're mistaken," I say adamantly and jump to my feet.

"Am I?"

I take a step, ready to run out the door, but Tank's and Vanessa's words, stop me dead in my tracks. No way. Kennedy is not looking for a baby daddy. Someone to take care of her needs. Correction: an NHL player to take care of her needs. She sees me as more than a hockey player, right?

You can sit there and look pretty.

Her words jump into my brain, but she was kidding when she told me that after I asked what I could do to help with the broccoli salad. There is more to us, and she told me she was on the pill. There's no way she would lie about that. Hell, why would she want to have another baby when she has so much going on in her life?

A girl like that, she's gonna get her claws into you man.

"Did she tell you that?" I ask.

"Not with her words, but yes."

My brain is too rattled to figure out his cryptic words. "You're mistaken. I'll prove it."

I head to the door, but Granddad jumps up and grabs my arm. I spin to face him, take in the tightening of his lips. "There's more."

I shake my head, not wanting to hear more. "No." I put my hands on my head to keep it from exploding as unease and panic grip my throat. My whole life, no one cared about who I was or what I was capable of outside of hockey. I was sure Kennedy was different. That I was more than just hockey, more than a career in the NHL. That I had substance. She told me that right? Or did she? "No, none of this is right."

"You need to walk away from her," he orders.

I grab the back of my neck as a headache begins. "No."

"I told you a million times, outside influences can ruin your career. *She's* going to ruin your career."

"I don't care about my career. I care about her."

"Then let me tell you this. She cares about your career. Not you."

His words stop me. "What are you talking about?"

"She's with you because you're going to make something of yourself. She was using you. Didn't I warn you about this kind of thing?"

"Sure, you told me women would gravitate toward any successful guy, but this, I don't understand any of this, not where Kennedy is concerned. Wait, why are you saying she *was* with me..."

"I offered her money, big money, to take care of her child and her...well, your baby. You were just a means to an end to her, Matt. Now it's all taken care of and you can forget about her."

I lean against the hotel door, air evacuating my lungs in a burst as blood leaves my brain. Lightheaded, I try to glance around, try to wake up from this nightmare, because this can't be happening.

"You think I'd walk away from my own child?"

Does my grandfather know me at all? I shake my head. Of course, he doesn't. He doesn't know what I'm capable of outside of hockey, doesn't see me as having any value in the real world. An NHL player, that's all I am to him, to everyone.

No way am I simply a means to an end to Kennedy, right?

He folds his arms, and blinks over milky eyes and for the first time in my life, I see his fragility. It's odd, he was always so larger than life to me. "She agreed to walk away."

I shake my head so hard, I'm sure my brain is banging against the sides of my skull. I refuse to believe him. I can't believe him. "No, she didn't."

"I'm not telling you this to hurt you." His soft voice is a sign he's changing tactics. Does he think turning on his warm grandfatherly charm will get through to me, make me believe him? "I'm telling you this to protect you."

The bedroom door creaks open and I turn to find a pale Liam staring at me. I nearly vomit when I meet his gaze, and realize what his life has become. I'm his big brother and a big part of the reason he's missing out on his childhood. "I don't need your protection. I'm a grown man and can stand on my own two feet."

He laughs, all softness gone. "Can you now? Who do you think is paying for your lifestyle, Matt?"

His words hit like a puck to the mouth, and I try not to let them reduce me to my teenage self where I'd never step out of line, never talk back. "You think because you pay, you can control what I do?"

"That's exactly what I think."

My words are shaky when I ask, "Why are you doing this?"

"Because it's the right thing to do." His head lifts, a sign this conversation is over, and he won. "Now, for your own good, put her out of your mind and get focused on your career. Liam is watching you, Matt, so pull yourself together."

"I know he's watching." Which is all the more reason I add, "And I don't want your money. I don't want anything from you. Never again." I pull the door open, and the hall blurs before my eyes as I bolt to the elevator. I need to talk to Kennedy and I need to talk to her now. She asked me to come over. She must want to straighten this out.

Either that or she's telling you it's over.

No, no, no that's not it. Granddad steps into the hall, and I glance back at his looming presence. "Don't you dare walk away from me, son."

"I'm not walking away. I'm running."

"You'll be back," he says, so completely sure of himself, there's a part of me that can't help but think he really does know something I don't. I suck in a breath, my throat so tight as I fight tears—I will not show weakness in front of him and give him any sort of satisfaction—I fist my fingers, letting my nails dig into my skin.

The elevator doors open and I jump on, pressing the lobby button a dozen times. Not that it will help me get there any faster, I just need something to do with my hands. The doors ping open and I jump off, moving through the lobby at break-neck speed. Outside, the cool night air washes over me but does little to cleanse the worry and anger and every other emotion I've kept pent up and locked away as I focused on hockey—always needing to be the best and live up to the expectations others put on me.

With a sense of urgency in my gut, I run to Kennedy's place. I lift my hand to knock and the door flies open. I hurry inside, and pull a crying Kennedy into my arms.

"Are you okay?" What the hell actually happened between her and my grandfather. She clings to me, and her stomach is gurgling so loudly I can hear it.

"I think I'm going to be sick," she groans.

The only think I can think of at the moment is to help her. "You need to get to the bathroom. Let me help you."

She breaks away, and says. "No, we need to talk."

I nod, and my gaze goes to the side table, and the room goes fuzzy as I focus in on the pregnancy test, nestled beside a bottle of antacids. Jesus Christ. I stumble back a bit, and Kennedy narrows her eyes, like she's confused by my reaction.

"Matt," she says and reaches for me.

Old fears and insecurities—fears that I'm nothing, a man of no substance, good for nothing but hockey, that no woman will think I have any worth outside of the sport—plow through me. They're so deeply ingrained in my brain and heart that I can't fight them.

My words are barely a whisper. "My grandfather was right. Everyone was right."

Her body tightens and she pulls her hands back wringing them together. "What?"

"Tank, Vanessa, they told me, they warned me. You wanted a baby daddy."

"Matt," she gasps. Shock and rage war with each other in her eyes. "That's what your friends told you?"

"Yeah, and look." I nod toward the pregnancy kit. "Now you're pregnant."

"First, it takes two to get pregnant, and it's not what you think," she says quietly, her cheeks paling, much like my brothers, the wind ripped out of her sails.

My God, if Granddad was right about this, maybe he was right about everything. Without hockey, I'm a man of no substance.

"My grandfather offered you money," I state.

Her demeanor changes, becomes cold and distant when she answers, "Yes."

"He said you took it."

"Did he?"

"You're not denying it."

"Would it matter?"

I shake my head, hardly able to decipher anything she's saying to me. "I thought you were different."

"I thought you were too," she counters, her words lacking any kind of emotion. She's either holding back, or I never really meant anything to her.

I back up, and grip the doorframe. "What's that supposed to mean?"

"You don't have to live up to anyone's expectations but your own, Matt. Maybe you'll like what you find when you stop."

I stare at her, and shake my head as I try to wrap my brain around what she's saying to me. Why is everyone being cryptic tonight?

"I was just a means to an end to you, wasn't I?" I ask.

"Was I just a fuck buddy to you?"

"No…yes…why don't you just answer the fucking question?"

"You're good at hockey," she says quietly.

Why the hell is she telling me something I already know. "I know, it's all I'm good at."

"There's more to you, Matt."

"What do you know?" I strike out.

She frowns, and there's a halo of sadness hovering over her. The weight of it damn near suffocates me. "Here's what I know. You're good at hockey. It's your life, it's all you've known."

"Yeah, your point?"

"It's all you've been *allowed* to know." I blink at her through watery eyes, completely dumbfounded, and she continues with, "You might have a hockey player puppet, but you'd be wise to figure out who's controlling your strings."

My grandfather has always controlled my strings, and maybe that's because he's been right about everything. "Were you even on the pill?"

She looks up at me, not with anger but with sorrow and pain, and I nearly collapse as it presses down on my shoulders. I stumble a bit, backing onto her stoop, not knowing where to walk, or run, or what to do next. My life—what little of it I've actually lived—has been turned upside down. I want her to tell me I'm wrong, that my grandfather is wrong, that we're going to be okay, but she speaks and it drowns out my voice.

"Ask your brother about Luna."

"What?"

She puts her hand on the door. "Ask him about Luna," she repeats and that's the last thing she says to me before closing the door in my face.

24

KENNEDY

I lean against the door and take deep, gulping breaths. I can't believe he went straight to accusations. I wanted to explain, but he wasn't going to believe anything I said—he didn't even want to listen. He's a good man deep inside, and I know it. He's going to have to take a long hard journey and figure out who he is, and that he's worth loving, before he can ever let anyone love him.

Tears spill from my eyes, and the minutes tick by slowly. I can't seem to push off the door, or make my legs work. Honestly, after everything we've been through, how could he think I could do something like this to him? It pains terribly, but I also know he's coming from a place of pain and hurt. I want him in my life, I want him in my daughter and mother's lives, despite the fact that his grandfather tried to pay me off.

Matt is a good guy and so is his brother, and at least now I understand why Matt felt like he was letting Liam down, setting a bad example. Everything makes so much sense, and there is absolutely nothing I can do for Matt. He has to fight his own demons, and I can only hope that when he comes out the other side, he's the man I know he can be.

Knuckles rap on my door and my heart leaps. No way could it be Matt. He has too much to work out before showing up at my door. I force myself upright, turn and slowly open the door. The second I set eyes on Piper, the tears spill once again.

"Kennedy," she says, and pulls me into her arms. She holds me as I sob like a baby. We're talking big, ugly, hiccupping cries here, and it's not fair that I'm doing this to her. After a long moment, she tucks me into her, closes the door behind us, and leads me to the kitchen. She sits me in a chair and glances at the costumes. Oh, right, that's why she's here.

"Do you want to talk about it?" she asks.

I take a huge breath and struggle to pull myself together. Piper and I are friends, although we don't share secrets, and while I would talk to Amy, she's busy with both our girls and I certainly can't go to Daisy or Sawyer. Matt is their friend first, and it wouldn't feel right talking about this behind his back. Wait, does that mean Daisy, Sawyer and I are no longer friends?

"Matt and I broke up." As soon as the words leave my mouth I snort. "I guess I can't say we broke up. We'd have to be a real couple before we can break up."

"I'm so sorry, Kennedy. Let me make tea."

"Forget tea. I need a drink. There's a bottle of wine in the fridge." Piper stands, pulls the bottle from the fridge, opens it and pours two glasses. I take a much-needed sip, and because I'm a lightweight, it instantly takes the edge off.

Piper blinks dark lashes over worried eyes. "I thought you two made a great couple. I've seen you together. I've seen the way you both looked at each other."

"I love him," I state.

"I thought so, and he loves you too. I know he does."

I nod, believing that's true even after the things he said to me, and accused me of. "I think he does, but he has to love himself and believe in himself first before he can let anyone love him."

She eyes me and swirls the wine in her glass. "What does that mean?"

"Well..." I begin and spend the next two glasses of wine explaining that puzzle known as Matt.

Soon enough, we finish the bottle, and I'm groggy. I thought about getting Madelyn tonight, and I wanted to bring Amy the pregnancy test, but she messaged me right after I bought it and got home letting me know she had spotting, and it was likely a false alarm. She seemed disappointed, and apologized for the panicked text. Apparently, it had only occurred to her tonight that she could be pregnant—they haven't been actively trying—which was why she freaked out and messaged me. I told her Matt was coming by, and I'd drop it off tomorrow, just in case. She was fine with that, and really, I don't think anyone else seeing me like this is a good idea. If Amy is pregnant again and happy about it, which I think she will be, I don't want to rain on her parade.

"Love, hate, it's such a complicated thing," Piper says quietly and I get the sense she's talking about her own life experiences.

"Want to talk about it?"

"Maybe another time. Right now, I need to tell you something you're probably not going to want to hear."

"I'm pretty sure nothing else can shock me tonight."

She reaches across the table. "I didn't come here tonight to help with the costumes."

I nod and lean closer. I'm not sure where she's going with this. I only know I'm not going to like it.

"I was at Storm House. There's a celebratory party going on."

"That's normal."

She winces and continues with. "What's not normal is Matt."

I grip my wine glass. "Matt's at the party."

"Yeah, that's why I came here. He's there, and he's acting like the old Matt." She pauses, like she's waiting for me to say something. I stay quiet and she nods and adds, "The old Matt, you know the loud, life of the party, drinking, and..."

"And..."

"The girls are all over him."

My heart clenches tight. I guess this is his way of dealing with things—by not dealing with them. But that's the old Matt. The Matt I know is so very different. I guess he's reverting to his old ways.

"He wasn't like that...when he was with you. He was different. He was a better man."

"I know." As much as I want to help him, as hard as it is to sit here in pain, there isn't anything I can do. "He's the one who has to figure that out, though."

She nods. After everything I shared with her tonight, she totally gets it, and unlike me, she's been at the parties with Matt in the past, and knows that other side of him I'd only ever heard about.

She lets go of my hand when I try to stifle a yawn, both physically and mentally exhausted. "I think you might need some sleep."

I nod in agreement. "Thanks for listening. Please keep this between us."

She nibbles her lips, like that might be hard to do. "Do you think Matt should know that you're not pregnant?"

"I think he should have asked me instead of jumping to his own conclusions."

A long moment of silence fills the kitchen as we go quiet, lost in our own thoughts. She breaks the silence with whispered words, "Men can be so dense."

Again, it sounds like she's talking from experience. "I'll drink to that," I say, and lift my empty glass. We both laugh, and then I stand, desperate to pass out so I don't have to think about the fiasco of my life—of Matt's. I just hope that tomorrow, he doesn't regret the decisions he's made tonight.

I walk Piper to the door, give her a hug and shut it behind her. I pull my phone from my pocket and check it. Not that I expect to hear from Matt tonight. I don't want to hear from him if he's drunk and partying. Matt has been known to do and say stupid things under the influence of alcohol—under the influence of his grandfather.

I head upstairs and get ready for bed. I fall into a fitful sleep, my sheets still holding Matt's scent, and memories of the last time he slept here with me. I wake to the sound of birds and force myself to get up. I have a busy day with Madelyn and I am not going to let my sadness interfere with that. Nor do I want her to pick up on it. I just hope I don't hear about any of Matt's antics from last night.

I head into the hall, and Mom's door is open, her room empty. She stayed at Leo's last night, figuring perhaps Matt and I would come back here after dinner with his grandfather. I realize she needs her own place, and having us here is a bit hard. I have to admit this, Matt was a big part of me moving. I wanted us to have a place where we could be together, without putting my mother out.

I head to the shower, but the water does very little to wash away the sadness enveloping me. The room is steamy when I finish and I swipe my hand over the mirror to clear it and take in the dark smudges beneath my eyes. I look like death. I pinch my cheeks to add some color. I really don't want to answer any questions today. Amy is going to take one look at me and know something is wrong, then she'll want answers. While I appreciate her concern, I just want a quiet day with Madelyn. I'll explain everything to her when I can. Right now, I'm just too rubbed raw inside.

I message Amy to let her know I'm on my way to get Madelyn. Down in the hall, I scoop up the pregnancy kit—a simple box that set off a storm—and drop it into my purse. The late October air is chilly, so I grab a coat and head outside. I'm glad I'm walking in the opposite direction of Matt's grandfather's hotel. I'd be okay to never set eyes on the manipulative asshole again. To think he tried to pay me off. Wow, that's how little he thought of me. And to think of the control he has over Matt's life. That's how little he thinks of his own grandson. I guess maybe he thinks he's doing the right thing, but there must be a part of him that realizes he's not.

I put on my best smile, yet Amy angles her head, her eyes narrowing the second she opens her door and sees me. No amount of makeup could hide my puffy eyes so I didn't even bother trying.

"I'm okay," I lie. I'm not. I'm not sure if I'll ever be okay again. I pull the pregnancy kit from my purse and hand it over.

"Thanks," she says and sets it down. "We're just getting breakfast. Come join us."

"Okay," I say, not really wanting to be alone. I find my girl in the kitchen, and give her a big hug. I set her on my lap as Doug comes into the kitchen, carrying Chloe.

"Morning, Kennedy," he says. "Where's Matt?"

Just the sound of his name sends need, and sadness spiraling through me. I work to inject lightness into my voice, "His grandfather is visiting from Alberta."

He smiles. "He must be so proud of Matt. Bet he's hoping he plays for Calgary or Edmonton some day. I heard he played a killer game last night."

"He's very proud of Matt's game," I say, and as my back gets up, I blurt out, "But there's more to Matt than hockey."

The room suddenly goes quiet and I curse myself for opening my mouth. I don't need to look at Amy to know she's staring, trying to figure out what the hell is going on.

"Ah, yeah sure okay," Doug says. "I like Matt. He's a good guy. He's great with the kids, and Amy told me he made you a casserole and stayed with you when Madelyn bumped her head." I realize he's a little lost and surprised by my sudden outburst and is trying to list his other good qualities.

"Yes, he's a good guy," is all I add, and Doug changes the subject.

"Coffee?"

I laugh, almost hysterically, because yes, I probably do need coffee and lots of it. I catch Amy's eyes and mouth the words, "Later." She nods, but the worry is still there. "I'll be okay," I say quietly. Heck, I was okay after Oliver walked out on us. But no matter how much I try to convince myself of that, it's harder this time. Matt meant more to me.

We finish breakfast, and I honestly just feel like I'm going through the motions, and Amy and I take the girls to the park. Afterward, I head home and put Madelyn down for a nap. Mom comes home, takes one look at me and gives me the smile that says she's there for me if I need her and I appreciate her not prying. I'm just not ready to deal.

Over the next couple of days, I do my very best to put on a smile, for my daughter's sake, and for my own sanity. I go to school, sing at The Lower Deck, and hand in my resignation at Storm House. I need the money, but I just can't be around Matt. I guess his house mates won't be too happy that he drove another cleaner from the place, but I have to do what is best for me.

As the week comes to a close, and Friday night is upon us, I leave Madelyn with Mom, and walk the long distance to the waterfront, hoping to summon up enough enthusiasm to sound somewhat decent singing and playing at The Lower Deck. I pass by the rental house I'd been coveting, the one I thought Madelyn and I could make a home in and welcome Matt into—even though I'd have to take another job to afford it—and see the rental sign has been removed from the window. Once again, my visions of grandeur are for nothing. When will I learn?

The Lower Deck is loud and rowdy when I arrive and take the stage. I pull my guitar from the case and strum it, but no one is paying me much attention, and I'm actually grateful, considering I can't seem to carry a note, tonight.

As I sing, I try not to think about the last week, how it went by so slowly, how every hour, every minute felt like an eternity. There is such a void in my life with Matt gone, and Madelyn's been so cranky, I'm sure she's feeling it too.

I glance up, and spot movement near the end of the bar. My heart jumps into my throat.

Is that...Matt?

25

MATT

I wake up after the crazy party last night, and wince as a jackhammer works its way from ear to ear, taking a direct path through my skull. Last night after leaving Kennedy's house, I didn't go back to my grandfather's hotel. Nope, I made a beeline to Storm House, where I got shit-faced drunk and partied hard. Yeah, what a great way to handle things, I know. This morning, I'm feeling every beer—every shot of tequila—I poured down my throat tenfold, and yes, I deserve it. But it became a drinking game of sorts. Every time someone asked about Kennedy, I took another shot. God, I am such an asshole.

Kennedy is pregnant.

As that thought rumbles around inside my brain, I roll to my side and stare out my window. My scattered thoughts slow, and something niggles in the back of my brain. *Is* she pregnant? I mean my grandfather told me she was, and I saw the kit, but she never came right out and said it, so maybe...

Christ, I'd been so caught up in my own demons last night that I hadn't even asked, I just assumed. Now, under the stark reality of day, where I can see a little clearer—even through the hungover haze clouding my brain—I can't help but wonder if things aren't as they seem. That's how fucked up I was after my grandfather basically told me I was nothing without hockey—a stain on this earth who couldn't be loved for who I was inside.

Jeez, I love you too, Granddad.

His whole life, he's been lecturing us about responsibility and setting a good example, and duties and responsibilities. Every member of the family felt it one way or another. Did my father even want to take over the dairy farm, or was it expected of him, the way it was expected of my grandfather to take over from his father?

I sit up and groan. "Fuck me sideways."

If Kennedy is pregnant, I didn't even hold her, or console her, or ask what she wanted. I made it all about me, and was a complete dick about it, which is especially bad because a part of me refuses to believe she's gotten pregnant on purpose. Did I really believe my granddad, Tank and Vanessa over her? I can forget about Kennedy ever talking to me again. My mind goes to the second scenario. If she's not pregnant, if this was some sort of mistake, and I didn't even let her explain, I can also forget about her ever talking to me again.

It looks like I'm fucked every which way I turn.

Well done, Matt. Well fucking done.

I slowly drop back down onto my pillow, and reach for my phone. There are about a dozen messages from my brother. Guilt swamps me, and I moan. I've let the kid down in so many ways. Not because I hadn't dedicated my life to hockey, but because I hadn't lived any sort of life because I was nothing more than a puppet and someone else was pulling the strings. Liam is probably back in the room being brainwashed by our grandfather.

Ask your brother about Luna.

I text Liam back.

Matt: Where's Granddad?

Liam: Last night he went out and got a bottle of rum after you left. He's sleeping it off.

Matt: Think you can sneak out without waking him?

Liam: Yup.

Matt: Meet me in the lobby. We'll grab some breakfast.

Liam: On my way.

Matt: I need about ten minutes.

I set my phone down, stand and realize I'm only in my boxers. I don't even remember getting undressed last night. I tug on last night's jeans and a fresh T-shirt and my brain rattles around inside my head as I slowly open my door, and spot a sleepy Vanessa coming from the bathroom just down the hall. Visions of me dancing with her and then her stripping bare in my room flash in my brain. Jesus Christ, did we?

"Hey," I say.

She snarls at me. "Hey." She goes into Tank's room and I breathe a sigh of relief. Thank God I had at least one working brain cell left last night.

I get ready quickly and rush outside. I wince as the early morning sun plays havoc on my hangover. Shading the sun from my eyes, I walk through the parking lot, and my head lifts when I spot movement at my truck. Is that... I get closer and no, it's not Kennedy. It's Piper. Why the hell is Piper standing by my truck?

"Hey," I say as I approach and my gaze drops to take in the nervous way she's shifting from one foot to the other. I see the piece of paper in her hand. "What are you doing?"

She flips the paper in her hand. "I was leaving you a note. I thought we should talk."

Piper and I never talk and surely to God this can't be about the costumes she was going to help us with. "What's up?" She looks around, her tired eyes darting to every corner of the parking lot. "Did you stay at Storm House last night? I saw you, right?" I wrack my brain, but don't remember much.

"No, I left shortly after you arrived. I went to see Kennedy."

My ears perk, and my heartbeat quickens at the sound of Kennedy's name. "How is she?"

She frowns and shoves the note into her pocket. "Not great."

I briefly close my eyes and curse myself for the way I handled things. "I'm an asshole."

"Yeah, kind of."

My lids fly open and I shake my head. "Why don't you tell me what you really think?"

"Okay, I will." I stiffen at that unexpected response and she continues with, "You love her."

"Yeah, I do," I admit without hesitation.

"You accused her of some pretty nasty things."

"Correct again." I'm being flippant, but there's a storm going on inside me and I'm clearly not good at handling real life. Probably because I've never had to deal with it before. That's on me, though. I have a voice, and I'm responsible for my own life and my own happiness. I realize that now. "I'm sorry. I don't mean to be a jerk."

"She wouldn't like me telling you this, Matt. She told it to me in confidence, but you two belong together and I just can't see both of you hurting like this."

"What?" I ask my heart jumping into my throat.

"The pregnancy kit. It's not what you think."

Okay, she's not straight up telling me Kennedy isn't pregnant —she probably doesn't want to betray her trust—and I can only conclude this is the next best way to tell me what I need to know. I exhale, and to be honest, I'm not sure whether I'm happy or sad. How fucked up is that? Some ridiculous part of me toyed with the idea that a baby would keep her in my life, and yes, I planned to be the best dad ever.

I rub the back of my tightening neck. "I didn't give her a chance to explain."

"She could have explained. She could have gotten the point across if she wanted to."

My head rears back. "What? Why didn't she then?"

"She let you believe what you *wanted* to believe, what you were ingrained to believe."

I was ingrained to believe that I was worthless without hockey, that I had no substance, that women would care only about my career, not who I am as a person. I guess I believed it because it was force-fed to me since I was first put on skates.

"Why did she let me believe that?" I ask quietly as my eyes sting, tears pressing hard.

"Because the decision on what you do next has to be yours, and yours alone. It has to be what you want. She'll fight for you, Matt. She loves you and will fight tooth and nail for you, but before she does..." she pokes me in the chest, hard. "... You have to fight for you first."

Her words jangle around in my head. "Piper—"

"This conversation never happened," she says quickly and walks away, leaving me to mull over her words of advice. I stand there for a long time, until a text from my brother comes in.

Liam: Where are you, bro?

Matt: Coming.

With Piper's words pounding in my ears, I drive through the quiet Sunday morning streets and pull up in front of the hotel. Liam comes out, looking tired and rumpled, and my heart clenches tight. I ruffle his already messed hair after he slides in beside me.

"Hey bro."

"Hey," he says quietly, that familiar sadness about him filling the truck and my soul.

"Let's get some food."

He buckles in. "And coffee."

That makes me smile. "Since when did you start drinking coffee? Don't you know that shit will stunt your growth?"

"Let's hope it does. I'm almost taller than you already."

I drive a few blocks and pull into my favorite pancake place. I park and we're both quiet as we head inside. The server takes us to a booth and fills our cups with a dark brew, and we both take much needed gulps.

"I'm glad you're here."

"Great game last night," he responds.

We love each other, and we might not be ones to display great amounts of affection, but Jesus, do we ever talk about anything another other than hockey? I'm not sure we do and it's time we changed that.

"Do you want a tour of the campus later, and maybe we can hit the waterfront for a walk and a Beaver Tail."

A smile lights up his face. "Sure. Um...what about Granddad?"

I try to make light of things, even though they're very heavy right now. "He can join if he likes."

"I'm not sure that's his thing." He looks down, picks up his napkin and starts ripping at the ends.

"Then it will be the two of us."

He casts me a fast glance. "I don't think he'll like that."

"Would you, though, Liam?" I straight up ask. "Would you like to spend the day exploring the city?"

He nods, and I take a breath. Maybe there's still hope for the both of us. The server comes back and we briefly scan the menu and we both order the special. After she leaves, and his gaze meets mine, I ask, "Who's Luna?"

He stiffens and straightens in his seat. "What?"

"Who's Luna, and please don't be mad at Kennedy for saying anything to me." He glances down, then looks over his shoulder, like he's worried someone is listening. "You can tell me anything, Liam. It stays between us."

"She's...this girl I like." He grins like he's remembering something nice. "She's a figure skater." He laughs, and I angle my head.

"What's funny?"

"She asked if I would be her partner in the doubles in figure skating. Can you imagine me doing that?"

"Actually yeah, I can."

Surprise leaps into his eyes and they go big. "Really?"

I don't miss the hope and curiosity hanging on that one word. "Is that something you'd like to do?"

"I...don't know. I've never given it much thought."

Why do I think he's fibbing? "Give it thought now." I pick up my coffee, sit back and sip. "I'll wait."

He glances into his cup like it holds all the answers in the world. "Granddad wouldn't like that."

"I'm not asking what Granddad would like. I'm asking what you would like."

A long, thoughtful pause and then, "I think it would be fun. We could do those twirly things where I lift her in the air." He holds his arm up and shows me his bicep. "I've been working out. I could lift her."

I can't help but smile. "If you want to do it, you should do it."

His smile falls. "But hockey."

"You can do both, Liam." I lean toward him, never more serious in my entire life. "You can have a life outside of hockey."

"Do you?"

Isn't that the question of the century? "I never used to, until I met Kennedy and it was the best, little bro. Now she hates me, of course."

"You're going to be a father huh?"

"No, I don't think so and after Granddad told me she was pregnant, and that he paid her off, I wasn't my best, and I hate myself for that. I went to talk to Kennedy, but I said some things, and I wouldn't blame her if she never talked to me again. One thing is for sure, if she was pregnant, I wouldn't be a deadbeat dad and walk away. I don't know how Granddad thought I could ever do that. I would be there for her and the baby, whether she wanted me or not."

"You're a good guy, Matt."

My heart misses a beat. His words mean the world to me. "I want you to live life, Liam. I want you to do things that are fun. I don't want you to end up like me, in your twenties, wondering where your youth went."

"But—"

"No buts. I mean it. I haven't been a good big brother." An invisible band tightens around my heart, and tears once again press against my eyes. "I've let you down."

"No—"

"I became what was expected of me. I lived up to that reputation, and I'm not sure I liked that guy. I want to be a better person. I want to be a guy others can count on."

He nods like he totally understands. "Granddad said he'll cut you off."

"I guess I'll have to get a job or two then." There's pride in his eyes as he smiles at me. "We can do this, bro. We can play hockey and have a life, with or without Granddad's support."

"I like that, but if I don't follow his rules..."

"You can always count on me. Don't you know I'm going to be an NHL superstar someday?" He grins. "And I'll never cut you off." The server comes and sets our plates in front of us. "There's something else I'd like to do today," I tell Liam.

He eyes me, and asks, "What's that?"

I think back to my conversation with Piper. She was right. The decision to fight for my life, and future has to be mine—and fighting for me means fighting for Kennedy—and I think I know exactly how to do it.

"Let's eat, and then I'll show you."

Is that...Matt?

I haven't seen him since last Saturday night, when he showed up at my door and said those cruel things. I haven't even seen him around campus either, and I thought maybe he went back to Alberta. It's been a hard week going through the motions of living and keeping things cheerful for my daughter.

A few more people enter The Lower Deck as I play, and my heart stalls when I see that it's Daisy, Sawyer, Piper, Brandon, Chase and Beckett. I'm surprised to see Beckett and Piper in the same circle, but what I'm really thinking about is Sawyer's wedding. I haven't seen her or the others since last Saturday night and now I'm not even sure we're friends, or that I'm still in the wedding. I'm not sure I want to be, either. How awkward would that be?

I turn my attention to my music and glance down as I finish my song. I've pretty much scrapped the song I've been writing for Sawyer and Chase's wedding. How can I put a happily ever after to it, when the truth is that it's based on Matt and me? Since I haven't heard from him all week, I'm assuming our happily ever after doesn't exist.

Matt's friends all grab a big table, and I find my gaze drawn to the bar again, to where I last spotted Matt—or at least I thought I did—but he's no longer there. Perhaps he was simply a figment of my imagination. I try to shut down my heart, and all the emotions flooding my veins as I finish my set. Once done, I pack up my guitar, tug on my coat, and take the few stairs off the stage. I'm ready to bolt out of the place and nearly make it to the door when Sawyer and Daisy block my path.

"Where are you going in such a hurry?" they ask.

"I uh...have to get home. Madelyn."

"Can we walk you?"

What the heck is going on? I haven't heard from them all week and now they want to walk me home? I glance over their shoulder and spot Piper lingering behind. Why the heck is she avoiding eye contact with me?

"Come on," Daisy says, threading her arm through mine, giving me little choice in the matter.

"Okay," I say as she yanks me, and Sawyer takes my guitar from my hands. I step out into the dark night, the late October air cool on my skin.

We walk the busy streets, pass lots of students out partying on their Saturday night, and I think of Matt. Is he at Storm House, getting drunk, with girls falling all over him? That's how Piper described it when she showed up at my house last week.

They all start talking about Halloween and the big bash Storm House will be throwing and my heart sinks. I guess I might as well toss Matt's costume. I walk in silence, lost in thought, and they all let me as they carry the conversation. With Sawyer on one side of me, and Daisy on the other, like they're worried I'm going to run or something, I glance over my shoulder at the others, who are trailing behind. Once again, Piper avoids my gaze.

I hold my hand out and flip it over, trying to be casual as a storm brews inside me. "If you guys have somewhere to be—"

"We don't," Daisy interrupts.

"I don't need an entourage," I joke.

"Get used to it," Sawyer says. "Once you're a famous singer, you'll have an entourage and groupies."

That makes me laugh. I love how supportive they all are. Matt was supportive of my career too. He was supportive of everything I did. When you really think about it, at first Matt seemed to be at war with himself when it came to sleeping with me. Was that because he was worried about falling for me, and that didn't fit into the life his grandfather had mapped out for him?

I look at Daisy and Sawyer and quietly ask, "Have you guys heard from Matt?"

Daisy nods. "Yeah, we talk to him every day."

While I'm happy he has friends and people he can talk to, there's an emptiness inside me. I miss our conversations. I miss him. "How is he?" I ask.

Both girls come to a complete stop. Was it something I said? "What?" I ask, my gaze bobbing back and forth between the two of them.

"Why don't you ask him yourself?" Daisy says quietly.

Really? Do they not know what went down? "Because..."

My words fall off as they turn me on the sidewalk, until I'm staring at the cute house I wanted to rent for Madelyn and me, the one that had been snatched up before I could figure out a way to afford it. "Why are we stopping?"

"So you can ask Matt how he is?"

"I don't get it."

The front door creaks open and Matt steps out, looking sad, sorry, and pained, not to mention so damn handsome it brings tears to my eyes and weakens my legs. I want to run, but I'm not sure whether it's to him or away from him. No, it's definitely to him, but I need to know he's the man he needs to be, for himself, and for the world. My legs give and I falter backward a bit.

"Whoa, easy," Daisy says as she tightens her arm in mine to keep me upright. I take deep fueling breaths as the others fall silent behind us.

"Matt," I murmur, struggling to choke back tears and sound somewhat normal. "What's going on? What are you doing here, in this house?"

Piper steps up to me and gives my elbow a squeeze. "Don't be mad."

"Mad, mad about what?"

Before she can answer, she scurries away, and Daisy walks me to the bottom of the steps and it takes all my effort to put one foot in front of the other. I stop at the bottom step and stare up at Matt, my heart pounding so hard, I can hardly hear anything around me.

"Can we talk?" he asks, his voice low and strained—tired. I take in his hair. It looks like he's been running his fingers through it for days, and when was the last time he'd gotten any sleep? I can relate to that. I've been a walking zombie for the last week.

"Yes," I say.

"Good. Go." Daisy shoves me and I nearly fall on my face. Matt jumps down a few steps and captures me before I lose my front teeth on the cement stairs. He helps me up, and the second his hands touch my body, I nearly sob. I've missed him so damn much.

"Daisy," Matt admonishes as he guides me to the stoop. "Be careful."

"Sorry," she says sheepishly. "Sometimes I don't know my own strength." She jerks her head toward Brandon and Chase. "Blame it on playing with these guys when we were kids. But I just really want this."

"What...what do you want?" I ask her as Matt keeps his arms around me, holding me close. Unable to help myself, I slide my arm around his waist, and let him support me the way he's been supporting me for months now.

Daisy grins at me. "You'll see."

Matt points behind him. "Can we talk...inside?"

His closeness messes with me and since my voice is lodged somewhere in my throat, I simply nod. His hand slides to my lower back and as my body absorbs the warmth, my heart flutters, a physical reminder of how much I love him. We step inside and he closes the door, locking everyone else out and us in. Once we're alone, I glance around the decorated house and notice some of his trophies sitting on the coffee table in the living room.

"Who lives here?"

"I do," he answers. "I rented it."

My brain races to catch up. Matt rented this place? I know he talked about moving out of Storm House next year. "But this is the place—"

"That you wanted to rent. I know. In fact, I was hoping you and Madelyn might want to be my roommates."

"Matt..." Oh God, is he asking me to live with him? I want that more than anything, but I haven't heard from him in a week and I have no idea what happened between him and his grandfather. Is the elderly gentleman still pulling his strings? Then again, if he was, Matt wouldn't be doing any of this, I'm sure of it, considering his grandfather wanted to pay me to exit his life and take my baby with me. "Whose idea was this?"

"Mine, and mine alone." There's something different about Matt as he straightens his shoulders and holds my gaze...a new kind of strength and confidence. No, not new. It's always been there, hiding and lurking, and he simply had to open the door to let it out. Joyful tears prick my eyes.

"I like that," I say.

Glossy eyes hold my gaze. "Come with me."

He takes my hand and silently leads me upstairs. We walk down the long hall and he ushers me into a baby's nursery, all decorated in neutral colors. My world tilts on its axis, and I press my hand against the wall to keep myself from falling, from being sick. Oh, God, he still thinks I'm pregnant. Is this why he's doing all this? Is it stemming from a sense of obligation, a need to stand up to be the man I always knew he could be—a man his grandfather no longer controls—and I love him for that, but I'm not pregnant. Would he have made this choice if he knew that?

"I love you, Kennedy. You're everything to me, the best part of me. I want you and Madelyn in my life. I'm completely lost without you. Last weekend..." He takes a breath and closes his eyes. "I hate myself. I hate myself for the way I struck out, for the assumptions. You didn't deserve any of that from me and I'm so damn sorry." He cups my face. "I spent all of last week missing you, but I wanted to have everything in place first. I want to be with you."

"I...Matt...." I shake my head and begin to back away. "This, no...no..."

He moves toward me, panic in his eyes. "I know you hate me. The things I said, accused you of...I'm an asshole."

"You're not an asshole." He blinks at me, the sadness in his eyes overwhelming me as it wraps around my heart and squeezes tight. "You're a lot of things, but you're not an asshole."

He comes closer. "A lot of things?"

I put my palm on the side of his face. "You're kind, and sweet, caring and compassionate. You care about others more than you even realize. You love life, and the world, and you haven't even begun to see or experience a quarter of it. You have so

much to see and learn, so much to give. But this...
I...I'm no—"

"I don't understand...if you feel that way about me—"

"This," I blurt out waving my hand before I put it on his chest. "Inside here, you're good and right. Your heart is full of integrity, but this...I can't be with you, move in with you because of a baby."

While I love that he wants to be a stand-up guy, I need Matt to love himself, before Madelyn and I can love him, and I want him to be with us, because it's what his heart wants, not because he thinks it's the right and just thing to do.

"I'm not," he says quickly, as he shakes his head.

"You did this because...you think I'm pregnant," I state.

He exhales and his shoulders relax. "I get it, Kennedy. The decision to fight for my life and future had to be mine, and I made the decision to do it. My grandfather cut me off, and I'm actually happy about that. He gave me an ultimatum."

"You picked me," I state quietly.

"Always." He tucks a strand of hair behind my ear. "You are the wisest woman I know, and helped open my eyes, helped me become a better man, a better example for my brother. I'm here asking you to live with me, to love me, because I love you and Madelyn." His hand falls and he places it over my stomach. "I know you're not pregnant, and that you'd never trick me or use me. You love me for me, and I love you for you."

That's when I realize why Piper has been avoiding my gaze and asked me not to be mad. She clearly spoke to Matt and I'm actually grateful for it. My heart wobbles and tears fall as

I stare at the man I've always been able to see. A man who is now in control of himself and his destiny.

"Someday though, I was thinking maybe we could have a child together. That's why I decorated this room. I wanted to show you that I want a future with you, and our friends outside helped me."

"Of course, they were all in on this," I say with a laugh.

"I don't know what the future brings, or where we'll be, or live, or if we'll be on the road, but I want a home base with you here, so Madelyn can grow up with stability in a place we both love. I wanted to show you how much you mean to me by renting this place, and the decorating was to show you I wanted a family, and that my future is in my own hands, but I also want it to be in your hands too."

"Matt…" I say, as he blurs before me.

Unshed tears, brimming with love and hope for our future fill his eyes, too. "I want a family, and I want it with you, Kennedy. You make me a better person, the person I know I can be and want to be. You were never just a cook or cleaner or a fuck partner. You've always been everything to me. I was scared to tell you. I was scared of rejection. I was scared of wanting what I wasn't sure I could have. I never wanted to be a man you couldn't count on. But I'm laying it all on the line right now and I promise to be everything you and Madelyn want and need."

"I want to be a part of your future too." As soon as the words spill from my mouth, he picks me up and starts spinning me around. A laugh bubbles out of my throat. He sets me down and kisses me deeply. Once we break apart, I ask, "So how are we going to pay for this place if your granddad cut you off?"

"We'll find a way, Kennedy. As long as we're together, we'll find a way and don't forget you're going to be a successful singer, and I'm going to be a kick-ass defensive player in the NHL. Until then, we could always take in a roommate, someone who is good with kids." He gives me a wink. "We have a spare room and Beckett has been looking to cut costs for the next semester. He comes from a big Cape Breton family and knows how to babysit."

Grinning, I hug him again, my heart so full of love and hope for our future. "You've clearly given this thought and I love you for that, Matt."

"I love you too, Kennedy." He grins. "Do you think we should go tell our friends? I'm sure they're busting to know how things are going in here."

"We could..." I say, and take his hand and lead him into the master bedroom. "Or we could christen this bed and talk more about the family we want to have. I just don't think either of us is ready to get started on it right now, though."

He scoops me up and sets me on the bed. "Agreed, and I like the idea of christening every room in this place." He's about to climb onto the bed, and I frown. "What?" he asks, worry invading his eyes, like he's afraid that I've changed my mind.

I push from the bed, unable to leave our friends hanging. He stares at me as I walk to the window.

"What are you doing?" he asks.

I open the window. "Hey guys," I yell, and everyone looks up. "Can we catch up with you guys later? We have a little making up to do."

"Make-up sex is the best," Beckett yells out as he fist pumps the air, and everyone laughs.

Daisy throws her arms in the air too. "You're the man, Matt."

I grin and turn at Matt. "Did you hear that? You're the man."

He grins back, scoops me up again and puts me back on the bed. "Now it's time for you to scream my name."

"The confidence," I say. "I love it."

He falls over me, his lips meeting mine. "And I love you."

I run my hands through his hair, my heart so full I'm sure it's going to burst. "Are you ready to deliver, Milk Man?" I tease.

"Yeah baby, I'm ready to deliver, tonight and for the rest of our lives."

―――――

EPILOGUE

―――――

I take my seat at the wedding reception and glance around the resort's majestic ball room, all decorated with ice sculptures and snowflakes—the perfect decorations for a Nova Scotia winter wedding. Ocean Mist Resort is a popular wedding destination in this Maritime province. It's located just outside of the city and has private chalets overlooking the Atlantic Ocean. I've never been to a wedding in February before, and while it's cold and blustery outside, inside there is a fire going and it's warm and cozy.

Maybe Kennedy and I will get married here, if she wants to. Then again, she has been talking about a destination wedding down south. Although I am getting ahead of myself. I haven't even asked her to be my life partner...yet. I touch my coat pocket, and lightly pat the velvety box inside. Tonight, when we're alone in our private chalet, I plan to pop the question and I can't wait to put a ring on her finger.

My phone buzzes and I tug it from my suit pocket and smile when I see a picture of Liam and Luna, huge smiles on their happy faces. They're on the ice and he's lifting her over his head. I think he put on even more muscle and grew another foot since he was here. I grin, and for the first time in my life, I feel like I've been a good influence on the kid. I'm thrilled to see Liam living life and smiling.

Grandad and I are talking, but things are different now. I no longer let him pull my strings and while he's offered to help out financially again, I declined, wanting to do things my way. This way I'm not indebted and don't have to answer to anyone. Okay, well I have to answer to Kennedy—not to mention Madelyn—and I'm okay with that.

Speaking of Kennedy...

I glance up to see her walking toward me, looking sexy and gorgeous in her off the shoulder sparkly blue dress, and I know in my heart I'm the luckiest man in the world. She's holding a very tired and very wiggly Madelyn, who is wearing a pretty white flower girl dress. She already tossed away the flowered veil she had on—I think she's going to be as headstrong as her mother. I guess we're lucky she managed to make it down the aisle with it still in place.

But seriously, Madelyn was the cutest flower girl I've ever seen—everyone thought so—but she's cranky now and Barb is coming to pick her up and keep her for the night so we can dance and slip into our private chalet, where I'll light a fire and we'll listen to the waves crash as I ask Kennedy to marry me. Maybe afterward, she'll sing the song she wrote for us and sang during Sawyer and Chase's ceremony earlier. The song brought tears to everyone's eyes and I'm sure it's going to be a worldwide hit once she gets it recorded.

Kennedy blows a strand of hair off her face, looking a little worn out and I can't wait to take care of her later. "Mom is here to pick up Madelyn. I'll walk her out."

"Let me take her. You sit, rest your feet and have a glass of wine."

She side eyes me. "Are you trying to get me drunk?"

I stand, and laugh and Madelyn holds her arms out to me, and my heart soars. There is nothing like my little girl reaching for me and snuggling into my arms. Yes, she's my little girl. Not legally, not yet, but once Kennedy and I get married, I plan to adopt her. Madelyn squirms until she gets in the perfect position, and I kiss Kennedy, letting her know I'll be right back.

"See you later, sweet girl," Kennedy says to her daughter and Madelyn gives her one of her backward waves. I bundle Madelyn up, head outdoors and find Barb waiting. "The roads are okay?" I ask.

"Yes, the snow is coming later, so I'd better hurry." She opens the back door and I buckle Madelyn in.

"How did she do?" Barb asks.

"Perfect."

She smiles and circles the car, and I walk back inside, my heart so full of love and happiness. I sit back down next to Kennedy and she puts her hand on my lap. She smiles at me, and I can't help but lean in and kiss her.

"Get a room," Beck says and smirks. Beck has been living in our spare room for a couple months now and it's working out perfectly. Madelyn loves him, and he even got me a job at the campus cafeteria where he works.

Kennedy grins at him. "We have a room." She leans toward Piper. "Sawyer's dress is absolutely gorgeous. You did an amazing job."

Piper smiles, but I don't miss the sadness there too. For a girl who is in the business program, she's awfully good at designing clothes. I don't know her well enough to ask what that's all about.

Sawyer and Chase finish cutting their cake at the head table, and they're flanked by their friends and family. It was a thrill to meet Chase's, Brandon's and Daisy's fathers, who were all NHL player for the Seattle Shooters. Of course, we all know Sawyer's dad. He's our coach. Soon enough, a slice of cake is set in front of us all, and I dig in.

"This is so good," I murmur.

"Delicious," Piper agrees, and takes another big bite. I grin as she gets icing all over her nose.

"You have," Beckett says and reaches for her face. She flinches and he ends up smudging the icing on her cheek.

"What are you doing?" she asks and her chair scrapes on the floor as she pushes back from the table.

"You had icing—"

"I did not. You just put icing on my face. Why would you do that?"

Beck opens and closes his mouth, the tension between the two so thick it's practically suffocating. Beck turns to us, obviously looking for allies. "You guys saw it, right?"

I hold my hands up, palms out, not about to get in between them. "I saw nothing."

Piper stands. "I need to go wash up." She glances down. "Great, it's on my dress too."

Beckett grabs a napkin and holds it out to her, but she bends and reaches for her own. Unfortunately—or fortunately, depending on who you ask—Beck ends up with his hand between her cleavage. He snatches it back like he just touched hot fire.

Oh boy!

Kennedy grabs my thighs again and I glance at her, take in her smirk. She knows shit's about to hit the fan, too.

"Sorry," Beck says quickly. "That was an accident."

A pink flush moves into Piper's face. "Yeah, sure, okay. I… uh…should go wash up."

"Let me help." Beck jumps from his chair so fast it nearly topples backward.

Piper shakes her head and it's clear she's flustered. "No, no. I'm okay, you don't need to help. I've got this. Where is the washroom?"

"I know where it is. I'll show you."

He puts his hand on the small of her back, and she sucks in a fast breath as he turns her toward the hall. She flinches from his touch, and practically runs, but he's close on her heels. Clearly, he feels bad and wants to help. Beckett is a small-town boy with a heart of gold. Actually, they both come from the same small Cape Breton town, and I have no idea what their history is. Beckett doesn't talk about it, and I only know they have one—and it's not good.

I shake my head. "What is the matter with those two?" I ask Kennedy.

"I don't know, but did you notice Beck hasn't brought a single girl home since he moved in with us?"

I take another bite of cake, and nod. "Maybe he's trying to be respectful. You know, because we have a child in the house."

"Maybe," she says, sounding unconvinced. "I wonder, though. If they don't get along and we all know it, why would Sawyer and Chase seat them side by side?" She glances around the huge ball room. "The place is packed, and they could have easily separated them."

I take a sip of water. "You think they know something we don't."

She shrugs. "Yeah, but I think we know it too."

"Meaning?"

She goes quiet for a second, and I can almost hear her brain spinning. "Remember when we got back together, and Beckett told us make-up sex was the best."

"Yeah."

"Maybe those two need to hate-fuck."

I grin at her. "I love it when you talk dirty, but they hate each other, Kennedy."

"And that, Matt, is exactly why a hate fuck is in order." I eye her and she continues with, "You felt the tension, right?" I nod. "They were glaring at one another, but they were also eye fucking. If something doesn't soon give, I think they're both going to spontaneously combust."

"Is that a thing?" I tease. She grins, and I say, "You're thinking we should do something about it, aren't you?"

She gives me a devious grin that I love. "Yes, and I think I know exactly what that something is."

. . .

***

Thank you so much for reading Kennedy and Matt's story. I hope you enjoyed it. The third book in the series, **Crash Course (Rebels)** releases September 6, 2022. Please read on for an excerpt of Crash Course, book three in my Scotia Storm series.

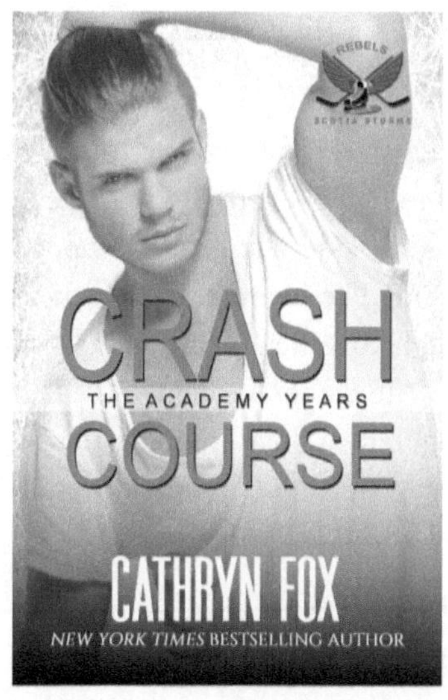

Crash Course
Piper

In Nova Scotia, April showers bring...snow. I'm not just talking about a light dusting here—like the weatherman called for. I'm talking thick, heavy flakes that are weighing down my hair and piling up fast beneath my Valentino's. Having grown up on Cape Breton Island, where they get even more snow than they do here in Halifax, you'd think I'd know better than to wear expensive shoes in April. But I had to talk to my fashion design teacher over at the community college and I always like to appear put together and professional.

I trudge across the street, my feet and ankles freezing, and note a few cars swerving as they take the corner. I guess they took their winter tires off too soon. At least I know better than to do that, and I'm glad I walked to the campus this afternoon instead of driving, even though only a fool would be traipsing outside in this kind of weather. I snort at that. I suppose I've been called worse...

I hurry across the street, on my way to my friend Kennedy's house, and as I round Beckett Moore's Jeep, I roll my eyes, because yes, he's the one who's called me worse. Not to my face, of course, but I've heard things back when we were in Cape Breton High together. Who would have thought we'd both end up at the same Academy in Halifax? I probably should have figured it out though, considering he's an amazing hockey goalie, and much coveted by the Scotia Storms, the academy's kick ass team.

Beckett and I even shared a few business classes in our Freshman year—keeping our distance in the classroom, of course—and while I'm enrolled in the management program, I'm also taking design classes because fashion is my passion.

I put my hand on Beckett's snowy jeep to steady myself as I round it, not wanting to land on my butt, as my feet slide, but the second I take the turn—big fat snowflakes blurring my vision—Beckett comes sliding out from underneath the car, the dolly's wheels getting stuck in the snow.

I gasp at his sudden, unexpected appearance, and try to jump out of the way, but I slip and contort, hurling my back, and end up with my legs wrapped around his head, as I straddle his face. Wait, is he grinning?

"What the hell, Beckett!" I try to stand, but only end up wiggling and gyrating, and dear God, never in my entire life did I imagine I'd be sitting on Beckett's face—and enjoy it. Okay, maybe I did once, a couple months ago at our friend's wedding, when he smudge cake on my cheek and dress and he accidently put his hand on my breast as he tried to help me clean it. Ridiculous right? Especially considering the fact that I hate this man with every fiber of my being, and would like nothing more than to wipe that smirk from his face. A man as horrible as Beckett should not be gifted with adorable dimples.

"Need a hand." He puts his big, rough hands on my hips to still me.

Ohmigod, he has no idea what his touch is doing to me. Or maybe he does. There isn't a girl on campus, besides me, that is immune to his charm. In my current predicament, as snow falls onto his face, his mouth so close to the needy juncture between my legs, I'm not convinced I'm immune to it either.

"What were you doing under there?"

"What are you doing up there?" he counters, and I'm pretty sure his hands are holding me in place.

"I'm trying to get off."

Ohmigod, kill me freaking now.

"Is that so?"

I give a fast shake of my head, and my wet hair clings to my cheeks. "It's not...I mean, I didn't mean it that way."

"You didn't mean you're not trying to get off me?"

"Yes. No."

I'm going to kill him for trying to twist my words, although maybe I'm the only one thinking it sounded sexual. How could I think otherwise when I'm talking about getting off as I wiggle on his face?

He lifts me, and lowers me on his body, and he sits up. His face is right there inches from mine, and his gaze drops and takes in my mouth as I try to plant my shoes on the ground. To anyone looking, I'm sure they think we're dry humping in the driveway, except I'm wet, and it's not from the snow.

What is going on with my life?

I put my hands on his shoulders for leverage, and he helps me lift myself off. "Good?" he asks as I get to my feet, my sex once again right there in front of his face. I grumble under my breath and keep my hands on his shoulders, as I carefully lift one leg and set it down on the ground by my other. Once I'm stable, I let go of his shoulders, and try not to think about how his muscles played beneath my fingers. But seriously the last thing I want to do is fall on him again.

Okay, maybe it's not the last thing.

I shake my head and shut down that ridiculous inner voice, making a mental note to give it a good hard lecture later. We hate Beckett.

He jumps up from the dolly, and snatches it up. "What are you doing?" I ask.

"I was fixing the muffler hanger. It was loose, rattling, making a terrible noise."

"In the middle of a snow storm."

His gaze leaves my face, leisurely traveling over my light stylish coat, tight jeans and ruined shoes. His brow arches in question as his gaze cuts back to mine.

"Yeah, okay."

I turn from him, and nearly face plant as I try to make it up the sloped driveway. I windmill my arms, nearly losing my backpack off my shoulder, but before I fall, his hand is around my waist, anchoring me to his body. I'm sure the touch is as painful to him as it is to me. I've heard the things he's said about me. Although he pretty much stopped speaking to me after my seventeenth birthday, walking around our high school like I didn't exist. I'm not really sure what I ever did to him. Shortly after my party, my car was vandalized. Someone spray painted slut on the driver's side door.

We all assumed it was Beck, and when my parents confronted his parents and Beck was call downstairs to answer, he vehemently denied it. Funny thing is, I believed him. Even after the cold way he treated me, I still believed him.

Our parents didn't associate with each other before the incident, they didn't really like each other. Probably because mine, own and run Cape Breton's elite golf and ski resort, and his are blue collar workers, and yes, it's also true—and sad—that mine think their way better than everyone else, and didn't want me associating with those from the other side of the tracks. After the graffiti situation they despised one another.

He might not have put those words on my car, and while I don't for one minute think he thinks I'm a slut, he no doubt assumes I'm a pampered princess, which in a way I am, but I don't hold the same beliefs as my parents. He just couldn't be bothered to see me as anything else, and because of it, I couldn't be bothered to show him. So now we're enemies, despite the fact that we share the same circle of friends.

"Thanks," I say, despite our past. He's helping me walk, and I'm grateful.

"Sure."

He helps me up the stairs, and pulls open the front door. Kicking snow off his boots, he wipes his face, leaving a big streak of grease on his forehead.

"Oh, you have..." I reach for his face and he flinches back. "Grease."

"Yeah, I know. I don't want you to touch it and get dirty. You're dressed nice."

Appreciating that, I nod, and he waves his big hand, a gesture for me to enter. I step inside and moan as the warmth envelopes me. Our friends Kennedy, Matt and their little girl Madelyn moved into this downtown house last October, and Beckett moved in with them shortly afterward, so I'm used to seeing him here. Or maybe a girl could never get used to seeing Beckett, especially since he likes to walk around without a T-shirt.

"Piper," Kennedy says as she comes running down the hall, a dish towel in her hands. "You're soaked."

"I fell," I say and steal a fast glance at Beckett, hoping he's not about to give the gory details of me riding his face.

"Come on, let's get you out of these clothes." I start shivering, almost uncontrollably as I take off my ruined shoes, and set my backpack on the floor. I hope the fabric inside isn't soaked, too. Matt agreed to be my model for my final project, and I don't want to drape him in wet fabric.

Kennedy glances at Beckett's wet clothes and hair and shakes her head. "Did you fall too?" Before he can answer, she says, "Get changed, you're dripping all over the floor and I don't want you to catch your death of cold."

"Yes, Mom," he says with a smirk, and Kennedy gives him the death glare. Honestly, they get along like brother and sister, and from what Kennedy says, he's amazing with her daughter. Me? Not so much. As an only child, I'm not used to siblings and I never really babysat. Nope, any spare time I had, I was working at the family's resort. My parents have been grooming their only child to take over for as long as I can remember. Too bad I hate the idea. Maybe even more than I hate Beckett.

I'm too afraid to tell my folks though. They've been so good to me, and they pay everything, from my food, and rent to my education and extracurricular activities. Heck they even sponsored the brand new Olympic sized pool for the academy, simply because I love to swim. I even have my own key to the facility, and can use it any day, any hour. I owe them, and the lodge has been in the family for generations. It's only right that I take over when they retire, right? I've consoled myself that I can design clothes on the side, but let's face it. Who has time for such things when running a golf and ski lodge year round?

"I just have to put this in the garage," Beckett says and holds up the dolly.

Kennedy nods and asks, "Did you get your Jeep fixed?"

"Yeah, and I'll get to your spark plugs, once the snow lightens."

"No hurry on that. I'm not planning on driving anywhere in this." She glances out the door, shivers and hugs herself.

"You're always so cold," Beckett says, and puts his one free hand on her arm, and rubs up and down to create warmth with friction. She smiles up at him, her gaze full of warmth and it's easy to see they have a special bond.

"Thanks."

"Good now?"

"Yup."

I don't like the guy, but it's so nice how thoughtful and caring he is with Kennedy. Is it odd that I have this weird knot of jealousy tightening in my gut? Yeah, I think it is. But it's so damn sweet. Honestly, I've had guy friends and boyfriends over the years, but I've never experienced a real closeness, or a special bond with any guy.

With that he nods, and disappears back outside. Kennedy loops her arm in mine and takes me to the stairs. We head up, and I say, "You and Beckett really get along well."

"Yeah, he's a sweetie." I almost snort, but don't want to be rude. "We really like having him here. He's handy too, and always willing to help out, anything we need."

If I spent the night would he help out with the ache between my legs?

Dear God, what am I saying?

"I'm a little worried about him though."

"Worried, why would you be worried?"

She frowns. "I think he's working too hard. I haven't seen him with a girl in...forever."

"You mean he's not parading them in and out of here every weekend?"

"Nope." We reach the landing, and she puts her fingers to her lips to let me know Madelyn is sleeping, and I almost breathe a sigh of relief. It's not that I don't like Madelyn, I'm just a bit nervous and uncomfortable around her. I never know what to say. All I do know is that I'm not a natural.

Inside the master bedroom, Kennedy grabs me a pair of sweats and a t-shirt and sweater, which I probably won't need because it's super warm in the house. "I have an extra pair of boots for when you leave, or you can stay over if it gets too bad out there. Hey, the four of us could make a night out of it."

Stay over, and be forced to spend more time with Beckett. No. Thank. You.

"Thanks," I say. "I'm sure I'll be fine."

"At least stay for dinner."

"Sounds great."

"I'll leave you to get changed. Meet me downstairs when you're done. I'll put on a fresh pot of coffee."

Ever grateful, as Kennedy makes the best coffee ever, I listen to her footsteps on the stairs and glance around, feeling a little uncomfortable getting changed in the master bedroom. I quietly open the door, and tip toe to the bathroom, shutting the door tightly behind me. I glance at my face in the mirror, and shake my head. With mascara dripping down my cheek, it's a wonder Beckett didn't scream in horror when I sat on his face. The girls I've seen him with, although I must say I haven't seen him with anyone since he's moved in here, would never be caught dead with their make-up running.

God, I sound like a jealous fool, when I'm anything but.

I peel off my coat, and damp sweater and wiggle out of my jeans. Not an easy task when their wet. I bend forward and grab the tub, having a hell of a time getting the legs over my ankle, when the bathroom door flings open. I gasp and straighten, and spin, and lose my balance as my gaze lands on a bare chested Beckett, his T-shirt draped over his shoulder, in that sexy, manly way that teases every erogenous zone in my body.

"Oh, ah...sorry."

"I...I was trying to get off..." I hop around on one foot, and that's when I realize I'm only in my bra and underwear, about to faceplant again.

He closes the distance between us faster than a world elite sprinter, and the second I'm in his big arms, his dimple appears as he smirks and says, "Again?"

* * *

If you want to find out what kind of trouble Piper and Beckett get into check out **Crash Course (Rebels)**

ALSO BY CATHRYN FOX

Scotia Storms

Away Game (Rebels)

Warm Up (Rebels)

Crash Course (Rebels)

Home Advantage (Rebels)

End Zone

Fair Play

Enemy Down

Keeping Score

Trading Up

All In

Blue Bay Crew

Demolished

Leveled

Hammered

Single Dad

Single Dad Next Door

Single Dad on Tap

Single Dad Burning Up

Players on Ice

The Playmaker

The Stick Handler

The Body Checker

The Hard Hitter

The Risk Taker

The Wing Man

The Puck Charmer

The Troublemaker

The Rule Breaker

The Rookie

The Sweet Talker

The Heart Breaker

In the Line of Duty

His Obsession Next Door

His Strings to Pull

His Trouble in Talulah

His Taste of Temptation

His Moment to Steal

His Best Friend's Girl

His Reason to Stay

Confessions

Confessions of a Bad Boy Professor

Confessions of a Bad Boy Officer

Confessions of a Bad Boy Fighter

Confessions of a Bad Boy Doctor

Confessions of a Bad Boy Gamer

Confessions of a Bad Boy Millionaire

Confessions of a Bad Boy Santa

Confessions of a Bad Boy CEO

Hands On

Hands On

Body Contact

Full Exposure

Dossier

Private Reserve

House Rules

Under Pressure

Big Catch

Brazilian Fantasy

Improper Proposal

Boys of Beachville

Good at Being Bad

Igniting the Bad Boy

Bad Girl Therapy

Stone Cliff Series:

Crashing Down

Wasted Summer

Love Lessons

Wrapped Up

Eternal Pleasure Series

Instinctive

Impulsive

Indulgent

Sun Stroked Series

Seaside Seduction

Deep Desire

Private Pleasure

Captured and Claimed Series:

Yours to Take

Yours to Teach

Yours to Keep

Firefighter Heat Series

Fever

Siren

Flash Fire

Playing For Keeps Series

Slow Ride

Wild Ride

Sweet Ride

Breaking the Rules:

Hold Me Down Hard

Pin Me Up Proper

Tie Me Down Tight

Stand Alone Title:

Hands on with the CEO

Torn Between Two Brothers

Holiday Spirit

Unleashed

Knocking on Demon's Door

Web of Desire

ABOUT CATHRYN

New York Times and *USA today* Bestselling author, Cathryn is a wife, mom, sister, daughter, and friend. She loves dogs, sunny weather, anything chocolate (she never says no to a brownie) pizza and red wine. She has two teenagers who keep her busy with their never ending activities, and a husband who is convinced he can turn her into a mixed martial arts fan. Cathryn can never find balance in her life, is always trying to find time to go to the gym, can never keep up with emails, Facebook or Twitter and tries to write page-turning books that her readers will love.

Connect with Cathryn:
Newsletter https://app.mailerlite.com/webforms/landing/c1f8n1
Twitter: https://twitter.com/writercatfox
Facebook: https://www.facebook.com/AuthorCathrynFox?ref=hl
Blog: http://cathrynfox.com/blog/
Goodreads: https://www.goodreads.com/author/show/91799.Cathryn_Fox

Pinterest http://www.pinterest.com/catkalen/